THE SUMMER WE ALMOST PAINTED THE HOUSE

THE SUMMER WE ALMOST PAINTED THE HOUSE

TOM COSENTINO

THE PAPER HOUSE
PUBLISHING

Copyright © 2023 by Tom Cosentino

All rights reserved.

No part of this book may be reproduced in any form or by any electronic or mechanical means, including information storage and retrieval systems, without written permission from the author, except for the use of brief quotations in a book review.

Disclaimer:

This is a work of fiction. Names, characters, places, and incidents are the product of the author's imagination or are used fictitiously. Any resemblance to actual persons, living or dead, business establishments, events, or locales is entirely coincidental.

For my wife Caye for all her support and encouragement and our children Genevieve and Dominic. To Niall Williams, the great Irish writer, for teaching me more about writing in his four-day workshop than I had learned in my entire writing journey.

To all my writing friends, both the new ones in my current Writer's Group and the ones who have been with me since the beginning, especially my readers that keep me on track. I couldn't do this without your feedback. Also, thanks to Stephen Black, my editor in Belfast and Art Fogartie, my editor for the final manuscript.

A special dedication to one of my best friends, Koda, the wonderful German Shorthaired Pointer that we lost right as we were going to publication. He was at my side or under my feet for every word that was written and every edit that was made. He is greatly missed.

CONTENTS

Prologue	1
1. In the Beginning	5
2. The East Side	11
3. The Duper	13
4. Breaking Point	17
5. Welcome to Lance's	21
6. Salmon P. Chase	28
7. Meet the Foleys	33
8. History of the Battle Wagon	37
9. Don't know much 'bout History	44
10. College Journey	47
11. Filling Out	50
12. Stealing Christmas	54
13. Christmas Miracle	58
14. A Christmas to Remember	65
15. No Need for Alarm	72
16. Calvin Upton	77
17. Saving	80
18. My Winning Season	85
19. The Championship	88
20. Interviewing	91
21. Mother Mary Comes to Me	97
22. The Surprise Woman	99
23. 96 ROCK Sign	107
24. Pepe	113
25. Mary's Third Appearance	119
26. Congratulations	121
27. The Goat	126
28. Challenge Accepted	132

29. Starting	138
30. Neighbor Beautification	141
31. Signs	143
32. Wait List	147
33. The First Keg	150
34. In the Dumps	159
35. Death Defying Act	162
36. Invitations	168
37. Graduation	171
38. The New Arrival	174
39. Introductions	181
40. The Second Keg	186
41. Ailis and the Faeries	195
42. Midsummer Night's Dream	200
43. If We Be Friends	202
44. Inquisition	210
45. Mary's Fourth Appearance	216
46. Ailis at The Super Duper	218
47. The Fourth of July Di Capra Family Picnic	222
48. Mr. Sherman's Date	230
49. Going Swimming	236
50. Trip to Liberty Hill	248
51. College Surprise	256
52. Noah's Ark Week	262
53. Movie Night	272
54. After Juliet	275
55. Mary Appears to Me	278
56. Moving On	283
57. Not Enough Makeup	288
58. The Offer	290
59. Mary's Command Performance	293
60. The Wedding	296
61. After Party	302
62. The NYC Plan	308

63. Finding Da	313
64. The Talk	319
65. Facing Mrs. Foley	323
66. Protecting Ailis	326
67. Broken	332
68. Last Week	334
69. Heading to the World	338
70. Pi Lam House, 1983	346
Epilogue	350
About the Author	353

PROLOGUE

The house where my life changed looked pretty much the same, smaller of course, as everything from childhood does when we're older. The original "seven" of the metal house numbers, somewhere lost to time, were replaced with a cheap stick-on version meant for a mailbox. The shingles we scraped, primed, and painted that fateful summer were now covered by cracked vinyl siding, the color faded to a generic gray. The ancient maple trees that guarded the sidewalk to the house were gone; no trace of their existence remained.

This was my first time back in my boyhood neighborhood, even though I had made visits to Genesee before. What did it say about my hometown that my trips were only for the occasional holiday or funeral? Even worse, what did it say about me? What made me so reluctant to revisit the past? I should be more grateful for how these streets made me who I am. I should have come back much sooner, especially to this place.

The Uber driver waited for me to get out as I stared

across the street at Lance's old house.

"You going to be okay alone in this neighborhood?" the driver asked as I finally pushed myself out of the back seat.

"Yes, I grew up here and someone is picking me up in a little while."

"Okay, be careful," he said, giving me a look as if he didn't believe I'd be okay.

I closed the door and waved goodbye; glad I was alone for this meeting with my past.

Sitting in the backseat of the sickly air-freshened Prius, I had transformed from a nauseous old man to the naïve teenager, waiting for my story to begin. I had seen the ghosts of our youth on the streets as we drove from the hotel to the places I knew so well. Standing and looking at the house where so much changed in my life, I knew one of those ghosts was me.

A light rain blurred my view, which didn't matter because I was seeing the neighborhood from 1979, my senior year of high school, the year I left Genesee for college, and, as it turned out, for the rest of my life. I hadn't planned on leaving for good, but it happened, and I bounced around the country while so many of my friends stayed right here.

I raised my collar and walked on the broken sidewalk to the memories across the street. I stood on the front walk, knowing an old man wouldn't raise much suspicion for staring at a house. The smell of the long-closed rendering plant that once permeated the east side on cold, drizzly days was thankfully absent. A city bus groaned, struggling to get up the hill, the familiar cue to get to the stop so we wouldn't miss our ride to school. It was all part of me.

I looked down the street toward Erie Boulevard and

thought of the night before she left. I pushed away those images, along with the recollection of the pain and tried to remember one of the thousands of funny things that happened inside Lance's. I laughed to myself, shaking my head in appreciation of how much we did that would be inconceivable in today's hypersensitive world. People now wouldn't understand what we did, why our parents gave us so much latitude, how we grew up faster than the kids corralled under the rotor blast of today's helicopter parents. A bunch of seventeen-year-old boys having a couple of beers and talking about girls? Their heads would explode.

"How did we do all that crazy stuff and get away with it?" I said to the spirits haunting me.

The answer came in a flood of memories that overwhelmed my attempts to reminisce quietly. My vision blurred on the periphery. I glimpsed the flickering movie scenes from my past being retold. My life played out before me, this part at least. I hoped it wasn't a sign that I was slowly dying.

The keg parties, all the beer we drank. The things we stole, all harmless foolishness. Christmas trees, Pepe, the radio station sign. The pranks and the jokes. How Calvin Upton didn't get us all arrested could be validated by the Pope as a miracle. We were constantly laughing and having a great time. Our year together was the struggle of the innocence of youth fighting hard against everything that was pushing us, unwillingly sometimes, into being adults.

I missed them all.

More of my past pulled me away toward my old house. From the top of the hill, the boarded-up windows of Our Lady of Sorrows on the corner of the street where I lived stood out against the carefully laid brick. The nearly one hundred-year-old stained glass windows the church commissioned from an artist in England, hidden magnificence beneath the weathered plywood. I used to marvel at the light playing through those windows as I sat through countless hours inside for Mass. The church used to be the heart of the neighborhood, but now it stood lifeless, no more than a tombstone.

I reached the corner and looked down my street to the curve in the road where my childhood home stood. I could close my eyes and walk to the front door from this point just from memory, but I could go no farther. I hadn't seen the house since my father died over twenty years ago. I summoned my courage, taking a couple of steps and then stopped, defeated.

Across the street was my elementary school, and those memories warmed me like a fireplace on Christmas Eve. So glad the building was still in use, repurposed as a community center, its heart still faintly beating.

I walked back up the hill past the bus stop, past Colin's old house; my body grew colder with each step. I didn't experience the fear that sometimes gripped me on these streets. They were still just as dangerous, probably worse, but I didn't care. The east side of Genesee had given me so much and I knew it could not take anything more from me. My childhood neighborhood was on life support when I left for college. After seeing Our Lady of Sorrows, no one could doubt it was nearly dead.

Shaking off the bad memories, I went back to the fun times, and there were so many. If I hadn't spent those crazy days with Lance and Colin, how much of my life would be different today? The question was too much for the senses, but I knew I had to tell our story.

CHAPTER 1
IN THE BEGINNING

My name is Joseph Vincent Di Capra. At seventeen I started my senior year; this is the story of my last year of high school and the summer before I went to college. My life story up to 1978 wouldn't have been the inspiration for an American family sitcom or made anyone envious of my experiences. My mother was forty-five when I was born; my father fifty-one. My four older sisters weren't overjoyed by my arrival. The oldest of my sisters was twenty-five, out of the house, and married when I came along. The youngest was seventeen and thoroughly embarrassed by her old mother walking around the neighborhood knocked-up. My other two sisters were somewhere in between and both out of the house, so they didn't have to help with diapers and warming bottles for their inconvenient little brother.

When I was in kindergarten my mother was diagnosed with breast cancer and before I was out of the first grade, she died. I remember the house being full of mourners and people coming up to me and grabbing my face so they could say, "What a poor boy." My father retreated to the life of a widower. My sisters took turns coming to the house and trying to be a mom to me by helping my father with cooking, cleaning, and offering to take me with them. My guess now is that my father didn't want to be alone, so he always politely said no.

Dad worked six days a week as the floor manager for a dying local department store. During the school year I was left to myself, getting dressed, doing my homework, and learning how to make a few simple meals but primarily knowing how to heat up the food one of my sisters made and put in the freezer. Summer vacation meant bouncing between my sisters, which I enjoyed because they went to great lengths to fill in for our mom.

I went to Our Lady of Sorrows Grammar School which was only a few doors up the street, and I watched Sister Catherine watching me walking to my house every day from the time my mother died until the end of fifth grade, when I guess she felt I was finally old enough to walk home without incident.

Quiet and appearing to be withdrawn, I plodded through my half-orphan existence. I wore the unfortunate news that I was Joe, the motherless boy. When my friends introduced me to a new kid, they said, "That's Joe Di Capra, his mother died."

When I entered high school, my father's store closed and he simply chose to retire since he was over sixty-five. He continued to work part-time at my uncle's shoe store, paid under the table. This gave him enough money to keep me fed and clothed. It also allowed him to spend his free time at the Genesee OTB, betting on the horses, and to help at Our Lady of Sorrows where he did light chores for Monsignor McCarthy.

When I finished Our Lady of Sorrows after the eighth grade, my father told me I had to go to the public school. All my friends were taking the bus to the suburbs to attend Bishop Slattery, the Catholic high school. I wanted to go with them but knew the tuition was too much for my father to afford.

My father knew that before my last sister graduated from the local public school, the great State of New York had purchased a huge apartment complex a few blocks from our house. In the spirit of the Great Society, urban progress, and the fact that the new interstate was going through the poorest neighborhood in the city, the state turned it into public housing. He saw what happened to the neighborhood; everyone did.

All these changes resulted in a torrent of middle-class flights to the suburbs. For Sale signs were everywhere to be seen, with a moving van on almost every block taking the fleeing families out to the planned communities and home-owner associations of suburbia. If someone, knocked into a coma in 1965, came back to the neighborhood in 1972, they wouldn't recognize the once quiet, friendly city streets.

Nothing changed the fact that we couldn't pay the tuition at Bishop Slattery. So, for my freshman year I walked up the street to H.W. Clinton Middle School.

From the outside it looked harmless enough but the kids from the public housing project made up a large percentage of the student body and to add to the fun, the juvenile delinquent home next to the junior high school had closed its own school and was now sending the "inmates" as they called themselves, almost all boys, to Clinton.

Every morning from my homeroom window I watched

the line of future residents of a penitentiary somewhere in the country trudge across the field separating the middle school from the delinquent home. They moved with the apathy of killers walking to the gallows. I looked the first week to see if there was a guard with a shotgun herding them to the classrooms.

After just a few weeks in ninth grade, I went to my father and begged him to let me go to the Catholic high school with my friends. He said no without explanation, but I could see he didn't like that he had to say no.

I told him about the kid from the juvie home getting arrested in my English class. I told him about the poor Hostess Twinkie driver at the Lebanese convenience store across the street from the school. The Hostess delivery truck pulled up and parked outside the old 7-11. The driver opened the sliding back door on the panel truck and loaded up a dolly with cupcakes and Twinkies and rolled it into the store. He had to be new to the route. He didn't realize what the east side of town was capable of doing.

The first kid ran across to the truck and jumped into the back. He grabbed an armload of sweets and ran down the street. His brazen act inspired three more guys to join him and get what they could.

The floodgates opened and within seconds the truck was jammed with dozens of the public high school's finest, helping themselves to all the iced, stuffed, and baked goods they could grab. The only thing I could think of was the feeding frenzy of sharks in the National Geographic film we saw in science class.

By the time the driver returned, his truck was empty.

After months of asking if there was any way for me to go to Bishop Slattery, my father took me down the street to the grocery store, where he introduced me to one of his racetrack buddies, the store manager. While they talked about betting tips and which horse was a sure thing, I filled out an application for a job I had already been given. When I signed my name at the bottom of the application, I officially became a stock boy at the East Genesee Super Duper.

I earned enough working after school and during the summer to pay the tuition at Bishop Slattery for my sophomore year. I had friends I already knew from my grammar school, but I was new and quiet, so I didn't make a lot of buddies outside of my established circle. I would sit in the back of the class whenever possible; I never raised my hand when I knew the answer, which was almost all the time, and I would never ask a question if I had one. I would try to figure it out later or ask my homeroom teacher, Sister Mary.

I'm sure my mother's death was somewhere in my file, which raised Sister Mary's concern for me. One day she approached me, probably to make sure the painfully shy kid was doing okay, and put her hand on my shoulder as I hurried with some last-minute homework.

"Is everything okay?" she asked.

"Yes, Sister, just doing homework that I didn't finish last night because I was working."

"Working, why are you working?"

"To pay my tuition, Sister."

It took a few seconds for this to sink in and then she smiled.

"Let me help you."

"No, thank you, Sister, it's easy. I just need more time."

"Let me look anyway; you are going too fast."

She pulled a desk up next to mine and looked at the

problem. She quickly saw the small mistake I made. I saw it at the same time and fixed it before her finger reached the paper.

"How are your grades?" she asked.

"Great Sister, my lowest grade is a ninety-five in Trigonometry. I was twenty-third in the class the last time the rankings were posted."

"Well done, Joe, you're a hard worker. Make sure you let me know right away if you are having any problems."

"I will, Sister, thank you."

She started to check with me every morning and soon I talked to her about my life, what I wanted to do, and the crazy idea of being a writer. She encouraged me to speak up in class and to try to break out of my small circle of friends and meet more people. I promised her I would try but could never get up the courage.

CHAPTER 2
THE EAST SIDE

My neighborhood on the east side of Genesee played a huge role in my youth. The turnover in the population overwhelmed our corner of the city within just a few years. We went from being known as a Jewish, mostly professional, neighborhood to a community with all races, new immigrants. At first, everyone was getting along.

I don't know the exact tipping point when the peace changed. The streets quickly became unsafe, especially for a kid like me. There was no one source of potential danger; it could come from anywhere. Nothing could be predicted along any lines, race didn't matter; food stamps and free lunches at school didn't matter. Lines didn't exist, which made it tough to figure out a survival plan. You could not make choices based on anything other than whether someone is a good guy or a bad guy. If you didn't know someone, you had to err on the side of bad guy to be safe. With the influx of all the new people, there were a lot of people I didn't know.

I learned how to move through the neighborhood.

Where I could go and where it wasn't a good idea to tread. I learned which backyards I could cut through, where to hide, where to double-back and take another route. I did a lot of running; I changed my path often. I tried not to walk alone at certain times but it was impossible to have a friend along all the time.

I also learned the body language of bad guys. How they walked in the street instead of the sidewalk. How they usually roamed in groups, and talked loudly as a way of proclaiming they were in charge. They had to prove they were bad guys. The opportunity to rough up a solitary boy as a surefire way to prove the neighborhood belonged to them could not be passed up.

A good guy was a treasure. If I saw someone I knew as a good guy in a group, I would go out of my way to say hello and find out who the other guys were. At least I could recognize them and say, "Don't you know so and so?" and potentially get out of a jam. I always said hello to the people I knew, maintaining contact. It was purely out of self-preservation and difficult for a shy kid.

My sister once asked me why I was so skinny. Did she need to make more food to put in the freezer? I told her that running for your life burned a lot of calories.

My goal being solely to reduce the potential for harm, nothing could be done to avoid it completely. My head was always on a swivel as I walked to a friend's house or to baseball practice. And we were always walking, everywhere we went, we walked. To the mall, to the bowling alley, to the movies, up to Seneca University for a basketball game, we were "hoofing it."

CHAPTER 3
THE DUPER

The job my father got me at the Super Duper enabled me to pay the $770 tuition for Bishop Slattery. Working left me with very little free time, but it got me out of going to the public high school, J.G. Armatas. It was worth every penny.

The Super Duper reflected the demographics of the neighborhood. It was an independent store catering to the Jewish residents that had left when the neighborhood changed and now made the drive in from the suburbs for the kosher deli and the aisle of Jewish specialty foods. The rest of the store was a regular grocery, small but very convenient for people on the east side. Next door to the Duper was a kosher butcher shop that was still dispatching cows and chickens when I was in elementary school. But by the time I started working at the Super Duper, they stopped when the number of practicing Jews left, and demand dropped.

The Super Duper was owned by Howard Leonard. It

was a widely accepted story that Mr. Leonard had burned down his store near the housing projects to get the money to buy the old Loblaws. It became the Duper. Mr. Leonard was not a happy man and treated his employees poorly. He treated kids that came into the store even worse. He viewed every young person as a thief. It didn't matter the color of the kid, he thought they were out to rob him. He would follow them around the store as he did to me once when the Duper first opened.

The Duper was full of stories. It was a kosher store in a lower-class neighborhood with a colorful staff. Working there was always interesting. Mr. Leonard's brother Marvin ran the Kosher deli along with the Jewish lothario, Bernie Robinowitz. Bernie openly flirted with every woman who came to the deli. It was common for me to hear the shrill laughter of a Jewish housewife coming from the deli as Bernie laid on compliments as thick as creamed herring.

The manager of the store, my father's buddy, was Mr. Olivieri. Mr. O was a chain-smoking, no nonsense boss who loved to teach lessons like making a stock boy clean out the stale, spilled beer from the cooler if he showed up on a Saturday morning with a hangover. The stock boys loved Mr. O for one good reason: he had the penchant for hiring only beautiful young cashiers. If a girl came into the store to put in an application, he would call all the stock guys to the front office to see if she met our standards.

Another good thing about working there was that Mr. Leonard and Mr. Olivieri both went home around six o'clock and left the store to us kids and the night manager, George DeLuca. George worked for the city DPW and since this was his second job, he didn't care much about what the stock guys did as long as we finished everything on the store closing list.

Mr. Leonard was a penny pincher. In my three years working for him, I only received one raise, when the government raised the minimum wage from $2.10 to $3.25. But the store was a block from my house, and I made enough to pay my tuition so I could put up with Mr. Leonard.

The staff at the Super Duper had shifted to a younger group. With George DeLuca's carefree style as night manager, work became fun, and we had time to become a group. The older guys who hung out on the loading dock smoking while telling me to do all the work had moved on to different jobs. The younger employees started hanging out in the parking lot after we closed up. We took turns buying a six pack and drinking a couple beers before everyone went home. I tried to do this as often as I could unless I had basketball practice or something to do with my friends from Bishop Slattery.

The stock boys were a great group and we all got along. We would speed through all of our tasks after Mr. Leonard and Mr. O left, leaving us time to play paper towel roll football, throw eggs at cars from the loading dock, or hang out at the front of the store, hitting on the cashiers. I looked forward to work and even found myself going in on my days off just so I wouldn't miss the goings on. I didn't want to hear about something great happening because I'd missed all the fun. The days of sitting at home were over.

I envisioned the college friends I would hopefully be meeting in a few months. From a small circle to a wider net of friends, I was very happy with my progress. My confidence grew, and I became less concerned that I would have trouble meeting new people at college. But there still wasn't the one friend I had longed for since I was young. The special lady that would be my first love. But I knew my shell was starting to crack.

CHAPTER 4
BREAKING POINT

We sat in Franklin's basement playing cards like we always did when it was too cold or there was snow on the driveway and we couldn't play basketball. I was restless. I felt we were in a rut, just doing the same things over and over. I wanted a girlfriend. I enjoyed talking to Patti DiPietro in homeroom, but I knew we were just friends and I appreciated that she talked to me.

No one in my group had a girlfriend, but it wasn't for lack of trying. Marty Reilly and I would walk around the hallways of Bishop Slattery hoping for the opportunity to chat to some girls before homeroom. We would walk to the mall and do the same thing. Unfortunately, the opportunity never happened. I'm not sure Marty and I would have known what to do if it had.

I lost a hand of poker because of my inattention, adding to my frustration.

"Don't you guys ever get tired of all of this? We do the same things all the time. We should try something different. Throw a party, invite some girls from school. Something, we need to do something." I was almost screeching by the end of my outburst.

"You done?" Franklin asked.

"Yes," I conceded.

"Who's deal, is it?" Chuck asked.

"Deal me out; I'm going to head home. I have Calc homework to do anyway," I said.

"I'll go with you, I have homework too," Marty said.

When we got outside, I felt like I was going to scream.

"Don't you ever get frustrated that we don't do anything else?" I asked.

"Yeah, I know what you mean. But what can we do. A party's not a bad idea but who would we invite, and would they even show up?"

"I know, my house is too small. Franklin wouldn't want to have one, neither would Chuck."

"My parents wouldn't let me have one either," Marty added.

"I know. What can we do, there has to be something."

"You talk to Patti in homeroom, try to find out if any of the other groups are having parties and if there's some way we can get invited. If we get invited, I'm going even if we have to take the bus," Marty said.

"Patti DiPietro? She says hello to me since we sit next to each other because we sit alphabetically. Maybe Sister Mary told her to talk to me, but I think she's just nice. But I like the way you're talking, that's exactly what I wanted to hear. There's got to be more to being seventeen than playing cards and basketball, although basketball is great. We have Thanksgiving break coming up, we should try to get something set up for at least Christmas vacation."

"Sounds good. We could talk to some of the CYO

cheerleaders too. We can do this. What about the friends you made in your freshman year at Clinton? We could try to get invited to a public-school party," Marty said.

"Man, you're coming up with great ideas. Let's do this. I'll talk to the cashiers at the Super Duper to find out if they have anything going on. We have more options than we realized. I'm sure I can get them to get us invited to a party."

"Sounds like we have somewhat of a plan, I guess that's a start," Marty said.

"Okay, I feel a little better. Thanks for understanding. I don't know what it is, maybe it's because it's our senior year. Or hearing the kids at school talk about all they're doing. And I know part of the problem is the neighborhood. Anyway, be careful walking to your house."

"Same to you, see you at the bus stop in the morning."

I walked down the hill, still preoccupied with the feeling that we were wasting our senior year. I should have been paying attention. I didn't see the group walking up the hill. When I looked up, one of them pointed in my direction.

Luckily, I was near the Our Lady of Sorrows convent. I cut into the driveway and ran to the backyard, jumped the fence into another backyard, and walked out to my street where I could see the corner.

I peered from behind a hedge, no one in sight. I scurried to the road and went into the backyard of the first house on my side of the street. I crisscrossed through the yards until I was home. It was a route I had taken many times. I got my keys out before I went to my front door so I would be ready to unlock it. One last look, up and down the street and it was clear.

I needed to be more careful. Even though a recent growth spurt had pushed me over six feet, I still had a long way to go to fill into my frame and I didn't stand a chance in most fights, zero chance against a group of guys intent on causing harm.

The adrenaline from the near miss combined with my bad mood kept me up for hours. Even the boring calculus homework wasn't enough to make me sleepy.

CHAPTER 5
WELCOME TO LANCE'S

I knew Lance Sherman and Colin Foley from the neighborhood and from the times they occasionally showed up at church. Colin's mother's cousin was married to my oldest sister. We always joked that we were related whenever we saw each other. I knew Colin and Lance were a little rougher than the guys at Bishop Slattery. They went to the public high school, and I had heard they liked doing things I had never dared to do because I was too concerned about getting in trouble.

I worked late shift the day after Thanksgiving. About a half-hour before closing, I was in the back room getting ready to take the garbage to the dumpster when I heard the intercom calling me to the front.

Great, I thought. *Now I'm going to have to hurry to finish the cleanup. What could they need me for?*

When I got to the front expecting a big order to bag, I saw Colin sitting back against the register, talking to Peggy the cashier.

"Hey, Colin, what's going on?" I asked, curious.

"I'll see you at school," Colin said to Peggy. He turned to me. "Can I ask you a question?"

Colin was a bruiser. He stood about five-and-a-half feet tall and weighed close to two hundred and fifty pounds. He played center and noseguard on the J.G. Armatas varsity football team because he plugged a hole in the line just by being there, proving to be impossible to move with his low center of gravity.

"Sure, go ahead."

"Can you buy beer?"

"I don't see why not. George is closing and he doesn't care. Do you care?" I asked Peggy.

"As long as you have money," she replied.

"Do you have money?" I asked Colin.

"Some."

"Well, follow me," I said, motioning Colin toward the beer cooler.

"Why don't I pay for one and you pay for one and we can bring them up to Lance's and drink them?" Colin asked.

I wasn't much of a beer drinker, but I began to acquire a taste from drinking with the night shift employees in the store parking lot after we closed. I didn't have anything going on and all my friends from Bishop Slattery were busy with family because of the holiday, so I accepted Colin's offer. I hadn't been inside Lance's house, but I heard stories about his father and other things that went on in the house. I knew Lance had also lost his mother to cancer a few years earlier.

"Sure, what do you want to get," I said as I opened the cooler and grabbed a six pack of Old Vienna.

"Make that two then," Colin said.

I grabbed a second six pack and handed it to him along with three dollars.

"Go ahead, here's my half. Peggy will let you buy the beer. Wait outside, and I'll be off in about fifteen minutes, and I'll walk with you up to Lance's."

We walked through the dark streets from the store, cutting through a small patch of woods to get to a dead-end street that cut the walk to Lance's in half. It was a route I wouldn't have taken alone, either day or night, but I knew if there was anyone in the woods waiting to jump us, Colin was fearless, and I could run faster than he could.

We made it through the woods and to Lance's house without any problems.

Colin walked into Lance's without knocking, going straight to the kitchen to put the beer in the refrigerator. I stayed near the front door.

"Yo, Lance, we got beer," Colin called out.

I heard someone running down the stairs.

As I waited, I looked around, surprised by the state of the house. My mother was gone but my father did his best to keep our house clean and my sisters would come over and help him on weekends. Lance's house was piled high with junk. The dining room looked like it hadn't been used in years with boxes reaching the ceiling and there was a smell I couldn't identify. I made a mental note to thank my father for all the work he did on his own.

"Joe, what are you doing here?" Lance asked as he rounded the corner from the stairs.

Before I could answer, Colin came out of the kitchen with three beers, handing one to Lance and then one to me.

"I met Joe down at the Super Duper; we each bought a six pack," Colin said.

"Thanks," Lance said. "Come on in and stay awhile." He motioned me toward the television in the living room.

I grabbed a big chair across from where Lance sat but had to move a pile of newspapers off the seat first.

"Welcome to my house," Lance said. "Anyone who brings beer is always welcome."

"I thought a few brews would be nice, so I took a chance to see if Joe was working," Colin said.

"So, you can buy beer?" Lance asked.

"Yeah, as long as the owner isn't there or the store manager. George is the night manager, and he doesn't care. If there's a cashier who won't rat us out and is also cool, then we're okay."

"That's great news," Lance said. "We have to do this more often, especially since you have a job and money."

"Well, I use most of that money to pay my tuition at Bishop Slattery, but I'm almost done paying and this is my senior year. But I'm also saving for college," I added.

"How are things at Bishop Slattery? You don't mind going to the sissy Catholic school?" Colin asked.

"No, I like it there, the teachers are great, and I'm really trying hard to get a scholarship for college. How are things at J.G. Armatas Maximum Security High School?"

"Football season is over, not much to look forward to," Colin replied, ignoring the jab at his school.

"School is school," Lance said. "Don't you have to wear ties every day?"

"Yeah, ties, shoes, no sneakers. But at least I don't have to worry about getting killed like you guys do," I said, trying again to dig back at Colin's sissy comment.

"It's not that bad," Lance said. "Most of the dangerous guys drop out before they become hardcore killers. So, all you really have to worry about is a random punch or something like that. Being on the football team helps. I'm more afraid walking around our neighborhood at night than I'm at school."

Lance also played football, as a skinny, second-string defensive back. He was fast and didn't mind taking a hit from a bigger player. He dusted himself off and got back in the play. I saw both of them on the field in October when Armatas played Bishop Slattery.

He was a little shorter than me, just under six feet. I wondered how he got a football helmet over his huge mop of wiry blonde hair.

"That's good to know," I replied. "Your dad doesn't mind you drinking beer?"

Colin laughed.

"No, he lets me do whatever I want to, really. If he was here, he'd try to bum one of these beers," Lance replied.

"So, if you wanted to have a party, with beer....and girls, you could?" I asked.

"Now that we have a place to buy beer, sure. That's a great idea. If we had the money for the beer," Colin said.

"And knew any girls that would show up to my house," Lance added.

"Girls will show up if they know there will be drinks. We should have a party over Christmas vacation," I said.

Colin looked at Lance.

"Sure, we can try that," Lance said.

"Are there any girls from your school you could invite?" Lance asked me.

"No, c'mon, they're Catholic girls. They spend their

time ironing the pleats in their school uniform skirts and chasing rich boys from Fayetteville. They absolutely don't drink beer and their parents wouldn't let them come to our neighborhood unless it was on a school mission to feed paroled car thieves," I said.

"Makes sense," Colin replied without turning from watching the television.

"Here's the deal then," I said, trying to keep their attention. "I'll buy the beer and you guys invite the girls."

Lance looked at Colin. Colin nodded.

"Okay, do you want to do New Year's Eve? That might get some people to show up," Lance said.

"Great idea," I said with more enthusiasm than I intended. "Start spreading the word at school on Monday. I'll even spring for some champagne if we can get someone to buy it for us."

"Girls do like champagne," Colin said. He looked over at me for the first time since we began the discussion.

"Great, we have a plan," I said.

"Who needs a beer?" Lance asked, breaking Colin's interest from both the television and the plans for the party.

"Me," Colin said.

"I'm good," I replied. I hid my nearly full bottle.

I began to think about how I would tell my Bishop Slattery friends that I wanted to throw a New Year's Eve party at Lance's house with beer and champagne.

"You're going to do what?" Franklin will ask.

"A party with beer and girls."

"You'll get busted and what are you doing at Lance Sherman's house?" Marty will say.

"But there'll be girls and beer and I told you guys I wanted to break out of my rut and experience more."

"You'll get in so much trouble, is that the experience you are looking for?" Chuck will say.

"But there will be girls, and it'll be fine. His father doesn't mind," I'll repeat to all their objections.

"Did you say something?" Lance asked.

"No, nothing, just thinking about the party," I replied as I pictured the living room, cleaned up, dimly lit, and all the girls with party hats and noise makers. Girls having a great time at our party and maybe even the chance of a kiss at midnight.

CHAPTER 6
SALMON P. CHASE

Trying to keep my promise to Sister Mary to talk in class and show people I wasn't just a shy recluse, I waited for the right opportunity to answer or ask a question, or, in an ideal world, crack a joke and make everyone laugh, becoming instantly popular. There were plenty of openings and I chickened out every time. Sister Mary would look at me as we waited in homeroom for the final bell, and I would shake my head letting her know I was still a coward. She would smile and fold her hands in prayer letting me know she was there to support me. I knew I couldn't keep letting her down.

Earlier in the week she waved me to her desk before the first bell.

"They are forming a Literary Magazine club," she said.

"Really, that's great. I can submit some of my short stories I've done for Sister Sylvia's class and maybe they'll get accepted."

"The first meeting is Thursday after school, in the

English Resource room," she said. She handed me the announcement.

"After school?"

"Oh, I'm sorry. Work?"

"Yes, Sister, I have to work. Also, I don't really have a way to get home other than the bus. There isn't anyone to drive me home."

"Well, I'll talk to Sister Sylvia, I'm sure you can submit your work without going to the meetings," she said.

"Thank you, Sister."

Still disappointed, I went to my first period, Mr. Norwood's Social Studies class. I didn't care for Mr. Norwood. An unfriendly teacher, he would write some snide comment on one of my essay questions even though I scored a "100" on every test.

History was my favorite subject, and I knew a lot of "facts" because on boring days, alone and waiting for my father to get home from work, I pulled out the huge encyclopedias my mother bought for me. I read them volume by volume, page by page. I went through every single letter of the alphabet, reading and remembering. I acquired a vast knowledge of what I assumed were insignificant facts.

I don't think my mother realized how much she would get for the money she gave to the salesman who sat on our couch and showed us poster-sized blow up pages from the volumes while chain smoking cigarettes and telling her about how much she needed to spend the money for her children's future. But I think it was her way of trying to do what she could for me because she knew she wouldn't be there to help me with my homework.

Her investment paid off because one of those facts finally gave me the courage to talk in class.

We were going over the monetary system and Mr. Norwood spoke about the President or otherwise important historical person on each American bill. I knew them all from the page in the "M" edition that showed pictures of each note with a brief description. I was such a geek. The men I didn't recognize, I would look up in the appropriate volume and read their story.

Mr. Norwood kept increasing the denominations along with his condescension toward the teenagers he was paid to teach. By the time he reached $100, no one knew the answer, except me of course, but I remained silent.

He started to make fun of the class because the room was quiet again when he asked about the $500 bill.

"Your parents are wasting their money sending you to Bishop Slattery," he said.

This hit a nerve with me because I worked at the Super Duper to pay my own tuition. I realized my fingers hurt because I gripped the seat of my chair with all my strength.

When he reached the $1000 bill, he confirmed that we were all stupid and ignorant. He didn't say it, but I felt his sincere disdain and became extremely angry because I knew all the answers but was too afraid to raise my hand.

When Mr. Norwood reached the $10,000 bill, he was really laying it on. He equated us with Neanderthals barely able to rub sticks together to make fire. We should go back and live in caves because we didn't deserve the roofs over our heads. We were uninformed and uneducated, unworthy of his skills as a teacher.

"So, none of you knows who is on the $10,000 bill? I had no idea I was given such a dumb class. I think I might just have to fail everyone."

Emily Eaton, the shoo-in for class valedictorian, raised

her hand, nearly jumping out of her chair. She fought, begged, and whined for every point in her grades. Failure was not an option.

"No, Emily, I really won't fail everyone," he said.

He circled the room with an accusatory glance while trying to regain his lost momentum.

"Ten-thousand-dollar bill?" he said slowly. "Anyone? Anyone out there?"

My anger boiled over; I was not a Neanderthal. I knew more about history than this bearded dolt, who thought he could belittle his class instead of teaching them. He hadn't taught anything all year beyond the facts inside the boxes of heavily bound books the chain-smoking salesman delivered to our living room from his rusted-out station wagon.

"No one? You Neanderthals? No one?"

"Salmon P. Chase," I said in a tone approaching a scream.

It wasn't me talking. The person answering the question sat at the desk while I hovered above my body. That person pounded his fist into his well-educated hand, disproving all of Mr. Norwood's claims about our lack of knowledge.

Mr. Norwood stood at the front of the class blinking.

I returned to my body. My face flushed with the heat of my anger and the embarrassment for having spoken in class.

Norwood was caught off guard. "Well, well…"

Everyone in the room looked at me. I envisioned all the students and teachers in Bishop Slattery as frozen in place in the hallways and in their interrupted classes to listen to what I said. Cars on I-481 next to the school stopped and waited. All of Genesee paused to listen.

The flush I experienced turned into a fever. Sweat

poured off my forehead. I loosened my tie and tried to breathe. The cartoon image of a thermometer exploding under a fire popped into my mind. I was the Looney Toon's boy in the boiling kettle with the headhunters dancing around me as I fulfilled the role of their main course for their dinner.

Mr. Norwood finally composed himself.

"Well then, who was Salmon P. Chase?" he asked with a sliver of regained haughtiness.

"He was Lincoln's Secretary of the Treasury," I thundered from my now bully pulpit.

Emily came running over to my desk. She furiously wrote in her notebook. Her head shook, and her eyes were wild like a dog that lost her bone to a smarter dog. She wasn't used to anyone knowing something she didn't know herself.

"What did you say? Who was he? How did you know that?"

I couldn't answer any of her questions because of the numbness in my body.

I don't remember what happened after that. I may have passed out from the exhaustion of the experience, or the class may have ended. I like to remember the event with my fellow students, except Emily, carrying me out on their shoulders and Mr. Norwood sitting at his desk crying with his head in his hands.

I beamed with new confidence as I walked to my next class. And again, I spoke. The door was now open, the shell was cracked, I could see the world.

CHAPTER 7
MEET THE FOLEYS

I knew Mr. and Mrs. Foley from Church and I would see Mrs. Foley sitting on the porch of their house whenever I walked to baseball practice or up to St. Benedict's to play football on the lawn beside the library.

They were an odd couple. Mr. Foley was a mountain of a man, at least six foot six and over three hundred pounds. Mrs. Foley was around five feet tall if her hair was up and she wore heels. What she lacked in size she made up for in spunk and spirit. She worked as a teacher's aide at my grammar school, and she kept perfect order with her booming voice and quick wit.

Once I began to spend time with Colin and Lance, I had the opportunity to get to know Mr. and Mrs. Foley much better.

"So, Joe, why are you hanging out with Colin all of a sudden," she asked me with no warning as I waited for Colin to get ready so we could head over to Lance's.

I couldn't think of an appropriate answer. The truth was

that her son approached me because he knew I could buy beer. She saw through me right away as I struggled for an answer to her question.

"So, I've seen you carrying beer to Lance's house," she said after watching me squirm.

I nodded and waited for the barrage of questions.

"Just take it easy," she said, "I don't mind a couple beers, just take it easy."

"We will, Mrs. Foley, nothing will get out of hand. I'm only bringing a six pack most of the time, that's two beers a piece. I don't think we'll be doing anything crazy after two beers."

"You're a good kid, I know you will be good."

Mr. Foley proved to be much harder to read. He loomed as an imposing figure because of his size but after a few beers he became a big teddy bear that loved to tell a story or a joke. I knew I was okay with him when I went to a New Year's Day party at Colin's house. Mr. Foley was telling stories to a gathered crowd in the living room about his job with the Post Office.

I hung on the edge of the group listening to Mr. Foley's stories, laughing at all the appropriate times.

"So, I was going down the Thruway in the postal jeep, going back to the main Post Office at the end of my shift. I was trying to see how fast I could get that piece of crap to go," he told his rapt audience.

"I got it up to ninety-five when it began to shake like my Uncle Declan going to confession for the first time in forty years. I'd just started to slow down when I saw the trooper's lights in the rearview mirror. So, I pulled over and when the trooper came up to me, I told him I was on my way to Community Hospital with a kidney I picked up from Syracuse. I had to get it to the hospital for a transplant. I showed him the cooler marked 'Human Organs' and flashed him some paperwork. He tells me 'Let's go' and gives me an escort all the way to Community."

By the end of the story, he laughed so hard, he could barely talk.

"So what was in the cooler?" someone in his audience asked.

"A six-pack for the end of my shift!" He roared with laughter.

When the merriment began to subside, the four beers in me asked about a story Colin had told me.

"Is it true that you moonlight at Barry's Tavern on the northside and that you drive your postal jeep over there and bartend in your Post Office uniform while you're on the clock?"

Mr. Foley stopped laughing. His expression changed. His eyes narrowed. The crowd became silent. Some looked at the floor and waited for Mr. Foley. He pushed aside the man next to him, got closer, and put his arm around me. He engulfed my slumping shoulders. He bent down. His mouth hovered right next to my ear. I shook with fear and looked around frantically for an escape path.

'Joe, Joe, Joe," he said.

The crowd took a step back to get out of the line of fire.

"Yeah. It's true," he said. He exploded into laughter, followed a second later by the crowd.

I blinked a few times until what he said finally reached my brain.

"You sneaky bastard," I said, the only thing I could think of at the time.

Mr. Foley laughed even harder, shaking the walls as he

slapped me on the back causing me to lose my balance. The crowd roared even more, and I roared along with them.

CHAPTER 8
HISTORY OF THE BATTLE WAGON

"It would be great if we had access to a car. All my money goes to tuition and my father can't afford to put me on the insurance or else I could drive," I said as we watched television.

"We did until Colin thought he wanted to be Evel Knievel, he's the one that ruined everything," Lance said.

"What do you mean, until Colin ruined everything?" I asked, now more interested in a potential story than what we were watching on TV.

"Go look out in the backyard at the evidence."

"You mean the beat-up station wagon? Yeah, I've seen it before."

"Well, that's Colin's car," Lance said.

"Don't call it a car," Colin said. He sounded like a barking Rottweiler.

"Okay, The Battle Wagon," Lance said, using air quotes and drawing out the word "battle."

"I love The Battle Wagon," Colin said.

"Okay, now I have to know the story."

"Colin got the car from his Uncle Jimmy…"

"It's the Battle Wagon, I'll tell the story," Colin said. "Everyone get a fresh beer, it's a long story. While you're at it, get two for me. Turn down the TV and get ready."

When we had our beers, we gathered around Colin like story time in elementary school.

Colin cleared his throat and looked up to heaven as if he remembered a long-lost friend who had died before his time.

"Lance and I went over to my Uncle Jimmy's over off of Valley Drive."

"I didn't know you had an Uncle Jimmy," I said.

"Are you going to let me talk?" Colin asked.

I held up my hands in apology.

"Like I said before I was rudely interrupted, Lance and I went over to my Uncle Jimmy's house. He isn't my real uncle, for those of you who won't shut up and listen. He's a close family friend that my father sponsored when he came over from Ireland. We call him Uncle Jimmy because we are very close to their family."

I nodded an apology.

"Happy now?" Colin said, leaning forward in my direction.

"Quite," I said.

"We went to my Uncle Jimmy's house because he needed his garage cleaned out and my father had volunteered me to do the job. So, I grabbed Lance, and we took the bus over to the Valley. Inside the garage was a lime green, 1970 Plymouth station wagon that belonged to my Auntie Rita. She died back in 1975 and Uncle Jimmy just let the car sit there. We pushed it out of the garage to get it out of the way."

"And he gave you the car?" I asked.

Lance laughed because he knew what was coming.

"I'll get there," Colin snapped.

"He's told this story a million times, you have to let him perform," Lance said.

"Lance and I took all day, but we made that garage look spotless and we had everything at the curb for the garbage pick-up. Uncle Jimmy was very impressed. He asked how much he could pay us even though my father told him not to pay us a dime. I asked him, 'What about the wagon?' He looked at me and then at the car and said, 'If you can get it started, it's yours.' I asked him where his keys were and if he had jumper cables."

"Which was a stupid question because everyone in Genesee has jumper cables," Lance said.

Colin rolled his eyes and waited a few seconds to let the latest interruption pass.

"We pulled his car up, put some fresh gas from his can for the lawnmower in the wagon and tried to do a jump start. After a few tries we sprayed in some starting fluid in the carburetor, and we got it going. I went to pull it back into the garage, but the transmission wasn't going into gear. I tried reverse and that worked. So, I shut it off and Lance and I pushed it back into the garage."

Colin finished his beer in one long swig and held out his empty hand. Lance and I looked at each other. I shrugged my shoulders, opened a beer, and put it in Colin's hand.

"I went home and told my father," Colin said. "He said that I'd have to get a job to pay for the insurance and to get the wagon road worthy. So I did, I got a job down on Erie

Boulevard working at the Mini-Mart next to the bowling alley."

"Colin had a job?" I whispered to Lance.

"Yeah, I couldn't believe it either."

"After a month had passed at the Mini-Mart, I had enough for a new battery, the first month of insurance, and the registration. Me and Lance went to the DMV, got the plates, and went over to Uncle Jimmy's with the battery."

"But you said the transmission was gone," I said.

Colin ignored me and went back to the story.

"SO, I KNEW THE TRANSMISSION WAS GONE. But that didn't matter. We put the new battery in and put in a five gallon can of gas. She started right up. We were taking the Battle Wagon to be looked at by Brian's Transmission up on Liberty Hill, Brian is a friend of my dad's. So, I put the wagon in reverse and drove it up to the shop."

"In reverse? All the way?" I asked. "That's crazy. That's like five miles."

"Yes, it was. I don't know how we didn't see a cop. We got lots of strange looks, but no cops," Lance said.

Colin scowled. "Luckily, we didn't see a single cop the entire way," he said. "Brian had the wagon up on the lift and fixed in a couple days. He only charged me for the parts. I was driving everywhere I wanted to go. Everyone at school was asking me for rides. I even had a car full of girls that I was driving home from school. It was glorious."

"So how did it become the Battle Wagon?" I asked after deciding not to make fun of Colin for using the word "glorious."

"That's one of the best parts," Lance answered, he knew the story by heart since Colin loved to tell it.

"The muffler started to go, and you could hear me

coming for about five blocks. It was tons of loud, mean, lime green smoke spitting wagon. It was only natural that people started to call it the Battle Wagon. I loved the nickname and even thought about having it painted on the side, but my dad wouldn't let me."

"That's awesome," I said. "Get to the part about why it's in the backyard."

Colin shook his head and continued.

"I loved riding up behind a bunch of kids crowding the street instead of walking on the sidewalk. You know how they won't move even though they know you're coming up behind them?"

I nodded.

"Well, I would get up close to them, put the Battle Wagon in neutral, then floor the gas. The sound would send them scattering. Everyone knew me and the Battle Wagon. Everything was going great until the dare."

Colin said "dare" like a kid cursing within hearing distance of a nun.

"The dare?" I asked.

"The dare," Lance said.

"Calvin Upton dared me to take the bump on Euclid Hill to see if I could get the Battle Wagon airborne. He said he did it in his father's BMW."

I knew all about Euclid Hill. Everyone in the neighborhood did. Euclid Street coming from Seneca University had a steep hill just before you got to our neighborhood. The road flattened out for about twenty feet before the hill continued. It was a paved ski jump.

Kids knew if you came down the road fast enough you could get airborne, going over the edge of the flat section and continuing down the hill. The gouges in the asphalt were a testament to how many times this had been tried.

"We got Joel Fleischman from the AV Club at school to bring a camera and film me going over the bump. After he had the camera set up, I went up the hill back to the light at Wescott Street. That's about a half mile. I floored it all the way and was going seventy when I hit the bump."

"And he went airborne, boy did he go airborne." Lance laughed.

"I went airborne and kept going at least two houses past where everyone else lands. I hit hard and I heard metal crunching. I slammed on the brakes and was able to keep control while I skidded to the bottom of the hill."

Colin looked away, reliving the flight, a tear in his eye.

"Well?" I asked. "What happened?"

"I cracked the frame. It took me, Lance, Dave Taylor, and Hugh Seeley to push it all the way over here, where I pulled it behind the house. I waited a week before I told my dad. I told him the Battle Wagon was at Lance's house because I didn't have the money for gas. He knew I got fired from the Mini-Mart for not showing up, so he believed me for a little while."

"Did you find out how much it would take to get fixed?" I asked.

"More than he'll ever have," Lance replied.

"What about Fleischman, did he get it on film?"

"We'll never know. His parents sent him to Genesee to live with his grandparents because he was getting beat up too much in Brooklyn. Right after the jump he went back to Brooklyn because he was getting beaten up more here in Genesee," Lance said.

"My father knows all kinds of body shop people but

he's teaching me a lesson by not helping me out," Colin said.

I couldn't think of anything to say except, "Wow."

Colin finished his second beer in another long swig.

"My buddy from Slattery, Will Schultz, just got a part-time job at that body shop across from the National Guard Armory on University Ave. Do you want me to ask him if that's something he could do?" I asked.

"Sure, but I don't have any money and I don't want to get another job to get fired from," Colin responded.

"I'll ask him anyway; he might want to do the work for the experience. The Battle Wagon deserves to roar again," I said, putting my hand on Colin's shoulder.

"It does, it surely does," Colin agreed.

CHAPTER 9
DON'T KNOW MUCH 'BOUT HISTORY

We walked the two miles to the Shoppingtown theatre to see the re-release of *Animal House*. It was the midnight showing and we had started going to the movies as something to do. The fact that Shoppingtown started the midnight movie series after Thanksgiving made it better, because we were all bundled up for the long walk. We were bundled up for two reasons. First, to stay warm for the walk. Second, to squirrel away more than a half a case of beer in our combined pockets. Colin and I wore old Army field jackets. They held six beers each. Lance had a hand-me-down parka three sizes too big with more capacity than our field jackets.

We missed the initial release of *Animal House* a few years before and had to listen to guys that had seen it, ramble on about this amazing movie. They would talk about the best scenes and laugh as they acted out the dialogue. When I saw in the paper that it was going to be the midnight movie, I told Colin and Lance we were going, and I would buy the beer.

The theatre was crowded for the special Saturday night showing. We found seats upfront and started unpacking our beers, settling in for what we had been told was the greatest movie ever made.

Twenty minutes into the movie I drank my beer in short sips after having spit out a mouthful on the unhappy guy in front of me wearing a "College" sweatshirt. I gave him the Belushi shrug of apology I had just seen on the big screen.

Our idiot friends in the neighborhood had not done the movie justice. It was hilarious, way funnier than their feeble attempts to recreate the scenes. I missed the second and third lines after the jokes because the laughing in the theatre drowned out the sound. People were also shouting out the good lines because they knew the dialogue by heart. All of that didn't matter because I was in love with the movie. With my impending trip to college the next September, I saw my destiny being played out on the big screen.

When the lights came on, I was exhausted from laughing. My sides hurt and the effects of drinking all the beers enhanced my enthusiasm. We rolled out of the theatre into the cold night laughing and retelling lines from the movie.

Colin was especially buoyant. Not only did he resemble Belushi in stature and hairdo, he now had his perfect role model.

"My goal is to be able to chug a bottle of Jack Daniels. Mark my words, I'm going to do it," he said with conviction.

"You've never even had Jack Daniels and besides, a bottle of Jack costs like twenty dollars," Lance said, knowing Colin never had any money.

"I know what I'm going to do," I said with one hundred percent certainty.

The guys stopped to look at me because of the seriousness of my tone.

"I know what I'm doing when I get to college."

I was the only one of the guys that hung out at Lance's with designs on heading off to college. The others never entertained the idea of going. They had no interest in high school, let alone college and they had no money to go anyway. I made it to the top of my high school class without even trying. I took a lot of ribbing for it, but I heard Colin brag about my success at school to a newcomer to Lance's house, so I knew they were only joking.

"When I get to college," I said, "I'm going to find the worst animal house fraternity and pledge."

I waited for the laughter and the jokes, but none came.

"Can we come to the parties?" Colin asked.

"Absolutely," I replied, "you guys can show those college guys how to party."

That was an ultimate compliment in our circle of friends, being the best at partying, and the guys puffed out their chests at the thought.

CHAPTER 10
COLLEGE JOURNEY

When I first went to my guidance counselor and told her I wanted to be a writer she laughed and said I'd never be able to find a job. Disappointed but still determined to follow my dream, I left her office and went into the Guidance Library that had hundreds of catalogs and other college and career guides. I had some ideas about which schools sounded interesting, but no real concept about what I should do.

I found a guide with the top ten schools for each major and located "English, Creative Writing." A school I always liked sat at the top of the list, the University of Virginia, founded by Thomas Jefferson. Of all the Presidents I read about in my *World Book Encyclopedias*, I found Jefferson to be the most fascinating. He was the definition of a renaissance man. I had a copy of the Declaration of Independence that Sister Robert gave me in seventh grade hanging on the wall behind my desk.

I went to the shelves and found the catalog for Virginia and signed it out so I could look through all the information. I put the catalog inside my math textbook and paged through it as Sister Ellen went over something I already knew. The campus was beautiful, exactly what I looked for in a prestigious university. They had tough admissions standards, but I scored above their averages for GPA and SAT scores. Then I saw the out of state tuition and froze. The estimated cost for tuition, room, board, and expenses for an out of state student was $17,200. Bishop Slattery's cost of $770 had been a huge hurdle. I had struggled to come up with the money. The tuition looked to be impossible for me. I had a free period after math, so I went to the English Department for some advice.

I headed to Sister Sylvia in the English Department. I really liked her, and she was very supportive of my writing. Sister Mary had made sure that I could submit to the Literary Magazine even though I couldn't attend the meetings.

Sister Sylvia delighted in the idea that I wanted to be a writer and told me the next time I visited Miss Gerherty in Guidance, I needed to tell her I wanted to be an English professor. That would make her more cooperative.

Sister Sylvia started naming off some of the schools she knew had great writing programs. I stopped her when she said the University of Virginia. I told her Virginia stood at the top of the writing programs in a college guide. She told me to get the catalogs for the other schools she wrote on a list so I could compare them and then decide where to apply. Maybe apply to all of them she encouraged.

"Your grades and SAT scores, how are they?" Sister Sylvia asked.

"Really good, I was way above the average for both at the schools I looked at."

"Tremendous. Your writing is some of the best I've seen here at Bishop Slattery. I wish I had you in more than one class."

"Thank you, Sister, I appreciate that."

Buoyed by my talk with Sister Sylvia, I made another appointment with Miss Gerherty the following day. This time I wanted to talk to her about how to pay for college and to tell her that I misspoke. I wanted to be an English professor as Sister Sylvia suggested.

"Great, there is ROTC," she said.

"What's that?" I asked.

"The military pays for your college, and you owe them four years of service after graduation. You are an officer; I think it's a really great deal and with your scores, you more than meet the scholarship qualifications. They pay for your tuition, books, and fees. You also get a monthly stipend for expenses."

Sold. My father and uncles were both World War Two veterans. My family had an extensive military tradition, even after only the two generations in America.

I showed her the schools I had copied from the guide of the best writing programs and the ones added by Sister Sylvia. She helped me find the catalogs, then we sorted through them and only kept the schools that also had ROTC. I had six catalogs to look through to help me make my choice. Most of the schools were in the northeast, a big plus. I grabbed one of the catalogs for St. Benedict's from the big stack on the table near the door. The school was a mile from my house and half of my class planned on attending. They didn't have ROTC, but I could afford the tuition and I could live at home to save a lot of money.

The journey was starting.

CHAPTER 11
FILLING OUT

The applications started to arrive within a week of my requests being mailed. I had all the schools ordered in preference on a checklist taped to my wall, and I filled them out but waited for UVA because I intended on mailing it first. There was also the matter of cost. The fees were going to add up to a week of earnings at the Super Duper. The list showed what I needed to send in with the applications and the fees. I also had the Army ROTC application. The Guidance office proved good for one thing. I made copies of everything I needed to send, the teacher recommendations and my essays. Miss Gerherty, impressed with my work, wished me luck with my choices. She also made sure she sent my transcripts and SAT scores.

Based on the information in the school catalogs I also ranked my chances of being accepted. I was confident I would get into every school, at least wait listed I hoped. I wrote letters to the head of the Creative Writing programs and asked for more details on their curriculum. I let them know that I had applied and would appreciate any additional information.

Once the replies to my requests for more information started coming in, I reordered the schools based on the details. UVA remained at the top. The reply from Donald Russo, the head of the program at UVA, was as magnificent as their catalog. The five-page letter included the exact aspects of the program, the syllabi from the core classes from the previous semester, internships, and workshop specifics. It was the first love letter I ever received.

I didn't excel at sitting and waiting. Even though I knew the responses were months away, I still jogged from the bus stop to my house after school every day and opened the mailbox with great anticipation. I considered myself lucky that I had a lot going on to keep my mind off all the unknowns about my future. My senior year wound down with an inherent sadness as my time at Bishop Slattery neared the end. It had been my salvation from the public school in my neighborhood, a costly one for me since I paid my own way. I also worked as much as I could at the Super Duper, trying to save up for school and everything I would need even if I did get the ROTC scholarship.

I tried to split what little free time I had with my friends from high school and my drinking buddies at Lance's house. Once summer came, Franklin and Marty would leave for their summer camps. Will was moving to Albany and Chuck, like me, worked, trying to make enough money for college. St. Benedict's and staying home, by far my last choice, loomed, but I put all my hopes into the ROTC scholarship and didn't want to have the burden of student loans if I intended to be an impoverished writer.

As Christmas approached, I wanted to forget about all the unknowns about my future, so Marty and I headed to Shoppingtown to buy presents and watch the girls.

"Thinking about buying a present for Anne Begley?" I asked.

Anne Begley worked with Marty on a project in Religion class. Then she started to say hello to him in the hallway. Then something amazing happened, she came and sat with Marty at our lunch table. They were quickly becoming a couple. I was jealous but happy for Marty.

"I really should," Marty said. "I need to make sure I don't ruin this. Do you think it's too early to ask her to the Prom?"

"Yeah, I'd say give it a little while longer. But congratulations, I did my Religion project with the B-O king, Lloyd Huggins, how did you get so lucky?"

"I slipped Father Guarini a twenty." Marty laughed.

"I wished I had thought of that. And had twenty dollars to spare."

"What should I get her?"

"Something that says I like you but not something that says I want to father your children." I laughed.

"So, an engagement ring is out of the question?"

"Start with the Prom and go from there," I said.

Two girls in festive Christmas sweaters walked by slowly and looked at Marty and me as we leaned up against the railing by the fountain in the main courtyard of the mall.

"Merry Christmas, ladies," I said.

They giggled.

"Merry Christmas," they said.

"So, engagement rings, let's go take a look," I said, mainly because the jewelry store was in the direction the girls were headed.

CHAPTER 12
STEALING CHRISTMAS

We were a week away from Christmas vacation and I was the only one at Lance's house. I had just gotten off work and I brought good beer over, a six pack of Heineken, for a little bit of Christmas cheer. It had snowed for the first time in weeks and the snow had me thinking about Christmas. After a few beers, I got the courage to ask Lance a question.

"Why no Christmas tree?"

"We haven't had one since my mother died," Lance said looking into his beer.

"You're kidding me, no tree?" I asked. "But I understand. It's actually one of the things my father is still enthusiastic about after my mother died. I'm glad he goes all out when it's tree time. So, I think you should have a tree too."

"Yeah, my dad wouldn't do anything and I'm sure he'd just say 'maybe' and then do nothing if I asked. But it would be nice to get a tree."

"Then we're going to get a tree; get bundled up." I said. "Do you have a saw?"

"Saw?" Lance asked.

"Just go get it, you'll see."

Lance went to the basement and got the bow saw. I had his coat, hat, and gloves ready when he got back upstairs.

"Let's go get a tree," Lance said. "Who's open this late and why do we need a saw?"

"Who said we were going to buy a tree," I said trying to sound like a criminal.

Lance raised an eyebrow, "How many beers have you had?"

"Two, just like you. But enough to think it's a good idea to steal a tree."

We headed to the high school; I knew the area behind the school was covered in pines. We would go sledding on that hill, so I also knew it was unlikely there would be anyone back there at this time of night. There were no lights on that part of the property and since the snow had turned into intermittent periods of near whiteout blizzard, there weren't many people on the roads either.

We walked around the field until I found a perfectly shaped tree just the right size. It only took a few seconds for the heavy bow saw to slice through the trunk. The tree fell into the snow. Lance and I both grabbed a branch by the freshly sawn trunk and started toward his house, dragging the tree in the accumulation.

We decided to go through the woods instead of taking the streets even though there wasn't anyone around. It was a lot more difficult than we thought and there were a couple times we were going to give up, but eventually we made it through the woods to Lance's house. Lance went into the attic and got the tree stand, lights, and decorations while I built a fire. Once the tree was in the stand, we placed it off to the right of the fireplace. Perfection. It was a balsam fir that hadn't been hedge trimmed like the trees in the lots. It was a magic tree, too perfect and I felt a twinge of guilt for cutting it down.

"Thank you, Christmas tree," I said.

We got the lights on and crossed our fingers. The bulbs hadn't been plugged in in almost a decade. We clinked our beers in celebration when they lit up. I turned off the lights in the living room, so we only had the fireplace and the lights on the tree. We brushed the dust off the ornaments as we carefully placed them on the branches. Lance and I hadn't said a word since the lights worked. We made sure each ornament sat near a light so it would pick up the reflection.

There weren't a lot of ornaments, and we didn't have tinsel. I worried the tree would be bare. We continued until all the boxes were empty. I stepped back and looked at the tree, surprised something happy like decorating a tree was slightly emotional.

The tree had the same effect on Lance; he hadn't said a word in almost a half hour. I felt his pain at the loss of his mother and the fact he hadn't had a tree since she died. I worried for a second how Mr. Sherman would react, but I let the thought pass because I knew this tree was magic.

When we were done, I sat on the couch and Lance took the big, overstuffed chair. We opened our last beers and marveled at our handiwork. It was the most beautiful tree I had ever seen.

The fire cracked and warmed the living room, making it almost comfortable. I fell asleep on the couch.

I woke up around 2:00 AM. Mr. Sherman had come back home from his night at the Mohawk Tavern. I could tell he had added more logs to the fire.

He saw I was awake.

"This was your idea I take it?" he asked.

"Yes, I hope it's okay. Lance and I had a few beers—"

He cut me off. "It's fine." He never took his eyes off the tree.

I got up, grabbed my coat, and started to get dressed to go home.

"It's the best tree I've ever seen Mr. Sherman, I hope you like it."

He turned his head and looked at me for a second before he went back to the tree. I slipped out and slid home.

CHAPTER 13
CHRISTMAS MIRACLE

Christmas 1978 would go down in the history of Genesee as the Christmas of the miracle snow. The holidays were tough in our quiet house since my mother died. My father tried his best to keep the traditions my mother loved going, but the more he tried, the more I could see him missing my mother. One time he put up the manger scene that my mother loved, and I saw him staring at the figurine of Mary. I went to my room to do some homework and when I returned an hour later to get a drink, he was sitting in the exact same position staring at the Blessed Mother.

The weekend after I helped Lance get his tree, we brushed off the station wagon and drove over to the VFW's Christmas tree lot. My father splurged on the tree even though it would take up most of our tiny living room. We always got a blue spruce, if they had one, or a nice balsam fir if they didn't. We went up and down each row of trees, my father inspecting them for flaws as I held the spruce or balsam after shaking off the snow. He would instruct me to turn it to the left or right and after a few "hums," he would either classify the tree as a "maybe" or "we'll" keep looking." I didn't mind the process because I knew he used to try to impress my mother with the perfect choice. But it didn't matter what tree we brought home, she would declare it "the nicest one we've ever had."

After three or four trips around the lot, my father would narrow the choices down to a couple of trees. When he really couldn't decide, I would drag the candidates to one spot so they could be compared side by side. When the choice was finally made, we paid the man in the plywood shed and my father and I would tie it to the rack on the station wagon and head home. My father had started a new tradition when it was just the two of us. We would stop at Orville's Diner for dinner. He always got meatloaf with mushroom gravy and mashed potatoes. I would get the fried chicken with french fries. Dessert had to be the rice pudding, which Orville himself proclaimed to be the "best in Genesee." To prove it, he had framed a copy of the write up in *The Genesee Herald* officially certifying the pudding as the best.

When we got home, we would put the tree in an ancient cast iron tree stand that was so heavy we never had the trouble of the tree tipping over. I had to put down newspapers as we let the remnants of snow melt off the tree and the branches relaxed in the warmth of the house. Our tiny bungalow soon filled with the scent of pine. It was nice even though I had to lean over to watch television around the bottom branches poking in front of the screen.

My sisters came over to help decorate for one of the few gatherings where everyone was at the house. My father watched all his kids from the kitchen, where he sat at the table listening to the radio. He never really graduated to television, preferring to sit at the kitchen table listening to the few existing programs he still enjoyed. The show he never missed played on Sunday mornings. It was an old Italian guy from the neighborhood who'd grown up with my father. He played his favorite songs by Sinatra, Dean Martin, and Louis Prima. He would talk about the old times in the Italian neighborhood, when the kids of the turn of the century immigrants filled the north side of Genesee played baseball in the streets and tried their best to become Americans. He would go on at times in Italian and my father would laugh and occasionally wipe away a tear.

On the night we decorated the tree, three days before Christmas, they were playing Christmas songs. My sisters were fighting over the placement of ornaments. I went into the kitchen for some eggnog. The weather report came on with the bad news that there was no hope for snow. For the first time in my life, we wouldn't have a white Christmas. All the snow from the previous storm (the night that Lance and I went to the high school) and earlier in December had melted. I never had to dream of a white Christmas because in the near polar regions of Genesee, New York, the one thing we never lacked at Christmastime was snow.

"Dad, do you ever remember a Christmas without snow?"

My father pondered my question for a moment.

"Just a few, not many really."

"I'm serving Midnight Mass this year. I know I told you I was done being an altar boy, but Monsignor came up to me after Mass last Sunday and asked why I wasn't on the list. I told him it must be a typo and he could add me anywhere he wanted."

"You lied to the monsignor?"

"I said what he wanted to hear. Is that a lie?"

"Probably not. Your aunts are going to miss you."

"Tell all my aunts I'm serving at Mass. That'll settle them down. Besides, we'll see them Christmas Day."

The aunts were my father's eight sisters. They still did a traditional Italian Christmas Eve with the seven fishes. I didn't mind missing the feast because I couldn't think of one fish I liked, and all my aunts would be pushing platefuls at me admonishing me for being too skinny, and telling me I needed to eat. I would miss doubling the opportunity for having money stuffed in my pocket because they had had a few too many whiskey sours with the feast, but I had Christmas Day to make up for what I would miss out on, and I knew that saying, "So sorry I missed last night" to each of my aunts would add to my score of cash.

By tradition, our family get together was held at my Aunt Vicky and Uncle Gennaro's house. We spent Christmas Day at my Aunt Eva's and Uncle Dominic's place. They both had spotless houses big enough for the family. Instead of potpourri, they had sauce on the stove all the time. They lived a block away from each other on the far northside, where most of the families from the Italian neighborhood moved after they made a little money.

On Christmas Eve, I kept the radio on to hear the weather reports. Nothing resembling good news, not the slightest chance for snow. I turned on the public television station. *It's A Wonderful Life* was on for the second year in a row. I had watched it for the first time the year before and instantly fell in love with the movie. It was set in upstate New York and could have been any of the small towns between Genesee and Rochester.

When the movie finished, I dressed to go to mass. I walked outside at eleven. My frosted breath was the only thing that blocked the stars in the cloudless sky. I walked down to the end of the street and went into the basement of the church to start all the preparations assigned to the older altar boys, tasks I knew by heart and enjoyed more than I would admit.

I always got there early so I would have my choice of the best cassock, one with snaps instead of buttons. I chose my favorite one, still warm from when the ladies that cleaned and decorated the church had ironed and starched them to perfection. Along with one of the other older guys I helped the younger altar boys get ready to make sure they looked their best. The talk among the guys as we waited for midnight was usually about the presents they hoped awaited them under the tree, but this Christmas Eve, we focused on the absence of snow. At 11:50 we herded all the servers up the back stairs to the narthex to line up. Monsignor gave us a quick inspection, but he knew the older altar boys had things squared away.

The sanctuary, decorated in pine garland and poinsettias, was standing room only. I looked around for people I knew, giving a slight nod of my head to my friends during the procession. My familiarity with midnight mass, my favorite of the entire year, helped me take my mind off the snowless Christmas awaiting me outside.

The first part of the hour-and-a-half service flew by because of all my responsibilities. I followed Monsignor through his blessings and the Consecration. I went into the vestibule to light the incense and piled it on in the thurible to make it extra smoky. I loved the way the smoke rose to the ceiling and combined with the flicker from the candles on the altar. I imagined a Catholic rock concert, a thought I kept to myself because the other guys would think I was crazy.

After Monsignor finished with the incense, I walked down the back stairs to dump the charcoal in the parking lot. As I stepped out of the back door, I slid on my heel a few inches. Snow! It was snowing – a real Upstate New York blizzard. I dumped the incense in the fresh accumulation and relished the sound of the sizzle as the snow extinguished the hot embers.

I wanted to stay outside in the blizzard, but I had to get back to the Mass. I ran up the stairs, put the censer on the counter to cool off and went back out to the altar. My friend Chuck Lucas looked over at me and saw my wet cassock.

"Don't tell me it's raining, that's even worse than not snowing," he whispered.

"Nope." I tried not to laugh.

It took Chuck a minute to think through my response. "Snow?"

"Yep," I said, again trying to hold in my excitement and keep my response to a whisper.

"No way."

"A blizzard."

It was hard to concentrate through the rest of the service. I wanted to go back outside and see how much it had snowed. After the service finished, and I had completed putting everything away, I ran to the basement and put on my coat and ran outside. The parking lot was still packed because people were busy brushing off their cars. There must have been six inches on the ground, and it was still snowing.

All my friends were standing in a group by the front steps of the grammar school.

"Can you believe it?" I yelled as I joined them.

"I told you it would snow," Franklin exclaimed.

"Right," Chuck said, "you're the regular Channel Three weatherman."

A snowball flew by us from another group of younger boys, and we quickly counterattacked. No one wanted to leave even at that late hour, but we didn't want to get in trouble on Christmas either.

I said goodbye to my friends and ran home. My father was back from my aunt's, the station wagon sat covered in snow, he had to be asleep by now.

I turned around and started walking. After a block I jogged, envisioning George Bailey running through Bedford Falls at 2:00 AM on Christmas Day in the unpredicted blizzard. I waved to the imaginary people and wished them all "Merry Christmas."

The snow had transformed the drab and replaced it with a dazzling cover of white. I ran for blocks until, finally exhausted, I turned for home. The warmth of the house welcomed me as I took off my coat and boots. I quietly walked up the stairs to my room and opened the curtains to my window overlooking the street. I didn't mind my cold bed. I was warmed by watching the miracle snow falling in the glow of the streetlights.

CHAPTER 14
A CHRISTMAS TO REMEMBER

I woke before dawn, excited by the prospect of a white Christmas and a trip over to my Aunt Eva's house for all the great food and the cash I missed the night before. I walked down the stairs from my bedroom. I could hear that my father had risen. He was in the kitchen listening to the news on the radio. I went to the front window and looked outside. The world had been transformed and it continued to snow. I don't think I ever saw as much snow as on the morning of the miracle.

The street hadn't been plowed and our station wagon sat buried in the driveway, the snow halfway up to the fake wood panels. I went into the kitchen just as another weather report began.

"We already have three feet on the ground, and we expect at least another foot before the front finally moves off to the east. There is a continuing blizzard warning, with wind chill temperatures below zero and drifts of over eight feet," the announcer said with official seriousness.

The news followed with more of the same reports. The

city remained shut down with almost all the roads unplowed. Because of the forecast of clear weather and the holiday, the Public Works had a minimal staff and now the snowplow drivers were stuck in their homes and couldn't get to the garage. The city used the skeleton staff to plow the streets to reach the stranded drivers and bring them in to work. Once they had enough drivers, the plowing would start with the major roads. It would take all day, so they were advising everyone to stay home.

"I already called your Aunt Eva," my father said when they went to a commercial. "Of course, everyone is staying home but we'll try again tomorrow because we can't let all that food go to waste."

"Is there anything here for us?" I asked, already missing my Aunt Vicky's baked ziti.

"We'll have to scrounge and open a few cans," my father said.

"For Christmas? The Super Duper is supposed to be open today. Mr. O has that four-wheel drive Dodge Ram and prides himself on never getting stuck. I'm going to get dressed and see if he opened the store."

"I doubt he made it, but if he did, that'd be great. I'm not looking forward to pork and beans for Christmas either."

I showered and dressed and headed down the hill to the Super Duper. Our street was not plowed, and I walked in the road because the sidewalks were in worse shape. Genesee Street was unplowed, but at least it had some tire tracks from daring motorists. I rounded the corner to the store. Mr. O's big orange truck was parked out front.

The doors were locked. A handwritten sign hung in the window: "Please Knock." I did as instructed, and Mr. O opened the door after a minute. He let me in and relocked the door.

"You're not scheduled today, what are you doing here?" he asked.

"Merry Christmas to you too." I laughed.

"Not very merry. We are snowed in, none of the deliveries are here of course and I'm waiting on Mr. Leonard to call to see if he wants me to stay. Everyone else scheduled for today called in and said they couldn't make it."

"Have you had any customers?"

"Just one person so far and he was only looking for the newspaper."

"I'll call my father and let him know I'm going to hang out here with you for a while in case you need any help."

"You don't have to do that," Mr. O said.

"We aren't going over to my aunt's house. I have nothing else to do."

I called my father, then grabbed a Coke from the cooler. Mr. O had opened a package of donuts and put them on the end of the register, so I scarfed up one of those too.

"I have to get some food for our Christmas dinner, so you'll have at least one customer," I said.

"I'm really hoping Mr. Leonard lets me shut the place down. This isn't worth my time. Plus, I have a bottle of Crown Royal under the tree that needs to be attended to."

"All my presents are at my sister's house. Since I'm not going to my aunt's that means I won't be seeing my sister, so no presents for me, not today at least. My father probably has one thing for me that he just remembered he bought and he's wrapping it now while I'm out of the house. I got him some pipe tobacco with a fancy pouch, I really went all out," I said. "I chipped in with my sisters and we got him a Lazy Boy; he's going to love that."

A city plow went down Genesee Street and left a huge snowbank at the entrance of the parking lot.

"Well, I guess we won't have any customers now," Mr. O said shaking his head.

"I can shovel a space big enough for one car," I said.

"No, don't bother, I'm calling Mr. Leonard and telling him that we are going to close. Why don't you go ahead and grab some beer, the good stuff, something for Christmas."

"Really? If you say so."

"For your dad." He winked.

I went to the beer cooler, straight to the import section. After looking through the different European beers and changing my mind several times, I settled on a six pack of Heineken and a six pack of Becks. My father rarely drank but I hoped he would make an exception for Christmas. I went to the bakery and got a fruit cake for dessert. I inherited the rare fruit cake gene from my father, we both loved it.

Mr. O made a bigger sign saying that we were closed for Christmas. I returned to the front of the store with my provisions. He also had a box full of food. I looked in and saw a couple of deli packages, a container of the store-made kosher dills, a loaf of the best rye bread from the local bakery that we sold at the deli, a bottle of Russian dressing, and a jar of sauerkraut. Mr. O pointed to the stuff in my arms.

"Throw that stuff in this box, it's all for you."

"Really?" I asked.

"The big package is corned beef; the other is some Swiss

cheese. You can steam the corned beef and make Rueben sandwiches. It's not a Turkey dinner, but it'll do," Mr. O said as I finished looking through the box.

"Thank you, they are one of my father's favorites. I can ring this up, which register do you want me to use?" I asked.

"Don't bother. Consider it my present. Merry Christmas. Go home and enjoy."

"Really? Thanks again. Be careful going home Mr. O. And tell that bottle of Crown Royal he never stood a chance. Merry Christmas."

It was tough going up the hill from the store with my box of supplies for our impromptu Christmas dinner, hardly the Seven Fishes or the trays of lasagna and antipasti in Aunt Eva's kitchen, but I still looked forward to a big sandwich, some great beer, and hanging out with my father.

I struggled to get in the door with the heavy load. Dad heard me coming in and helped me before I could put the box down.

"What's all this?" he asked.

"A Christmas present from Mr. O. The fixings for hot Reubens and good imported beer." I smiled.

"Well, I'm hungry, what about you?"

"Mangiamo."

"I'll get the corned beef warmed, you get your coat off and find something good on TV."

I tried all the channels for something worth watching. We had gotten cable the year before, so we were lucky there were choices. I found *Going My Way* on TBS and set up the trays for our Christmas feast.

My father brought the plates in, the corned beef

steaming and glistening with fat. The sandwiches were huge, Mr. O must have given us a couple of pounds.

"I'll get the beer, sit down Dad," I said as I ran into the kitchen.

I opened two and returned to the living room with the beer. My father picked up the bottle and read the label.

"German beer? You know that during Christmas 1944 I was in Belgium. The Germans were trying to kill me."

"Oh, I'm sorry, I didn't think about that. I'm sorry Dad."

My father took a sip.

"Tastes good, I'm just busting your chops, Joe,"

I smiled and picked up my bottle.

"A toast then, to a great Christmas, the miracle of the snow and to my father for not letting the Germans shoot him and making them realize they should stop fighting and go back to making beer."

We clinked bottles.

Since I had applied for an ROTC scholarship, and my father had mentioned the Army, I decided to ask him about the war. I had tried bringing up the subject a couple times before, after reading something in the encyclopedia or seeing a movie, but my father would only say that the war was a "long time ago".

"So, Dad, what was that Christmas like in Belgium?"

He chewed his corned beef slowly. I expected the same answer.

"I had just turned twenty and had been away from home since Christmas of 1942 when I had my last leave before we were shipped to England for the invasion."

"D-Day? I asked.

"Yes, but that's another story. The German attack

before Christmas 1944 was unexpected. We were sitting back, looking forward to a real meal for Christmas. We thought they were about to surrender. It was tough. I don't know how we held the line with what we had. It was so cold. We didn't have enough food or ammo. But we held."

He started to say something then stopped and took another bite.

I knew a lot about the Battle of the Bulge, so I changed the subject, happy with what little he had said.

"Great sandwich, isn't it?"

"Yes it is. This has been a nice Christmas," he replied, his eyes shiny from what had to be his thoughts of the war.

"You know Dad, I think you have done a great job and I like this Christmas with just the guys."

"Thanks," my father said, looking a little surprised.

"But next year, let's definitely go back to all the food, you playing cards with Uncle Gennaro and the guys, and me having money stuffed into my pocket by your sisters."

"Sounds like a plan." He chuckled.

We ate our feast and watched the movie. My father seemed somewhere else, but he did that a lot. The war? Thoughts of my mother? I never knew for certain.

The huge meal left me stuffed. My father fell asleep before the end of the movie.

He was asleep when Bing Crosby surprised Father Fitzgibbons with the visit from his mother. I thought of my own mother and couldn't hold back the tears. I went into the bathroom until I finished crying.

CHAPTER 15
NO NEED FOR ALARM

My complaints to the guys about how Mr. Leonard was always screaming at me, telling them how bad a boss he was, always giving me dirty looks seemed to be a daily occurrence. Colin looked at me and went immediately to his hero for inspiration, Bluto from *Animal House*, "Delta gets even."

"What can I do to get even with Mr. Leonard? I need the money for my tuition, and I can't do anything to get fired. I'm surly to the customers and I goof off as much as I can get away with, again without getting fired. In some ways I have already bested him."

"But does he pay you enough to take the abuse?" Colin asked.

"No, but what can I do? I really don't have a choice. I can't get a job where I have to take the bus. There's no way I could play basketball, get my schoolwork done, and spend half the day on the bus."

"Egg his new Lincoln Continental?" Lance suggested.

"Naw, that's not a good one, he'd probably make a

stock boy go out and wash his car and that stock boy would probably be me," I replied.

"How about we run into the store with masks on and rip off his cheap toupee?" Colin asked.

"I like where you're going with that, it's public and embarrassing," I replied.

"What does he really hate?" Lance asked.

"Besides his employees and customers?"

"Yes, we know he hates you, that's why we are wasting our time talking instead of slashing his tires," Colin said trying to imitate Belushi.

"He hates when we have to call him after he leaves the store," I said. "We're supposed to call Mr. O first. Leonard in a last resort call."

"What would he come back for?" Lance asked.

"A problem with the alarm was the last thing, he was furious. We had woken him up," I replied.

"Then we break in and set off the alarm." Colin jumped up, "Let's go." He ran out of the room still channeling Belushi.

"And get arrested and I lose any chance at a college scholarship?" I shook my head.

"Is there any way to set off the alarm without breaking in?" Lance asked.

"I pounded on the windows once and George yelled at me that I would set off the alarm," I answered.

"That's it," Colin said as he came back into the room. "We get up on the hill on the other side of the road."

I immediately understood where Colin's thoughts were heading. The hill opposite the Super Duper was all woods before an open space of fifty feet at the bottom before the road. It was our favorite place to throw snowballs at cars because if anyone stopped, we would run into the woods. We'd played there all our lives. We would split up and run down different trails we knew even in the dark before we met up behind Dave Taylor's garage. Same routine every time. No one could find us if they even made it up the hill to the woods.

"We throw snowballs at the windows, not hard enough to break them, no ice balls you idiots, just hard enough to set off the alarm," Colin said. Lance and I were already grabbing our coats.

We went over the plan once we reached the edge of the woods and peered at the big windows of the Super Duper. Genesee Street looked to be clear of traffic, so we took our positions where we could reach the windows with a good throw.

"Here we go," I said as Lance and Colin took their designated spots to look down Genesee Street for the police.

I made a snowball and let it fly. It fell about ten feet short of the front door.

"Maybe we should have had a man throw the snowballs," Colin said,

"Eat me," I said as I made another snowball.

This time my trajectory held true, and the loosely packed snow made a perfect "plunk" when it hit the window dead center.

"I guess we should have asked if it was a silent alarm," Lance said, this time without calling me a name.

"I think it is silent because we always have to run out of the store when George sets the alarm. Even when we take too long and don't lock the last door in time, I never hear anything. I haven't seen anything in the store that resembles a real bell like you see in the movies. There are sensors on all the windows though. That I know because I see them when I'm lowering the shades at night."

"Okay, let's give it a minute and see if the first one worked," Lance said.

We all waited. After a few minutes of nothing happening I broke the silence.

"This time let's all throw one. I'll take the window I hit, Colin you take the one to the right and Lance you take the one on the left."

No more instructions were needed. We made our snowballs.

"Okay on my command," I said. "One…two…three…throw!"

The snowballs flew in slow motion and hit their mark in succession: mine, Lance's, then Colin's. We were certain that did the trick.

"Okay, let's get back about twenty feet into the woods so no one can see us, and we can still watch the store," I said.

We only had a wait a few minutes before a city police car came down Genesee Street from the direction of downtown. It pulled into the parking lot of the Super Duper, made a slow lap around, and then pulled back onto Genesee and went to the loading dock. A cop got out and inspected the loading dock doors. He drove back to the front of the store to check the main door. As he walked along the row of windows, Mr. Leonard's Lincoln pulled into the parking lot, sliding to a halt in the snow. He got out in his bath robe. On his way to the policeman, he slipped and fell on his backside.

"GODDDAMMMMMMMMMM-

MOTHFFFFFFFFFFFFFFFFFFFFERRRRRRRRR," echoed through the parking lot. Mr. Leonard struggled to get back on his feet.

I stuffed my gloved hand into my mouth to keep from making noise. The policeman was laughing.

I looked to my side to tell Lance and Colin we should leave quietly but they were already running down the trail to the garage. I got up and broke into a full sprint without looking back.

CHAPTER 16
CALVIN UPTON

Calvin Upton was one of the more unusual characters who hung out occasionally at Lance's house. His parents were professionals, his father a professor at Seneca University and his mother a doctor, although she had gone part-time to home school Calvin.

Calvin's parents didn't think he should waste time doing things regular kids did, so they loaded him down with schoolwork and rarely let him outside. He excelled at taking advantage of what little freedom he was allotted and when he visited Lance's he always wanted to do something crazy.

He wore t-shirts from bands none of us had ever heard of and spiked his unruly hair to mirror his contempt for all rules. He was the tallest kid in our group but instead of being gangly, he moved with the stealthy confidence of someone who owned the world.

We did outlandish things at Lance's because of the complete lack of parental supervision. Once he was released, Calvin's home incarceration manifested into lunacy.

Calvin even dared to sneak out in the middle of the night and drive his father's BMW around the neighborhood. He bragged about this, but he didn't have any way to prove it, but he got Colin to believe that he had jumped Euclid Hill in his father's car, which led directly to the demise of the Battle Wagon.

The first time I met Calvin, he showed up at Lance's house with a grocery bag full of egg cartons.

"Who deserves to get egged?" he asked without saying hello.

Of course, Colin and Lance had a long list of suggested targets.

Before the eggs were halfway gone, we were being chased by a coach from the neighborhood Little League we all disliked because his teams always won. Houses, cars, schools and even the sign of the Lebanese convenient store were disfigured with yellow stains.

Back at Lance's we opened a couple beers.

"Where do you live?" I asked Calvin.

"You know that big house that backs up to the church yard? The one with the turret?"

"Yeah, my mother loved that house," I replied.

"Well, that's where my parents keep me prisoner."

"Prisoner?" I asked.

Calvin then filled me in on his situation, how he finished school at fifteen and spent his days going up to Seneca University with his father and auditing classes.

"My parents want to wait another year till I'm seventeen before shipping me off to Harvard."

"Harvard, really? Wow," I replied.

"Where's Harvard? Lance asked.

I ignored the question and jumped in with another for Calvin.

"How did you get hooked up with these delinquents if you're going to Harvard and didn't go to public school?"

"I was looking for trouble one night and asked around. Everyone had the same answer: go see Lance Sherman," he said. "What about you?"

"They found me, I work at the Super Duper, and I can buy beer. I'm handy to have around," I said, holding my beer up as proof.

"Great, that's good to know. Hey, I have a new one planned; I want you guys to be the first to know."

"What?" Colin asked. "I really hope something explodes."

"Tell Joe about the time you convinced the emergency room that you just got back from Africa and then gave them all the symptoms of dengue fever," Lance said.

"Yeah, I still want to know how you faked a hundred and four temperature so I can use it to get out of school," Colin said.

"A true magician never reveals his tricks," Calvin said with a smile.

"I really want to see something explode this time; what are you going to do Calvin," Colin asked.

"Nothing like explosions, but I'll keep researching that idea. You guys keep an eye out, you'll see. If I do it right, I think it has the potential to turn a pedestrian city like Genesee on its head." Calvin smirked. "I need to get back home before I get caught. See you guys later."

CHAPTER 17
SAVING

We received a rare invitation from Olivia, a girl Lance and Colin knew from school to a party at her house. Olivia's mother planned to be out of town, and she had the house to herself. She had permission to have a few of her girlfriend's sleepover so she wouldn't be alone but after a week of talking about it at school before Christmas break, it had turned into a house party with the entire junior class of Armatas High School.

I got to the party late because I had basketball practice. The walk from the gym was terrible because the wind chill came in close to zero. I pulled my wool cap down as far as I could over my wet head, but I could feel the ice forming on the hair that stuck out.

The party was well underway, the crowd bigger than anyone expected, because word had continued to spread even though it was vacation break. Olivia had blocked off the upstairs and the formal living room, so we were jammed mostly into three rooms on the ground floor.

Somehow, she managed to get the smokers out onto the covered front porch.

As I walked up to the front door, the smokers eyed me suspiciously, a kid they didn't know with icicles hanging off his hair.

Colin called to me from the doorway to the dining room where he was talking to a couple girls. He had a huge smile, and I could tell something was up. He waved to me to hurry. When I got to him, I could see he was holding something behind his back.

"What are you hiding?" I asked.

"Something I got with some of my Christmas money."

"Don't tell me you bought liquor."

"Yep," he said as he pulled the bottle out. "Jack Daniels".

"Where did you get that?" I asked.

"Like I said, I took my Christmas money and had Mr. Sherman buy it for me," Colin said almost giggling.

"Why haven't you cracked it then?" I asked.

When he started laughing, I realized what he was thinking.

"No, you can't do that," I said. "I'll pay you for half of the whiskey. We'll get some shot glasses and pass them around."

"No, I'm going to chug it, I'm just drinking a couple beers to get warmed up."

"You've never had JD before and you think you can chug the whole thing, you're crazy."

"If Belushi can do it, I can do it."

"That was a movie and that was iced tea."

"Belushi is my hero and when I do this, I'll be a legend

in the neighborhood. I've dreamed of this ever since we saw the movie, you know that."

"I don't want you to."

"I'm going to chug it, I already told everyone I was," Colin said. He yelled into the crowded room. "You guys saw *Animal House?*" He held up the bottle. "I'm going to chug this bottle of Jack in honor of my hero John Belushi. When I do this, you guys have to call me Bluto."

The crowd cheered. Colin walked into the middle of the room, the kids creating a circle around him. He held the bottle up again and unscrewed the cap. He took a sniff.

"Ahhhhh," he said to even more cheers.

"Here it goes," Colin said. He lifted the Tennessee whiskey to his lips and started to drink.

I expected him to last only a couple swallows, but he kept going. A quarter of the bottle, then almost half. Then he wobbled and stopped not even half of the way through. Everyone still cheered and started patting him on the back. I took the Jack Daniels from his hands and put the cap back on. His eyes were glazed over and he lost his balance. The people behind him were barely able to support his bulk as they helped me get him to the couch in the family room.

He looked up at me and slurred. I think it was, "Arrrrrggggg."

"Next time, Colin," came the calls from the partiers.

I sat down next to Colin and turned his head so I could see into his eyes.

"Are you okay?" I asked.

"Yeth," he replied.

"Okay, just sit here for a while and I'll check on you."

I mingled, made my rounds through the people, checked on Colin every ten minutes or so. He snored. I imagined the Battle Wagon's engine racing with a failing muffler. I grabbed a beer and went to talk to some of the girls I knew from the Super Duper. When I went to go get them more beers, I cut through the family room to check on Colin. Three kids sat on the couch.

"Where's Colin?"

They didn't know. I asked the people next to them; they didn't know either. I went into the kitchen. No one had seen him. I went up and checked the bedrooms, hoping he had woken up and headed for an empty bed, but he wasn't there either. I checked every room in the house and then turned off the music and yelled, "Has anyone seen Colin?"

"There's his coat, so he must still be here," Lance said.

I don't know why, but I grabbed my coat and headed outside. It was even colder than when I left basketball practice. I ran through the snow towards Colin's house. After passing about ten houses, something caught the corner of my eye. I started to run faster. Colin was passed out in the bushes in front of a house a block from the party. He only had on a t-shirt; he shivered in the snow. I picked him up and shook him. His eyes fluttered for a second. I opened my coat, and tried to cover him as much as possible.

"Home," he slurred.

It took all my strength to get him to his feet. I barely weighed one-hundred and sixty pounds and Colin outweighed me by almost a hundred. I dragged him the remaining block and a half to his house. As I started to try to carry him up his front steps, he woke up.

"No, my dad, you can't take me in, take me back to Lance's."

I tightened my grip and headed towards Lance's house, two and a half blocks away. I opened the front door and somehow carried him to the couch. I ran upstairs to Lance's bedroom, took all his blankets, and went back down to the living room.

I covered Colin in everything I could find. I made sure he was breathing and on his side in case he got sick. I built a fire and dragged the couch closer to the fireplace until I could feel the warmth. When the color started to return to his face I collapsed into a chair.

"Do you need a beer," someone asked. It was Lance. He had come from the party after he realized Colin and I were gone. Dave Taylor and Hugh Seeley were behind him in the doorway.

"I need an entire case. I found him passed out in the freaking snow a block from the party. He didn't have his coat. He would have died if I hadn't realized he was gone. Lance, we can't be this stupid," I said before my emotions bubbled up and I couldn't talk.

Lance left and returned with a beer. He sat next to me and put his arm around my shoulder.

"Anything we can do?" Dave asked.

I shook my head no.

"What made you leave the party?" Hugh asked.

"Something, I don't know. I just knew I had to go," I said, taking another drink from my beer.

"You're a hero Joe, a real hero," Lance said.

Colin snored loudly and twitched. His snoring grew louder, and we all began laughing. I laughed until my sides hurt.

"What a night," I said.

CHAPTER 18
MY WINNING SEASON

I played CYO Basketball for Our Lady of Sorrows all four years of high school. It was a lot of fun playing in the Catholic League and we had pretty good teams. My friends Marty Reilly, Will Schultz, and Chuck Lucas were also on the team, which added to the enjoyment of playing.

We won our division my first three years, but we managed to fall somewhere along the way in the playoffs. The previous two seasons we had made it to the championship game but lost on a last second shot and then failed in a late comeback the following year. The pain of those losses lingered into my last season, but it was tempered by the fact that we had all our players coming back for our final year. We were optimistic about our chances to win the championship.

Our coach, Don Cook, wasn't much older than his players. We enjoyed playing for him because he didn't yell at us or scream when we made a mistake. His punishment consisted of time on the pine, which I clocked quite a bit, but not because I made a lot of mistakes. I just wasn't that good. I tried as hard as anyone on the team, which won me some respect. At the start of my last season the team elected me captain. I reveled in the great honor and felt the importance of the pre-game meeting with the referees and the other team's captain. For most games this consisted of my only meaningful trip onto the court.

Since we were so good, I mostly saw playing time at the end of games when we were up by forty or fifty points. "Garbage time" as we called it, began with the subs like me leaning forward from our spots on the bench when the clock was winding down and it was obvious that we were going to win. Coach Cook even took the extra step of calling a time out to save those last few minutes and make sure the scrubs like me got a chance to play.

We rolled through our senior season undefeated in our league. We had an average winning margin of over twenty points, but we hadn't yet played our rival, St. Athanasius. Athanasius was a parish five times our size and their best player was a brute. He played starting linebacker for one of the city high schools and had secured a trip to college on a full scholarship to play football. We couldn't stop his strength, but they had a very hard time stopping our speed. We were a running team, taking advantage of fast breaks, making a lot of steals, and generally just out scoring our opponents.

We also had a couple fearless guys that would take a charge from the brute, so part of our strategy was to get him in foul trouble. We also had the advantage of a home game, so our bleachers would be packed. We didn't need much motivation beyond the fact that we genuinely didn't like them. If I had been a tougher guy, I would have asked the coach if I could go in and try and pick a fight with the brute to get him kicked out of the game, but I didn't have a death wish.

The gym was standing room only well before the start, as we expected with a game against our hated rivals. The contest progressed, close throughout as the lead changed hands back and forth. The crowd louder than any we had ever had. Everyone stood throughout the entire game. Near the beginning of the fourth quarter, a scuffle broke out. It nearly turned into an all-out brawl. Coaches and officials caught it just in time. But the spark lit our fuse.

As Coach Cook walked back to the bench, he waved the crowd into a frenzy. I started kicking the bleachers and soon everyone joined in, stomping up and down. When play resumed, we grabbed that energy and ran them off the court. We faltered for the last two minutes as they tried a futile comeback, but in the end, we won by nine points.

We all rushed the court and hugged as a team, followed by the crowd. We celebrated on the court for a long time. It was, at that point, the greatest sports moment of my young life.

CHAPTER 19
THE CHAMPIONSHIP

The first two rounds of the playoffs were easy wins. I even got to play in both games. The semi-final proved to be our toughest contest short of when we faced St. Athanasius. We were plagued by poor shooting and a lack of energy. Once again, a near fight sparked us into a run after our best player received a cheap shot when he went up for a layup. We succeeded in running them off the court after the foul.

We stayed to watch the second semi-final game to see who our opponent would be. We had a choice of who we wanted to play. They ended up losing by forty points. We left at the end of the third quarter, knowing we would face the toughest team in all the Catholic Youth Organization, St. Jude Thaddeus. Everyone knew St. Jude Thaddeus was the patron saint of impossible causes; the impossible cause being beating their basketball team. They had crushed St. Athanasius. No one said it, but I know we felt we didn't have a chance.

The game, scheduled to be played at a former Catholic high school gym, by far the biggest gym we had ever played in, added to the magnitude of what we faced. Our fans never travelled well, but surprisingly we had a better representation than everyone expected.

We stayed close in the first half but at the start of the third quarter we fell behind. We were down twelve points by the beginning of the fourth quarter. We huddled before the start of the final period that would be my last fifteen minutes of organized basketball. The coach looked around the huddle.

"You guys have had a great season. You have fifteen minutes to make it greater. Dig down and grab whatever you have left. Throw it all out there. There is no tomorrow. We can win this, so go win it."

We had the ball to start the quarter and went down the court and scored. They missed a shot and we scored again, the margin now within single digits. Then the greatest play anyone ever witnessed in the long, prestigious history of Genesee basketball happened. Our best player, Mike Gerald, stole the ball.

Mike sprinted down the court, the two opponents chasing were well behind him when he jumped. In my mind the play happened in slow motion, which makes it a better memory. He rose above the rim and slammed it in with a two-handed dunk. Mike wasn't much taller than me, but he could jump through the roof. He had never tried to dunk before, and I'm one hundred percent certain there had never been a dunk in the Genesee CYO League.

Our bench went crazy. The crowd went crazy. The other team became frazzled. They called time out when we tied it up. We were up by ten with twenty seconds left when Coach Cook looked down the bench and looked at me. He didn't say Joe; he said "Captain".

I ran to the scorer's table and went in for Mike Gerald who received a standing ovation. I knew the cheers were for him, but they still made me feel as if I walked on air. I don't remember what happened in those ten seconds. I counted with the crowd until the final buzzer sounded.

As the captain, I was the one called out to center court to receive the trophy. I remember trying as hard as I could not to tear up, but I lost that battle. I returned to the bench with the trophy over my head and handed it to coach. After being so close so many times, we were finally the champs.

CHAPTER 20
INTERVIEWING

The letter from the Army ROTC office at Seneca University arrived in late February. The instruction said to call the secretary and schedule an interview for the scholarship application process. I called as soon as I finished reading the letter.

The appointment scheduled for 2:00 PM, the following Thursday. I had no idea what to expect. I didn't have a suit yet, which I planned on buying closer to graduation. I took the bus to Shoppingtown and bought an off the rack, navy blue, three-piece suit. I didn't know anything about a good brand or good material for a suit, but the salesman said it fit well and it was something I could afford.

When the day arrived, I left school early, taking the bus downtown and transferred to another bus back to my house, where I changed into my new suit. It was a cold, dreary rainy day, so I asked my father if he could give me a ride. He dropped me off about a half-mile from the ROTC office because the roads on campus were restricted. I walked in the rain, holding an umbrella, trying to follow the campus map I took from the Seneca University catalogue I got in the guidance office.

Stopping to ask someone directions once, I found the office with thirty minutes to spare. I went into the bathroom and tried to dry off the best I could, mad at myself for not bringing a hairbrush or a comb. I wanted to make myself presentable; I needed to calm my nerves.

After a few deep breaths and one final inspection, I went into the office and introduced myself to the secretary. She took me to the student lounge to wait until the officers were ready. I studied the posters depicting various jobs within the Army, histories of famous units and a uniform guide next to the full-length mirror. There were students coming and going, some in uniform. I immediately felt at home, both at the university and with the cadets. My desire to be a part of all of this was increasing with every minute that passed.

I became more nervous than I had been for anything in my life, more than anything with school, basketball and even the close calls walking the neighborhood. I put both hands on my knee to stop it from bouncing. I tried to concentrate and focus to get rid of my nerves. It seemed like I had waited an hour but when I looked at my watch it had barely been ten minutes.

The secretary finally came and got me, and I followed her into the colonel's office where he waited behind a desk. A captain and a major sat in chairs off to the side. I had known all the ranks since I memorized them as a little kid from the Army section of *The World Book Encyclopedia.*

The colonel motioned for me to sit on a couch, which I sunk into, making it seem like they were towering over me. This was my first real interview ever. The one at the Super

Duper lasted a minute. I looked over the wall of the office at Mr. O before he went back to talking to my father about the horses.

The questions went around the room. I answered, numb. I tried to say the right thing. The officers were stone faced and I had no idea if my answers were what they expected. I tried to fit in the fact that my father was a D-Day veteran and his brother had fought in WWII, the Korean War, and did two tours in Vietnam. He retired as a command sergeant major after thirty-three years of service. I told them I had always wanted to be a soldier. I emphasized how my family's service served as a source of inspiration and that I would be honored to wear the uniform. I hoped they would be impressed by such a statement coming from a teenager just a few years after the tragic end of the country's involvement in Vietnam. I hoped they could tell I was sincere because I really did feel that way. But they had probably heard the same lines from all the other candidates.

Sweat ran down my side. I just hoped my forehead wasn't drenched. I told them about paying for my own tuition at Bishop Slattery, working, playing sports, and keeping my grades at the top of my class. This seemed to impress them. I went into more detail about how I went to a public school for one year and knew right away it would be a hinderance to reaching my goals, so I got the job and went to Bishop Slattery. I continued about how I played CYO basketball and even though I rode the pine the team voted me the captain in my final year.

I didn't bring up wanting to be a writer in case my career goal didn't fit into what they were looking for in future officers, so I told them I was undecided and was still considering several majors for college.

"So, I see you have excellent grades and on top of that you played sports and held down a job to pay your own tuition?"

"Yes, that's correct," I answered.

"That's very impressive, but remember these scholarships are very competitive, but congratulations on all that you've accomplished so far," the colonel said.

They finally lightened the mood and asked some easy questions. At the end they asked if I had anything for them, I had no idea I would be able to ask, so I thought quickly.

"How do the different branches work and how do you get assigned to a particular one?"

The answer was a confusing mix of Army terms, but I smiled and nodded in faux understanding.

I asked, "How does the Army determine where you are stationed?" Then, I inquired about current morale in the Army since they had gone to the all-volunteer force, because I had seen a story on the news about the problems they were having. They were honest and told me about the challenges. The post-Vietnam Army tried to find its footing, so it could move forward after all the division in the country. The colonel had been in Vietnam, and he thought things were getting better but they still had a long way to go. He told me that the ROTC program at Seneca University had come within one vote of being kicked off campus in 1970. The current corps of cadets was small but solid. I asked about the program at the University of Virginia. They said that around the country it was pretty much the same except for schools close to military installations where a lot of the students were children of active duty or retired personnel.

"What are the next steps in the process?"

"This interview is the last step. We have your SAT scores and your high school transcripts. We'll add a write up summary of the interview with our recommendation after we discuss your full application," the colonel said.

"It has been my lifelong goal to be in the military and I hope you gentlemen will recommend me for a scholarship," I said with all the confidence I could muster.

The officers nodded.

"The decisions would be made on May first. You will be informed by mail of your status," the colonel said.

They stood and thanked me. I got up off the couch, but the strength had gone from my legs, and I hoped they didn't see me wobble a little. I shook all their hands firmly and looked them in the eye. They wore name tags, which allowed me to thank them each by rank and name. They seemed impressed by this added touch.

The secretary showed me out and I walked down the stairs and out onto campus. It had stopped raining and there were a few breaks in the clouds. I saw a snack bar and bought a Coke and a bagel with cream cheese to replace some of my depleted energy from the stress of the interview. I grabbed a seat on a bench and watched the students walking through the quad on their way to class or just going back to the dorm. Even though I hadn't spent more than a few hours on an actual college campus, other than St. Benedict's, this felt so right to me. It felt like home. The John Denver lyric, "coming home to a place he's never been before," came to mind. That was me – sitting on a bench, surrounded by the ivy-covered buildings where I didn't have to watch the people coming towards me and wonder if I had to run.

I walked the two and a half miles home instead of trying to catch the bus. I cut through the neighborhoods, old houses chopped up into student apartments, big Victorians that had seen better days and finally to my neighborhood where I just walked and didn't bother to notice if there was anything to worry about. I don't know what would have happened if a group of bad guys had seen me in a three-piece suit and carrying an umbrella. I wonder if I could run in my dress shoes. I made it back to my house without incident, glad to have taken such a big step toward my future.

a lot of the students were children of active duty or retired personnel.

"What are the next steps in the process?"

"This interview is the last step. We have your SAT scores and your high school transcripts. We'll add a write up summary of the interview with our recommendation after we discuss your full application," the colonel said.

"It has been my lifelong goal to be in the military and I hope you gentlemen will recommend me for a scholarship," I said with all the confidence I could muster.

The officers nodded.

"The decisions would be made on May first. You will be informed by mail of your status," the colonel said.

They stood and thanked me. I got up off the couch, but the strength had gone from my legs, and I hoped they didn't see me wobble a little. I shook all their hands firmly and looked them in the eye. They wore name tags, which allowed me to thank them each by rank and name. They seemed impressed by this added touch.

The secretary showed me out and I walked down the stairs and out onto campus. It had stopped raining and there were a few breaks in the clouds. I saw a snack bar and bought a Coke and a bagel with cream cheese to replace some of my depleted energy from the stress of the interview. I grabbed a seat on a bench and watched the students walking through the quad on their way to class or just going back to the dorm. Even though I hadn't spent more than a few hours on an actual college campus, other than St. Benedict's, this felt so right to me. It felt like home. The John Denver lyric, "coming home to a place he's never been before," came to mind. That was me – sitting on a bench, surrounded by the ivy-covered buildings where I didn't have to watch the people coming towards me and wonder if I had to run.

I walked the two and a half miles home instead of trying to catch the bus. I cut through the neighborhoods, old houses chopped up into student apartments, big Victorians that had seen better days and finally to my neighborhood where I just walked and didn't bother to notice if there was anything to worry about. I don't know what would have happened if a group of bad guys had seen me in a three-piece suit and carrying an umbrella. I wonder if I could run in my dress shoes. I made it back to my house without incident, glad to have taken such a big step toward my future.

CHAPTER 21
MOTHER MARY COMES TO ME

Every morning for as long as I could remember, my father sat at the kitchen table in the mornings listening to WGEN, the news station on the radio. I would come down to get ready for school and find him reading the paper with the radio volume turned up loud due to his hearing problems. He always had my bowl of cereal filled and the milk sitting next to it when I got out of the shower.

"Anything new?" I asked.

"The mayor is going to jail for taking all those kickbacks."

"And that's supposed to be a surprise in Genesee, New York?" I asked.

"Another mysterious statue of the Virgin Mary was found yesterday morning at the Blarney Stone Restaurant on Liberty Hill," the announcer said, cutting short our discussion of Genesee politics.

"This is the second statue that has been found in Genesee in the past month. No one has claimed responsibility for the prank, but the appearances might just be miraculous." The announcer laughed at his own joke.

"Speaking with Blarney Stone owner Gerry McGowan, he told WGEN News that when he arrived to open the restaurant Mary was sitting on top of table twenty-three facing the door. We've reached out to the Diocese of Genesee for comment, and we'll bring that to you once they return our call."

"What's that about?" I asked.

"Somebody probably thinks it's funny, leaving statues around town, just some kids."

"What if it isn't." I laughed. "You should talk to Monsignor and tell him to change the church's name to Our Lady of Blarney Stone."

"Very funny Mr. Comedian, hurry you're going to be late for the bus."

CHAPTER 22
THE SURPRISE WOMAN

Lance's older brother Andy had moved back home after a stint in the Army and a few forays into different jobs out of state. Ten years older than Lance, he attended a county technical school, studying to be an electrician. He looked exactly like an older version of Lance with a huge mop of pre-electrocuted hair that seemed appropriate for the profession he had chosen. We hardly ever saw him because he worked when he didn't have class. We looked forward to the few occasions when his friends gathered at the house, especially when we were able to join in their party if Andy was in a generous mood. It helped his mood if we bought beer to be added to the tub of ice on the back porch as a price for access to his friends.

We would hang on the periphery and try to look cool holding our beers, listening in on the conversations, waiting for the chance to jump in and say anything. They used the huge, screened back porch for their parties, because it was the nicest part of the house. We liked watching the girls. They were way too old to be interested in us, but their conversations were completely different from the high school girls we knew. They were unattainable and mysterious, almost a different species. We could not help being drawn into their personalities. They had a surprising level of independence created by the luxury of not having to be home before eleven.

One girl in particular consumed my interest, a petite redhead. She smiled at me once. Just the acknowledgement that I was a person sent my heart soaring. Anytime Andy's friends stopped over, I always looked for her and kept telling myself that I would talk to her if I got the chance.

On the first wonderfully nice day of the spring, a cool breeze, sunshine, and the smell of the world blooming again signaled another tough Genesee winter was finally over, Lance, Colin, and I were sharing a six-pack I brought from the Super Duper after I got off work. We were sitting on the back porch enjoying the weather, talking about nothing in particular.

"Beers?" Lance asked.

Colin and I chugged what we had left as a signal to Lance that we were ready for another round. Lance stood up and grabbed beers from the tub of ice and tossed them to us.

"Hitting the head," he said as he walked inside.

I opened my beer and gave the bottle opener to Colin.

"Someone's coming," Lance said when he returned from the bathroom. "I think my brother is here with some friends."

"I hope those friends are girls," Colin said.

"That would be nice," I said thinking of the redhead.

I tried to act nonchalant as Andy and his friends came out onto the porch.

"Lance, go grab more chairs," Andy said to his brother without saying hello.

I watched the arrivals file through the door. My heart sank until the redhead finally walked in, the last person to come out on the porch. They added a case of beer to the tub of ice, another good sign. It meant they might be staying for the rest of the evening.

We learned they had just come from a happy hour at R.J. O'Toole's. Andy appeared to be a lot more accepting of our presence. Lance went inside and turned on some music. He put a speaker in the window of the porch.

They continued with their party without Andy objecting to our presence. I was happy that we successfully kept our spots on the porch, our first hurdle to being tolerated as part of the crowd. We slowly made our moves, each of us leaving our corner of the porch and mixing in, trying to join in on the different conversations.

A seat opened near the redhead, and I waited for the other girl that left to come back, but when she did, she sat on the railing with another group. I gathered my courage and took the empty seat. She looked up and smiled when I sat down.

"Who are you?" she asked.

"Joe, I'm Lance's friend." I tried not to twinge from my stating the obvious.

"Hi, I'm Gwen. You still in high school?"

Again, I had to try hard not to react to a question that could ruin my attempt to talk to her.

"Yes, but I'm a senior, so I'm finishing soon. I'm going to go to the University of Virginia," I said even though I hadn't heard whether I'd been accepted.

"Wow, that's a great school, you must be really smart."

I shrugged a shy yes. "I'm going to be in the Creative Writing program, I'm want to be a writer."

"What are you going to write about?"

"I don't know yet. I like to read, mostly the classics right now, you know the required books for school. I got a reading list from one of my favorite teachers. I submitted some short stories to our literary magazine but I was kind of hoping they would teach me what to write at Virginia. What about you? What do you do?"

I wanted to ask if she had gone to college but didn't know if that was a good question. Knowing Andy's friends, her chances weren't great, and I didn't want her to think I was trying to be snobby. I knew I had a lot to learn about talking to girls. I was also incredibly nervous, but the beers helped.

"I work up at Seneca University for the free tuition. I'm slowly making my way through school a couple credits at a time."

"That's great, what's your major?"

I heard this was the first and best question to ask a college girl.

"I'm an Art Education major. I want to be an art teacher. I'm pretty close to finishing. I'm also a waitress at O'Toole's up on campus. I have to save up for when I student teach and take a leave of absence from my day job for the semester."

"Where do you want to teach, here in the city?"

"Not really, probably one of the suburbs because they spend a lot more on their art programs."

"Right, the city's tough. You don't want to teach where I go. We have art at Bishop Slattery but it isn't much."

"Bishop Slattery, that explains going to Virginia."

"Yeah, I went to Clinton for a year and then got a job to pay for the tuition at Slattery myself. My father couldn't afford it."

"Really? That's impressive. You're full of surprises. What are you doing hanging out with this crowd?"

"I think I could ask you the same question."

"The girl in the red tank top is my sister," she said pointing across the porch. "I go out with her to keep her out of jail."

"Really?" I asked.

She started laughing.

"Don't believe everything I say."

"Okay, thanks for the good advice."

"You're cute for a high school kid."

"That I'll believe because it's true." I said quickly, surprising myself with my courage. I hoped in the dim light of the porch she couldn't see my flushed face and the perspiration on my forehead that had popped up like the spring flowers outside.

"So do you have a girlfriend, cutie?"

"No, I don't. I'm very shy."

"You don't seem that shy now."

I held up my beer to show the source of my power.

"So, what type of art do you do? Are you a painter?"

"I try to paint, some ceramics also. I just like working with the kids; it's a lot of fun."

"I'm sure it's a great job. I think writing will be enjoyable, I hope. I'm afraid I won't make any money at it though. I haven't told my father I want to be a writer, but I think he's just happy that I'm going to college."

"You could teach English while you're writing, but try for the college level. Stay in and get your master's degree.

There's more money and time to write if you teach at a college. The professors at Seneca that teach in the Creative Writing program have published novels. I saw the display they have outside their offices."

"That's a great idea," I said, holding my gaze at her a beat too long. I felt a blush start again.

"So, what else do you do besides hanging out at Sherman's and drinking with your friends?"

"I work at the Super Duper on Genesee Street to pay my tuition like I said. I played CYO basketball; we won the county championship this year. Actually, I sat on the bench most of the time, but I was the team captain. I also applied for an Army ROTC scholarship, I'm supposed to hear if I got it soon."

"Really, how did you get so motivated?"

"I don't know. I just know that I want something more. I can't explain it, but I see the kids at Slattery. Their fathers are doctors and lawyers. They drive new cars. I'm not envious, but I can tell getting to that level will take a lot of work."

"Then why be a writer instead of one of those doctors or lawyers?" she asked.

"That's a great question. I'll make a final decision once I get to college and have more information. Who knows? I may take a required class in something like economics and find out I was born to be an economist."

"I can't see how anyone would be born to be an economist." She said, laughing. "Can I buy you a beer?" she said, pointing to my empty bottle.

"I can do it," I said taking her bottle and trying not to run over to the tub while I looked out of the corner of my eye to make sure no one took my seat. I hurried back and opened her beer before handing it to her.

"Thanks. How about a toast, to our futures. You'll have to put a character named Gwen in one of your novels. Of course, she'll have to be beautiful and smart, just like me." She winked.

"That's a deal," I said as we clinked bottles.

Gwen's sister walked up.

"I told Mary I would meet her at the Lost Horizon at midnight after she gets off work."

"Joe, this is my sister Joanie. Joanie, Joe."

"Hey, kid."

I winced.

"Hi, Joanie, nice to meet you."

She nodded and turned back to her sister.

"Are you going to come with me?" Joanie asked.

"I guess I have to. Are you sure you don't want to stay here?"

"I told Mary," she said.

I said a quick prayer that Gwen would stay.

"Go get her and bring her back here. This is a nice party, and the beer is free," Gwen said.

"Let's go," Joanie said. She looked at her watch.

"Okay, I'll go."

Gwen turned to me and put her hand on top of mine.

"It was nice talking to you Joe. Look forward to seeing you next time Andy invites us over."

She stood and kissed me on the cheek. Out of the corner of my eye I could see her shirt fall open a little when she leaned forward. I could see the top of her lacy, baby blue bra. It was the most beautiful thing I had ever seen, and I tried not to stare.

"We are always hanging out here. You guys should come over more often. We have some good parties," I said.

"Deal," Gwen said.

I watched her walk away. She turned and looked back at me and smiled.

CHAPTER 23
96 ROCK SIGN

Lance received an unexpected present from his oldest sister at Christmas, a decent stereo system with an equalizer and big Bose speakers. She won it at a raffle at a bar and didn't need something so loud in her house, so she gave it to Lance. The stereo was a big step for all the parties we were planning on throwing and because it added to our increasing credibility as a place to hang out.

There was a new rock station in Genesee, 96 ROCK. It was the first FM station to play Led Zeppelin, Lynyrd Skynyrd and the other music we liked. A 96 ROCK button on your gym bag or bumper sticker on your locker door gave you instant coolness. Lance's stereo was always going, tuned to our new favorite station. If the weather was nice, we would sit outside with the speakers in the windows.

We were sitting on Lance's front stoop talking about our usual meaningless subjects, lamenting the lack of female acquaintances and other general nonsense when a city bus went by. The buses now carried advertising on the side panels, big plastic ads in metal frames. We hadn't noticed the signs before even though one went past Lance's house every twenty minutes. We never paid any attention until the bus with the 96 ROCK sign splayed across the side drove past us in a cloud of diesel smoke. We jumped up from the stoop and ran after it for a few houses, just to make sure it was real. We immediately began to plan how we were going to swipe a sign and put it up on the back porch.

"How are we going to steal a sign from a moving bus?" Lance asked.

"Obviously we'll have to get it when it stops," I replied.

"But it only stops for a few seconds to let people on," Colin said.

"Then we need a good plan," I said.

"What if we find out where they park the buses at night and steal one then?" Colin asked.

I cocked my head. "The parking lot is on the other side of town; it's near my uncle's shoe store. How are we going to get there and back with a fifteen-foot sign? Take the bus?".

"Colin can lie down in the road and block the bus. He can pretend to be tying his shoe or something. That'll give us enough time," Lance said.

Colin nodded his head.

"Even though I have Colin gets hit by a bus in the pool on how Colin dies, I don't want to win," I replied.

"Well, we need a plan, we just don't know yet. Let's just keep thinking," Lance said.

The next day at school I prepared for my part for our plan. Bishop Slattery was situated out in the suburb of East Genesee, about five miles from my house to the front door. Since we didn't have our own school buses, we relied on chartered city ones to pick us up and take us home.

The buses lined up in front of the school. I stood by the door of my homeroom waiting for the final bell, ignoring Sister Mary as she told me to sit back down. I stared at the clock and tried to will the second hand to go faster. The moment the bell rang, I sprinted down the hall and went to the first bus with a sign.

I inspected the bracket. I ran my fingers along the bottom of the aluminum without finding a latch or anything. I looked at the top of the frame, hurrying while the buses were loading up. Again, nothing. The left side of the frame looked different. I took out my house keys and tried to pry up the metal. With just a minimum of effort the left side popped up. I put my hand on the sign and slid it about an inch out of the frame. The sign was a hard plastic, maybe a quarter inch thick, but flexible. It would be easy for two people to carry. I couldn't wait to tell the guys.

§§

Colin and Lance were right where I expected them, on the front stoop watching the buses. I sat down without saying anything and waited for the next bus.

I didn't have to wait long. Colin and Lance got up and ran alongside looking at the sign for clues. They tried to keep up, but couldn't after a while. I sat on the stoop laughing.

"What, you don't want the sign anymore?" Colin huffed as he sat down next to me.

"Catholic schoolboy chickened out," Lance said.

I laughed at them which only made them angry.

"I knew you'd be too afraid to steal a sign," Colin said.

"Nope," I said.

"Nope what?" Lance asked.

"Nope," I said again.

"You better say something else other than nope or I'll knock out your teeth," Colin said.

I looked at them both and continued to laugh.

"That's it," Colin said standing up and cocked his arm.

"I know how to get the sign," I said. I ducked out of the way just in case Colin didn't hear me before he threw the punch.

"What? How?" they said together.

I explained my actions at the end of the school day, telling the story in every detail. A minute in, as I told them how Sister Mary yelled at me, Colin got up to hit me again. I fast forwarded to the part of looking the bracket over and about how the left side of the frame flipped open and the sign slid out.

"You're sure that's how it works?" Colin asked.

"Positive," I replied.

Colin and Lance looked at each other.

"Okay, what do we do?" Lance asked.

"Two guys to get the sign and maybe two guys to stop the bus somehow," I said proudly. I was now the authority on the subject.

We set up the plan for a Saturday. It gave us the most time and the best chance for a bus to go by with the sign. Colin and I waited at the bus stop. Lance sat down on a wall bordering a driveway about forty feet from the corner where we stood.

We enlisted Hugh Seeley and Dave Taylor to help. They were positioned on Lance's stoop. Their job was to give us a signal if the next bus carried the sign on the sidewalk side. We did a couple of dry runs to test out the timing. We went over the sequence of events and made sure everyone knew the signals.

The first six buses didn't have the 96 ROCK sign. We were about to give up for the day when Hugh and Dave jumped up off the stoop as a bus approached Lance's house, giving us the signal. This was it. Colin and I walked to the edge of the sidewalk like we were going to get on the bus. Hugh and Dave came down from Lance's house to help get the sign out of the frame.

The bus stopped for Colin and me, and the plan sprang into action. I stepped up onto the first stair of the bus.

"Does this bus go to Shoppingtown?" I asked.

"No, just came from there," the driver said.

"Where's the stop for Shoppingtown?"

"On the other side of the road, kid."

"Okay thanks," I said. I stepped off the bus and Colin stepped up.

Lance and the other guys had the frame open and were sliding the sign out.

Colin stood at the coin deposit searching his pockets for the fare. First his front pockets then his jacket.

"Either pay or get off," the perturbed driver growled.

"I got it here somewhere," Colin said.

"I have an extra quarter," I said. I gave Colin the signal that they had the sign.

"Naw, I can't owe you man, thanks anyways," Colin responded.

"Get off the bus, kid," the driver said. He started to look into the rearview mirror just as the guys were about to duck behind some bushes with the sign.

"ROXANNE," I sang. "You don't have to put on the red light, ROXANNE."

Both the driver and Colin turned to look at me. Out of the corner of my eye I could see that the guys were almost out of view.

"ROXANNE," I sang again just to make sure.

"Is your friend okay?" the bus driver asked.

"He's just a little brain damaged," Colin responded. "Sorry, I don't have the money, maybe next time."

Colin stepped off the bus and we waited for the driver to turn onto Salt Springs Road. When he was out of sight. we ran over to where the guys were hiding.

I looked over the gleaming black and yellow block letters. "We did it."

We hung the sign over the spot where we kept the beer tub.

We stood back to admire our handiwork. "Everyone is going to think we are so cool," Lance said.

"I think we need to go get some beers at the Super Duper and invite a few people over so they will know we are so cool," Colin said. He ran his hand over the smooth plastic, then gave Lance an impromptu high five.

"And by 'we,' you mean me," I asked.

"Of course," Lance and Colin said together.

CHAPTER 24
PEPE

Across Genesee Street stood the neighborhood of Drumlin Hills. The houses were majestic and expensive. The man-made barrier of the major road and the prices of the houses protected the neighborhood from white flight. We would cross over Genesee and stroll into Drumlin Hills, usually late at night, when we felt like taking a walk without having to worry about being confronted, fighting, or running for our lives.

The higher you went into Drumlin Hills, the more expensive the homes became. The tiny 1200 square foot house I lived in with my father seemed like a shack compared to these homes. It seemed that way because it was true.

We got to a dead-end street we hadn't ventured up before, I looked at Colin and Lance and they both shrugged, 'Why not?'

The higher we got on the hill, the more the houses resembled mansions.

"If someone sees us, they'll call the cops," I said. "We have no real business being here."

"It's a free country, we're just walking," Colin replied.

"I'm just saying, look at us and look at these houses. Ray Charles could see that we don't belong here," I said.

"I have every right to walk down this street, and no one is going to stop me," Colin said, his voice rising.

As Colin and I escalated our argument, Lance kept walking, ending up a few houses ahead. I began to counter Colin's last statement when Lance stopped us by saying, without emotion, "Look, guys".

We jogged up to Lance and looked where he pointed. In the yard, perched on an ornate base, a statue, an old-fashioned lawn jockey. I laughed. Colin said, "Cool."

"I want him," Lance said.

"What?" I asked. "Want him in what way. Are you in love?"

"No, Lance's right, I want him too," Colin said.

"Okay, let's think about this," I said. "It's a statue, it probably weighs a couple hundred pounds. We don't know how it's anchored in the ground. That base alone could be a couple hundred pounds of concrete. We are at least two miles from Lance's house. How can we carry all that weight that far and make it all the way back without someone seeing us especially the cops. No officer, we found him on the side of the road."

My logic had no impact on Colin and Lance. They had ventured into the yard to look over the lawn jockey.

"Guys, get out of the yard, now we have nothing to tell the cops because you are actually doing something we aren't supposed to be doing," I said.

"We are doing something. You are still a pussy in the road," Colin replied.

Colin pushed on the statue; it didn't budge. Lance joined him. It still didn't move. Colin kicked at the dirt around the base. They were talking but I couldn't make out what they were saying. I kept looking up and down the street for the police and then at the house, waiting for a light to come on.

Finally, Colin and Lance left the yard and joined me in the street. They started walking down the hill.

"We going back to Lance's?" I asked.

"Yep," Colin said.

"Good," I said, "we were pushing our luck standing in that yard."

We crossed over Genesee Street, back into our neighborhood. Colin and Lance started talking as if crossing the boundary made it safe to talk out loud.

"I have a heavy rope at my house," Colin said.

"I have that old crowbar in my basement," Lance said.

"What about a sledgehammer, do we have one of those?" Colin asked.

"Dave probably has one, but we can't go over to his house now," Lance replied.

"You guys want to go back and steal that lawn jockey," I said. "You aren't going to carry all that stuff back over there, then carry it back along with the statue. We'd need ten guys."

"We don't need ten guys, just a car," Lance said.

I knew right away what he meant. We were going to take Lance's father's car back up to the house, knock the statue off its base, and put it in the back of the station wagon to bring it back to Lance's house. The guys in our group didn't fully adhere to the laws that governed driving and vehicle registration. When Lance briefly had a paper route when he was fourteen, on a very cold winter morning, he and Colin decided they didn't want to walk all the blocks of the route, so Lance took his father's car keys and drove his beat up station wagon around the neighborhood. While Lance drove, Colin threw the papers from the back seat.

"You guys are crazy," I said.

"Yes, we are," Colin said.

We reached Lance's street after 3:00 AM, the bars had closed and when we turned the corner we could see that Mr. Sherman was home, the station wagon parked askew in the driveway. Colin turned toward his house to get the rope. Lance and I continued to his house. Once inside, Lance went to the basement for the tools he needed. I waited in the living room trying to think of a way to talk them out of this caper. Lance came back into the living room loaded down with supplies.

"I'm going to put everything in the car, then I'm going to go get the keys," he said as he looked up the stairs to his father's bedroom.

I could hear Mr. Sherman snoring. After a night at the Mohawk Tavern, I knew he was passed out drunk and that Lance had a very good chance of getting the keys without waking him. The floor above me creaked every few seconds. I pictured Lance sneaking up on his sleeping father. Finally, I heard Lance coming back down the stairs. He didn't say anything, he just shook the keys in front of my face.

Colin came in the front door with a coil of rope.

"Ready?" he asked.

"Yep," Lance said.

They both looked at me.

"Coming?" Colin asked.

"I'm in, just to do what I can to keep you guys from doing something crazy," I said.

"Too late," Colin replied.

Lance started up his father's car. As it rumbled to life, we looked at the bedroom window for the light to come on. After a minute we felt assured we hadn't awakened Mr. Sherman. Lance slowly backed the car out of the driveway. It took us only minutes to get back to the house with the statue. Lance drove past it, turned around, shut off the engine, then coasted down the hill, stopping near a huge maple tree in front of the house. Colin and Lance took the tools to the yard. I stayed in the car.

They tied the rope to the lawn jockey and started to dig and pry at the base. It didn't look like they were making any progress. They both grabbed the rope and started to pull without any luck. Colin walked about thirty feet away from the statue. He got down into the football three-point stance he used as a lineman for the high school team. He took off as fast as his squat legs could carry him and hit the statue at his full speed, putting a shoulder into the statue with all his force. The lawn jockey flew off its base and Colin fell to the ground holding his shoulder. Lance stood in shock. I jumped out of the car and opened the tailgate.

"Let's go," I said just loud enough to be heard.

Colin staggered to his feet. "That's how it's done."

I ran over and the three of us tried to pick up the statue. It took us a couple of tries to get the right balance and a good five minutes of stopping to rest to get it to the station wagon and in the back. We threw the tools in the back seat and rolled down the hill to the stop sign before

Lance started up the car. The trip back to Lance's house remained silent until we pulled into his driveway.

Colin still rubbed his shoulder. "I can't believe we did it."

"You guys wanted him. I have to give you credit for your determination," I said.

"Let's at least get him in the house," Lance said.

The three of us pulled the lawn jockey from the back of the station wagon and onto the screened porch.

We leaned him up against the wall under the 96 ROCK sign and stepped back to look at our accomplishment.

"It looks like he's belonged there all his life," Colin said.

"Perfect," Lance said.

Colin lifted his shirt. He had a large, dark bruise spreading on his right shoulder.

"Well, we need to have a party while I have this or no one will believe the story," he said inspecting his bruise.

"He needs a name," I said.

We looked at the faded paint, his red and white jockey's uniform, his hand held out to hold a long-missing lantern. His face had been painted white to cover a previous and no longer acceptable darker face. It gave him a strange complexion.

"Pepe," Lance said, mispronouncing it as "pay pay".

"Perfect," I said because my suggestion was going to be Pedro since we were all huge fans of Cheech and Chong.

"He needs something," Lance said. He ran back into the house.

He returned with a snug red knit cap like Cheech wore in the movies and put it on Pepe's head.

"Perfect," I said again.

CHAPTER 25
MARY'S THIRD APPEARANCE

We heard about the third appearance of a statue of Mary at an assembly at school. Father Cronin made the announcement at the beginning of an assembly.

"The Blessed Mother was found at the Putt-Putt behind the McDonald's on Genesee Boulevard. She was blocking the windmill on the Par 3, 18th hole," he said. "While we are gladdened by the outpouring of the faithful that have been going to the sites of where the statues are being left, we don't condone the use of the likeness of the Virgin Mary in a prank. This is your one get out of jail free card. If any of you have been involved in this in any way, I want you to come to my office and confess. If this happens again and we find out it's one of our students, then you will be dealt with in an appropriate manner."

I looked over at my friends sitting next to me on the bleachers and shrugged my shoulders. I leaned over to Marty.

"Good prank but I won't turn you in until there's a reward."

"Same to you," he said.

"Do you think it's someone from school?" Chuck asked.

"If the next one shows up as a hood ornament on Father Cronin's car, we'll know it is," Franklin said.

"It really is getting crazy though," Will said. "My father said that there were buses of people all the way from Buffalo that came to pray to the statue."

"I heard we'll make the national news if it happens again," I said. "Monsignor McCarthy told my father that all the parishes got a letter from the Bishop, and are supposed to talk about the statues at all the masses this weekend."

"Well, maybe we should go downtown to the Catholic Shop and buy a bag of one hundred plastic rosaries. They only charge five dollars for the bag," Chuck said.

"To do what?" I asked, even though I knew exactly what Chuck intended to do.

"A hundred for five dollars, that's really cheap," Will said.

"Sell the rosaries to the people getting off the buses. It's five cents a rosary," Chuck said trying to regain control of the discussion. "If we sell them for a quarter, that's twenty cents profit per rosary, that's twenty bucks."

"You'll have to split it with Marty," I said.

"Marty, why Marty?" Chuck asked.

I started laughing. "Because I'm pretty sure he's the one putting the Mary statues around town. Now I get to turn Marty into Father Cronin for the statues and Chuck for the selling of indulgences."

"And I thought this was going to be a boring assembly," Franklin said.

CHAPTER 26
CONGRATULATIONS

I'd sent my applications for the University of Virginia and the Army ROTC scholarship months ago. I had made it a habit to check the mail when I got home from school. Four other schools had responded: accepted at three and wait listed at my second choice. This made me very worried about my chances with UVA. On the weekends I was always away when the mail came, either working or out with a group of my friends. I disliked the growing exercise in frustration because the closer I got to the end of the school year, the level of disappointment from an empty mailbox grew.

The officers at the ROTC office at Seneca University had told me the decision on who would get the scholarships would be made by May 1. The date had come and gone weeks ago.

I called the same number where I had arranged my interview. The secretary said the decisions had been made but there must have been some delay. The staff usually got a list of potential cadets around the same time, but the list had not arrived at the office. I thanked her for the information even though the news made me worry about the outcome.

I had talked over the three schools where I had been accepted with my father, Sister Mary, and Miss Gerherty. None of them made sense without an ROTC scholarship. More determined to go to UVA than ever, I began to wish that I had only applied there.

The letter from UVA came on a Monday. I got home from school and opened the mailbox, expecting the same disappointment I had been getting for the past several weeks. The first thing I saw was an envelope with the seal of the University of Virginia. I almost screamed.

I grabbed the letter and examined it closely. There was some rule about letters from colleges that I couldn't remember at the moment. Was a single page letter bad news? Was a big envelope with a lot of information supposed to be good news?

I grabbed the letter and ran out of the house, too afraid to open it up. I had put all my hopes into Virginia and if I didn't get in, I might be going to St. Benedict's up the street, which to me amounted to four more years of high school, living at home, and doing exactly what I was doing now.

Not that I would be unhappy with what I was doing. I had a great time hanging out at Lance's, also hanging out with my high school friends as the school year wound down and working at the Super Duper. With basketball season over, I had a lot of extra time, but compared to all my friends who didn't work, I seemed to be really busy. I had more to do in a week than they did in a month.

I went up to the Our Lady of Sorrows school parking

lot, to the cement base around the flagpole where my friends and I used to sit and talk about what we were going to do with our lives. I never had any idea what I wanted to do other than I didn't want to work in a department store like my father. The notion of being a writer was still a dream.

    I held the envelope to the sun and tried to read the letter inside. I began to open it when I saw a group of about ten guys walking up the hill. I didn't recognize any of them, which wasn't good. I watched for a minute then knew by their body language that it would be better if they didn't see me sitting there alone. There was a big guy in the center of the group. He seemed to be the leader because the others were orbiting around him. He had on a Los Angeles Dodgers baseball cap, something I hadn't seen in Genesee before. This group screamed trouble and I was an easy target.

    I walked away at an angle to make it more difficult for them to see me. I shook my head in disgust that I had to do such things, but I had learned lessons the hard way about getting caught alone when a group of guys like this came my way.

    The first time, they pushed me around when I rode my bike up to the plaza where the Lebanese guys now had their store. There used to be a small drug store that sold models and I loved to use any extra change to get a military airplane model or a car, the Mustang was my favorite.

    I circled behind the church, so I had the option of cutting through backyards to my house or going into the church itself. The church provided a great place to escape but because of the growing crime in the neighborhood, it wasn't always unlocked, so I had to act quickly if I couldn't get in.

I thought I heard voices. Maybe the guys were going down my street, I couldn't chance it any longer, so I went into the back door of the church by the rectory. I put my fingers in the holy water font and blessed myself, looking to heaven and saying thanks for the unlocked door.

I went into the basement where they kept all the cassocks in lockers and the tables where the ushers counted the donations after mass. I considered the church basement a good place. I remembered my first-time serving Christmas Eve midnight mass. My job was to walk in with a candle then walk out with the same candle at the end – nothing in between. Even with my limited responsibility, I worried about making a mistake. I could envision tripping on the hem of my cassock, falling, setting some old lady's wig on fire.

I grabbed a chair and sat down at the table. I took a deep breath, opened the envelope, and unfolded the letter. I took another deep breath and began to read.

Right after Dear Joseph was the word" congratulations." I had to wait to read the rest because I couldn't see with the tears in my eyes.

I had to tell somebody.

I cracked the side door of the church for a view of the school parking lot. The coast appeared clear. I walked out to the sidewalk and took a quick look to see if anyone might be within sight. Again, no one near the church. I ran up the hill to Franklin's house.

I could hear a basketball being dribbled in the driveway as I got closer. When I turned the corner of Franklin's house, I could see my friends were playing a game of two on two.

"I got in," I yelled when I was close enough, waving the letter in front of me and causing them to stop.

"Where," Marty asked.

"UVA, I got in," I said with a slight catch in my voice.

"Congratulations," Franklin said. "Your dream school, that's quite an accomplishment."

"I still need the scholarship though," I added.

"You'll get there, somehow, someway," Chuck said.

"Well, I'm going back to the church later to light a candle then."

"One step at a time, congratulations," Marty said.

"What's next then?" Franklin asked.

"The ROTC scholarship," I said putting the letter back into the envelope. "I'm going to put this inside so it's safe and then I've got winners."

CHAPTER 27
THE GOAT

"Get up here right now," Colin said when I answered the phone. He didn't say hello or wait for my reply.

I was surprised and tried to say something, but Colin had already hung up. Why would he call me up to tell me to come over to Lance's house when he knew I went there every day anyways. There had to be something going on that was crazier than the everyday strange happenings.

I dressed and jogged the couple blocks up to Lance's house. I went inside but no one was in the living room. I called out but no one answered. I went out into the big screened in back porch but that was empty too. I almost went inside, but then I heard a strange sound, then Lance and Colin laughing.

I looked out into the back yard. There, in the driveway, was what looked like a goat tied up to the Battle Wagon. I shook my head. I thought it had to be a dog, but it wasn't. It was a goat. I ran out the back door. Lance and Colin were feeding the goat some Cheetos. The goat had a strange orange smile.

"What the hell is this?" I asked.

"A goat," Colin said.

"I know it is a goat but what the hell is the goat doing in Sherman's back yard?"

"My dad brought him home." Lance was laughing. "Colin and I had to get him out of the car and tie him up back here. You should have been here."

"Okay," I said. I knew Colin and Lance wouldn't get to the point unless I asked direct questions. "Why did your father bring this goat to the house?"

"One of his buddies from the Mohawk Tavern is turning fifty and my dad bought the goat as a gag birthday gift," Lance said.

"The party's tonight," Colin said. "We're going to hang outside the Mohawk Tavern to see what happens. Maybe they'll even let us in if we say we're there to take care of the goat."

"We do a lot of crap at the house that should get the cops to show up. I think this one will get them here for sure. The neighbors aren't going to let this one stand," I said. The goat stuck his head deeper into the bag of Cheetos.

"Mr. Castleman has already been here," Lance said. "He asked why there was a goat tied up to the car."

"I said 'so he won't get away.'" Colin said, then snorted.

"I'm sure that didn't piss him off," I said. "Is he calling the cops?"

"Don't know," Lance answered. "But if he does, we'll just tell the cops the truth. They'll probably tell us we have twenty-four hours to get rid of him and he'll be gone anyways."

"Where did your father get a goat?" I asked.

"Some farm up on Onondaga Hill. I can't believe the farmer would sell my father a goat. I can't wait to hear what lie my father told him."

"Probably just told him the truth and had the farmer cracking up and then invited him to the Mohawk Tavern," I replied.

"You're right, that's exactly what he did," Lance said.

Colin started to giggle.

"We should" was all he could say before he started to laugh to the point that he fell off the hood of the Battle Wagon. Lance and I watched him and knew it was pointless to ask him what he laughed about until he stopped.

"What's so funny?" I asked when he slowed down enough.

"I think the goat needs to go for a walk."

"No," I said.

"No," Lance said.

"But he *really* needs to go for a walk," Colin said.

"Okay," I said.

"Okay," Lance said.

We untied the goat and headed to the front of the house. News of the goat had gotten around because there were a bunch of kids waiting for us.

"Where did you get a goat?" some kid asked.

"That's not a goat," Colin replied, "it's a dog, a Bearded Mountain Retriever."

The kid looked the goat over skeptically.

"That ain't no dog, you're crazy."

"Yes, he is crazy," I said, "but that's another topic. This is a dog. At least the guy who sold it to us said it was a dog." I could barely keep a straight face.

"Did that guy rip us off?" Lance asked. "I'm a beat his ass if he ripped us off."

"It's a dog," Colin said again, "watch."

Colin took the goat's lead and walked him onto the front lawn. The goat started munching away at the grass.

"SIT," Colin commanded. "SPEAK. ROLL OVER."

"If that's a dog, that's one dumb ass dog," the skeptical kid said.

"Whatever he is, he needs a walk," Lance said.

We started walking, then turned down a quiet side street. With each block we gained a couple more followers until we had over twenty people. When we turned on Candee Road to head back to Lance's house we saw a cop coming down the street.

"Let me do the talking," Colin said.

"Because you have had so much success talking to cops?" I asked.

"At least I have the most experience."

Lance and I conceded the point to Colin. The cop stopped his car, but he didn't turn on his lights, a good sign. We stopped and smiled as the cop looked at us for about a minute before getting out of the car.

"Good afternoon, fellas, is that goat yours or did you just happen to find him walking around the neighborhood?"

"He's ours," Colin answered.

"Does he have a name?" the cop asked.

"Toby," Colin answered without missing a beat.

"And what are you planning on doing with Toby? If you don't mind me asking."

"We were just taking him for a walk, just stretching his legs," Colin answered.

"Did you ever consider there may be laws against livestock in the city?"

"He's not livestock, he's a pet."

"C'mon now, boys, what's really going on?"

Colin proceeded to tell the policeman the entire story, even the part about Mr. Sherman bringing the goat to the bar.

"The Mohawk Tavern? Tonight?" the cop asked.

"Yes, be there around nine for the show," Colin smiled.

The policeman looked at us until his thoughts were interrupted by the goat's bleating.

"Okay, then, take him home and make sure he stays tied up until tonight. Where's your house?"

"On Comstock, 736," Lance answered.

"Okay, I'll swing by tomorrow just to make sure he's gone. A goat as a gag gift. If that doesn't bust someone's balls, I don't know what will. And tell your father not to get worried if a bunch of off duty cops show up at the Mohawk Tavern tonight."

"Will do officer." Lance smiled.

We walked the goat back to the house and tied him back up to the Battle Wagon. Colin went inside and called everyone he could think of. By dinner time we had a big group of guys there, beers, and a party out in the backyard.

When Mr. Sherman finally woke up and came outside, I saw him coming and tipped a beer towards the goat who happily drank from the bottle.

"What the bloody hell are you guys doing with the goat?" Mr. Sherman asked.

"Just getting him primed for the party tonight," Colin replied.

"Well take it easy, I don't want to have anything happen

before I take him to the bar. And if he pukes in my car, you'll be cleaning it up," he said looking at each one of us in turn.

"No problem," Lance said.

Colin reached into his pocket and produced a tube of Brylcreem that looked older than the three of us combined. He squeezed a little onto his hands and rubbed it into the goat's head and goatee. Then he pulled out a comb and stylized the goat for the big night.

"You guys are too much," Mr. Sherman said.

He laughed and walked back inside.

CHAPTER 28
CHALLENGE ACCEPTED

We were all lying around the living room, watching our daily re-run of M*A*S*H when Mr. Sherman stumbled down the stairs, hacking and coughing with each step. He took one look around the room and shook his head.

"You boys are a bunch of bums. You should be out doing something other than lying around watching TV."

"Like what?" Colin asked. He was never afraid to take Mr. Sherman on.

"You should be knocking on doors looking for odd jobs, cutting lawns, or cleaning up this house." All this coming from a man that hadn't held down a steady job in a decade, sponged off his girlfriends, and drank himself into oblivion every day.

"Have you looked around the neighborhood lately?" Colin asked. "I don't think anyone cares about their lawns and half the houses are falling apart and need to be painted but their owners don't give a rat's ass."

"You should still be out there trying," Mr. Sherman answered. "If not this neighborhood, walk over to Drumlin

Hills. Those people don't do any yard work for themselves. There're tons of potential jobs over there."

"I work at the Super Duper," I said.

"Someone would call the cops within five minutes after we knocked on the first door in Drumlin Hills," Lance said without turning away from the episode where Hawkeye made up an imaginary person.

"You're right because you kids deserve to have the cops called on you," Mr. Sherman said moving away from the point he tried to make.

"We deserve to have the cops called on us most of the time," Colin said.

"You guys are worthless," Mr. Sherman grumbled as he began to walk away.

"Why don't you pay us to do something if you are so fired up about us working?" Colin asked.

Mr. Sherman turned around.

"I don't have the money to waste on you guys," he replied. He shook his head at us and walked into the kitchen to make himself his pitcher of breakfast whiskey sours.

We turned our attention back to Hawkeye and Captain Tuttle until Mr. Sherman came back into the living room with his drink.

"I'll pay you to paint the house," he said.

We all turned to look at him.

"I'll pay you with a quarter keg per side. You can get them one at a time or I'll get you a full keg when you finish the entire house."

The first thought that popped into my head, all of us hosting a rocking keg party. It would catapult us into the partying royalty in the neighborhood.

"Okay, we'll do it," I said before Colin or Lance had time to think about it.

"That's a lot of work," Lance said.

"That's true," I said. "This house is a big colonial with lots of nooks and crannies. The paint is peeling on all the windows and trim. The shingles are in just as bad of shape. The other problem is who was brave enough to get up on a ladder and do the peaks of the dormers. I was only thinking about a keg party full of girls when I said we would do it."

"You make it sound worse," Colin said.

"He'll renege even if we do the work," Lance said about his own father.

"Go to hell," Mr. Sherman said to his own son. "If you guys do the work, I'll pay you."

Lance looked at Colin who looked over at me.

"We need to talk this through," I said.

"Okay, but think about how big a job this is," Colin responded.

Lance continued to watch Captain Tuttle.

"Let's go in the other room and decide," I said.

We convened in the breakfast nook to discuss the proposition even though I had already agreed but I knew that didn't mean anything if my friends had no intention of doing the work.

"Everyone has to be committed to this," I said. "No one can shirk. We have to be here every day unless it is raining. We can start with the front and leave the side by Castleman's for last because we'll need some serious ladders for that side."

"Where's he going to get the money for all the paint, brushes and all the other things we'll need?" Lance asked.

"Plus, it'll take us all summer just to scrape the front of the house."

"But think of the pluses. Think of all the girls that'll come if we invite them to a keg party," I replied.

"Joe's right," Colin said, "a keg is different."

"What the hell does that mean," Lance asked.

"A keg means there will be more beer than we can drink," Colin said. "We have to have people here or else it's a waste."

"That's true, but that doesn't mean people will show up. Or people will show up and we'll have fifty dudes here and no chicks," Lance said.

"There's always a chance that no girls will show up if we throw another party," I said. "But with a keg at least we have a possibility of taking it to a different level, a kegger. Do you know anyone we know who has had a keg party?"

"No," Colin and Lance said together.

"It'll be worth it," I said even though I was trying to convince myself.

"Who's going to get up on the ladder to do Castleman's side? That's got to be a hundred feet up to the peak," Lance asked.

"I'll do it, I'm not afraid," Colin replied.

"I'll get up there if it means we get a keg party," I said with as much confidence as I could muster. "Lance, do you have a paint scraper?"

"Yeah, I'm pretty sure there's one in the basement," he replied.

"Go get it and the step ladder. If I can scrape the dining room window in less than a half hour, then everyone's in. Deal?" I asked.

The guys looked at each other, then back at me.

"Deal," Colin replied first.

"But you only have thirty minutes and we'll time you," Lance said.

§§

Lance handed me the paint scraper after I set up the ladder. I expected an old, rusted scraper but this one was still in its cardboard sleeve. Mr. Sherman bought it for a project he never started. I ripped off the carboard and inspected the edge. It was sharp and brand new.

"I'm ready." I nodded to Lance who looked at my watch.

"Ready, set, go," he said as he dropped his hand like he was starting a race.

I ran the scraper along the sill and the flaking white paint came off like Jill Bell's panties or at least like Lance claimed they did. Two minutes in I had the entire bottom of the casement done. The ground underneath the window looked like there had been a fresh, thirty-year-old, lead-based snowfall.

"Do I need to go on to prove my point," I asked them after fifteen minutes and only the top of the frame to go.

"Yes," they answered at the same time.

"I'm about to bet you ten bucks you can't do the next window in ten minutes," Colin said. "A couple more bets and we'll have watched you do all the work and we'll be drinking beer without doing a thing." He laughed.

"Screw you," I said. "I'll finish this window then one of you chumps will go get me a beer for my hard work."

I finished the window easily and we went back inside to take Mr. Sherman up on his offer.

"You renege and we'll tell the Mohawk Tavern you have a disease and need to be banned," Colin told him.

"Don't worry, you guys do the work and I'll buy the beer." He was slurring a little. "Now who wants to come with me down to the paint store. I'm thinking a nice New England gray with a white trim."

"That's what it is now. How about something new?" Lance asked.

I whispered in Lance's ear that we could miss a lot of spots if we went with the original color.

"Gray it is," Lance said, and we headed out to Mr. Sherman's car for a trip to the paint store.

CHAPTER 29
STARTING

My alarm went off at 6:30 AM the first Saturday after Mr. Sherman laid down his painting challenge, an easy time for me to rise since it was the time I usually got up for school. I wanted to get a couple hours of scraping in before I had to go to the Super Duper at ten. I dressed in old clothes I pulled out of the closet and threw my work clothes into my gym bag. I ate a bowl of Fruit Loops, then brushed my teeth before heading out of the house. The mornings were still chilly this early at the end of May in Genesee. I only had my old t-shirt, so I started jogged to Lance's to try to warm up.

Lance and Colin had agreed to get up early so we could get a lot done before they stopped to watch the M*A*S*H rerun at 3:00 PM. I wasn't surprised to find the front stoop empty when I turned the corner. Instead of going in and waking Lance up, I just grabbed a ladder and scraper and got to work. I started on the front just above the living room window. I worked hard to stay warm. The old peeling paint flew off the clapboards without a lot of effort.

After an hour, I stopped to sharpen the scraper and reposition the ladder for the fourth time. Lance came out of the front door, stretching and yawning, eating chips from a bag of Lay's BBQ flavor. I saw Colin walking slowly toward the house, over an hour late.

"About time, you lazy bums," I said.

"Wow, you got a lot done," Lance said ignoring my insult. "Let me get changed."

Colin walked up to the stoop.

"Get to work," I said.

"What do you want me to do?" Colin asked.

I stopped for a second, wondering how I was now in charge, but I didn't mind if it got all this done faster.

"Start scraping under the windows on the other side of the stoop. Make sure you sharpen the scraper first. And don't gouge the wood," I said. I grabbed control. "Before you start, get the extension ladder from the side of the house. You can move up near the second-floor bedroom windows once you finish with the lower ones."

I helped Colin set up the ladder and he was up and scraping before Lance finally emerged.

"Dang, I can go back to bed, you guys have this all under control," Lance said as he sipped from a cup of coffee, the corners of his mouth still stained from the BBQ chips.

"Are you going to start working sometime today?" Colin asked.

"No, I'm good," Lance said. He sat down on the top step of the stoop.

"I'm going home," Colin said climbing down the ladder.

"Kegs," I said.

"Okay, kegs," Lance replied.

He put down his coffee and grabbed a scraper.

"Where should I start?" Lance asked.

"Get the other extension ladder and start on the bedroom windows over the dining room," I said.

"We are going to be ready to prime in a couple days at this rate," Lance said.

"Let's just keep focused on this part. We have a long way to go," I said. "We still have the windows themselves. They are going to have to be reglazed, which will take us a week at least."

When it was time for me to change and go to work, I gave Colin and Lance a list of what they should do while I was gone.

"Who put you in charge?" Colin asked.

"You guys did this morning when I showed up and you didn't."

"We got this, go bag groceries and flirt with the old ladies," Lance said.

"Okay, but I'm going to call before I leave work and if you can't swear you finished the list, I won't bring any beer. I'll go over to Franklin's and play cards with my real friends."

"Yeah, yeah, we got this," Lance said again.

I left for the Super Duper, looking back to see if they were still working until I reached the corner. I shook paint chips out of my hair and pictured Colin and Lance already on the couch watching Saturday morning cartoons.

"We'll never get a keg," I said to myself.

CHAPTER 30
NEIGHBOR BEAUTIFICATION

There was a two-family rental house kitty-cornered from Lance's and usually rented out to old ladies. We were mixing paint on a drop cloth in the front yard when a gold Olds Cutlass pulled into the driveway. A petite blonde who looked to be in her thirties got out with a bag of groceries.

"Hi Lance," she called from across the street.

Lance returned the greeting and Colin and I waved.

"She's smoking hot. Who is that?" I asked when she was safely inside and out of earshot.

"That's Jennifer, she moved in a couple months ago, she works nights at the GE plant out on Thompson Road, so we hardly ever see her." Lance replied.

"There are two other bad reasons why we never see her," Colin added. "First, Mr. Sherman started to hit on her when she moved in like Pete Rose going after a hanging curve ball."

"Eww," I said retching.

"Yeah, it was not pretty. It was after his first pitcher of whiskey sours, so he was already greased. To make matters worse, his fly was down, and she noticed. She turned her head and couldn't look at him," Colin said.

"What's the other reason," I asked.

"She just got a live-in boyfriend," Lance answered before Colin.

"That's too bad," I said.

"Well, I've heard a lot of yelling coming from over there, so I don't know how long it'll last," Lance said.

"Well, she definitely adds to the neighborhood beautification project, if we had one," I laughed.

"The boyfriend's a dick, he doesn't work and there's a twelve pack of empties out in the garbage can every night," Colin added.

"Yeah, I was talking to Jennifer on the sidewalk last week and her boyfriend came out on the porch and just stared at me," Lance said.

"That sucks, what'd he think you were doing? It's obvious she wouldn't go for someone like you," I said.

"Thanks," Lance said, feigning gratitude.

"We should try to invite her over for a beer if her boyfriend is gone and your father isn't home," I said.

"We can try," Lance said. "She's really nice, she doesn't have to take the time to be nice to me, but she does."

"Hopefully there's some sunbathing in the yard in her future." Colin smiled.

"If she did, we'd never move from painting the front of the house," I said.

"It'd be worth it," Lance said, looking over at Jennifer's house.

Colin and I nodded in agreement.

CHAPTER 31
SIGNS

Since we didn't have any experience painting, we were having a hard time getting organized. We kept switching jobs, starting and stopping, never establishing any momentum. I didn't want to be in charge and Colin and Lance seconded that opinion even though they kept asking me to run things. We started out strong but had stalled because we needed a workable strategy; we needed a routine so everyone would know what to do without being told.

"Okay, we're chasing our tails," I said after we finished up another day without any real progress.

"Right, I would really rather be chasing tail instead of doing this," Colin said.

"Yeah, me too," Lance said.

"What should we do then?" I asked.

"Maybe tomorrow all we do is spot prime, nothing else," Colin said. "I think everything we need to scrape is done. Keep a scraper in your back pocket if you see a spot that needs it."

Lance and I stared at Colin.

"Wow, that's a great idea," I said.

"Yeah, how did you think of that?" Lance asked.

"Let's just compliment Colin on his managerial ability and leave it at that," I told Lance.

"Yeah, whatever that means. Great idea, man," Lance said to Colin.

The next day, we put Colin's plan into place. The priming was done shortly after lunch. We stood at the front walk and admired our work.

"It's missing something," Lance said.

Lance went back up on a ladder and painted "Led Zeppellin Rules" over the dining room window. When he was done, he joined Colin and I at the front walk.

Colin congratulated him. "That's awesome."

"I like it for two reasons: we're painting over it tomorrow, and you spelled Led Zeppelin wrong," I said.

"Crap," Lance said. He rolled his eyes.

"Well, if we are painting over it tomorrow, I'm doing something," Colin said.

He climbed the ladder, thought for a few minutes, and finally painted "ARMATAS BULLDOGS FOOTBALL."

Colin rejoined us and handed me the paint brush.

"Your turn."

I couldn't think of anything to write other than a quote from Thomas Jefferson, but I knew that would only get me a beating.

"I'll pass," I said,

Lance took the brush from my hand and from the top of my ladder, he wrote his initials, "L. S."

The moment Lance's feet hit the ground, Colin snickered his way up the ladder, paintbrush in hand. He filled in the spots between the letters: "LOSER."

Colin and Lance continued taking turns until the front of the house was almost covered in slogans written in primer. I refused when they wanted to keep going and open a new can.

"Relax, you need to relax," Colin said while I was fighting them off. "We are going to paint over all of it tomorrow anyway."

Colin and Lance finally relented because it was time for M*A*S*H re-runs.

The next day it rained, all day. The day after, rain.

Lance's phone started ringing the third day, some of the calls were from people we knew who loved the new paint scheme, but most were from concerned neighbors inquiring if we planned on painting over the signage.

It rained for five days straight. The entire neighborhood got to see the graffiti covered house until we finally got a break in the weather and pushed ourselves to paint all the siding on the front of the house in a single day.

"I liked the other way," Lance said as we took down the ladders.

"Well, we have three more sides to do," I said.

"But you won't be able to see it from the street."

"Exactly," I said.

"I'm going home," Colin said. "It's Sunday spaghetti night, the only night I get to eat as much as I want. Lance, you coming?"

"Of course," Lance replied.

Mrs. Foley took every chance she could to feed Lance given the inconsistency of his father's food shopping. I started to bring a sandwich from the deli along with the nightly six pack for the same reason.

After school the next day, I changed into my painting

clothes and headed to Lance's. As soon as I turned the corner, I saw Colin and Lance across the street looking up at the house. I worried that we missed a spot or someone had stolen the ladders. I began to jog and joined them.

"What's wrong?" I asked.

"Look what our friend did," Colin said, pointing at the house.

I didn't have to search long to see the twenty-foot-tall letters "L.S." painted on the roof.

"I didn't leave any room for either of you to make my initials a loser this time," Lance said.

"No doubts there," I replied.

Colin shook his head.

"You know that's going to be there for a long time." I said.

"Yep, that's why I did it."

CHAPTER 32
WAIT LIST

I stopped running to the mailbox to see if the decision letter on the Army ROTC scholarship had arrived after a month passed from the deadline. I gave up hope of going to Virginia.

Finally, just before the end of my senior year, the letter was there. My hands shook as I opened it and read. I saw "congratulations" and my knees went weak. Then I saw the next sentence, "first level alternate." I didn't know what that meant other than my plans to go to the University of Virginia or any school other than St. Benedict's were most likely over. I would have to live at home and continue to work while I went to school. I wouldn't be leaving Genesee or joining a fraternity as I had envisioned.

This heart-breaking level of disappointment was new to me, even with the passing of my mother. I worked so hard for everything, and I thought my plans were sound. I read the letter again to make sure I didn't miss any good news. But there was none.

I went up to my room and closed the door. I was

supposed to go over to Franklin's house to play basketball but didn't even leave my room for dinner. In the morning I showed up at the bus stop. All the guys were already there when I slow walked up the street.

"What's wrong?" Franklin asked. "You didn't come over yesterday. We only had five guys so we could only play two on two."

"I finally got the letter; I didn't get the scholarship. No University of Virginia. I am a first level alternate, so I guess there's still hope, but I don't know how much."

'Sorry man," Chuck said.

Marty put his hand on my shoulder. "Sorry, that's too bad."

"I know how much you wanted it but it's not the end of the world. Make the best of St. Benedict's. Half of our class is going there," Franklin said trying to cheer me up.

"I'll be there," Chuck said. "You can be in our carpool."

That was a great offer from Chuck because I didn't have a car.

"Thanks, Chuck. I don't know what I'm going to do. Maybe go there for a year, save my money and transfer. I don't know."

"Going to St. Benedict's and saving your money to transfer isn't that bad of an idea. But you'll have to do really well. Transferring is harder than being accepted as a freshman," Franklin said.

Franklin's father was a doctor. Franklin had three siblings that went to great schools, with two of them following their father and becoming doctors. He was going to the University of Pennsylvania, and he deserved it.

"Well, it's almost graduation," Franklin said. "Let's enjoy these last few days. You should try to have some fun and take your time to make up your mind. Plus, you're an alternate, that might still come through."

"You're right, thanks guys."

I appreciated their help but it didn't do anything to lessen my disappointment.

CHAPTER 33
THE FIRST KEG

The front of the house was finished, scraped, primed, caulked, and painted. Even the trim was done with the glass scraped of any drips. The ladders were moved to the next side of the house. It looked like we did a great job but since the house was in such disrepair, we could have thrown buckets of paint on the siding to make it look better. But we'd done a good job and had every right to be proud.

We fully expected that Mr. Sherman would renege on his promise to get us a keg. But on the day of the party, we loaded into his beat up 1967 Ford Country Squire station wagon and drove down to Party Source. We got a quarter keg of Old Vienna. The guy behind the counter handed me the tap without what I thought should be the appropriate level of ceremony. It was the first tap I'd ever held, with its gleaming chrome and spigot of wonder. It was going to be the dispenser of our magical beer this evening. I resisted the temptation to hold it high and shout "Excalibur," sure that wouldn't have gone over very well with the store's staff or my friends.

We couldn't believe how much the keg weighed and we did a terrible job of lifting it into the back of the station wagon. Mr. Sherman insulted us at each and every misstep. We did an even worse job of getting it out of the car, almost dropping it a half dozen times before we were able to find the right grip.

We saw Jennifer pull up in her Cutlass while we struggled with the keg.

Lance called across the street. "We're having a keg party tonight. My father won't be here, you're welcome to come over."

"Great job Lance," I whispered.

"Sorry can't, but thanks for the invitation," she called back.

That's when Jennifer turned so we could see her face and what we saw stopped us in our tracks. She was sporting a fresh black eye.

"It had to be that dick boyfriend," Colin said.

"The three of us should go over and give him one from us," I said.

"He's huge and he could kick all of our asses," Lance replied.

"We should do something," I said.

"We should get the keg on ice," Colin said getting us back on task.

We crab walked the keg onto the porch where we put it in our big tub we usually filled with beer bottles. We packed it with ice and then wrapped it in an old blanket since we had a couple hours until the start of the party.

"Don't even think about tapping this early. You have to wait until we are all ready," I said.

"I won't," Lance said, but I could tell that he was thinking about something.

I stared at him with squinted eyes, trying to see if he was lying.

"I said I wouldn't, jeez," he said again before turning around and going into the kitchen.

I had to trust him. I yelled through the doorway. "I'm going home to shower and get changed." Lance waved without looking back.

We tried to invite as many people as we could but as a backup, Lance told his brother that he could invite a few friends. I made the suggestion with the hopes of seeing Gwen again. I invited a few people from Bishop Slattery even though I wasn't sure they would show up. I told them they could come for a few minutes at least and if they felt uncomfortable, they could leave. I was hoping the word would get around Slattery that I was having a kegger, but I doubted anyone would show up. I doubted even more that if my classmates heard the news, they would believe Joe Di Capra was throwing a keg party, especially since no one stopped to ask me for the details.

I arrived at Lance's house well before the appointed time to tap the keg. As always, I was the first to arrive. Dave and Hugh had pitched in to help us get the house cleaned up and presentable. The main rooms had been organized, the kitchen and bathrooms were clean, and no weird smells emanated from any corner of the house.

We tapped the keg right at 8:00 PM sharp.

Either from our manhandling the keg in and out of the car or our attempts to figure out how the tap worked, the beer that came out was all foam. We filled up the three pitchers we were able to scrounge and waited for it to settle.

"Any idea how long it'll take to stop getting foam?" I asked.

"Your guess is as good as mine," Lance said.

"The only thing to do is start drinking," Colin said. He poured a beer into a plastic cup.

By 8:30 PM, Lance's and Colin's friends from the public high school were there, but no girls and none of the people we invited from outside our group.

My neighborhood friends from school showed up shortly after the guys from Armatas. They looked around and saw that there were only guys in the house.

"I thought you said there'd be girls here," Chuck said.

"I really hope there will be some, but you know girls, they like to be fashionably late," I responded.

"You don't know girls and neither do we," Franklin said.

"True," I said, "but you guys need to stick around just in case. At least go get a beer; the keg is out on the back porch. It finally stopped pouring nothing but foam."

My friends looked at each other in a silent conference about my suggestion and headed to the porch.

At nine Andy's friends showed up but Gwen wasn't with them, much to my disappointment.

At nine-thirty some of the girls Lance and Colin invited from Armatas showed up in a big pack. The beer had finally settled completely and poured clear and Canadian. I recognized a few of the girls but there was no one I thought I should take the chance to talk to. Stragglers started showing up in dribs and drabs. By ten we had a decent crowd, at least enough people to finish the keg, which was one of our main goals. We all knew if we didn't finish the keg, we stood a good chance that Mr. Sherman wouldn't buy us another one no matter how much painting we did.

The Slattery guys were huddled in a corner by themselves with what I suspected were the first beers they had poured over an hour earlier.

Andy's group was playing quarters and having a great time out on the porch. One of his friends talked up one of the high school girls. Drunk and feeling a little queasy because of all the foamy beer I drank, I tried to steady myself.

I went out on the front steps to get some air. A few more people came for the party, and I pointed them to the back porch for the keg. I turned towards the living room to show them where to go. When I turned back to face the street, Gwen came up the front walk.

"Well, I was hoping you would show up," I said with way too much enthusiasm.

"I wouldn't have missed it for the world when Andy told me there was going to be a party. But I'm here, fashionably late." she said.

"That's what I told my friends. Girls like to make an entrance. I'm glad you made it before I passed out," I said. I was only half joking.

She laughed, which made me feel better.

"The keg is on the back porch, please help yourself. Andy and all your friends are out there too. I'll come find you in a minute if that's okay?"

"Sure, I'll be mad if you don't," she said with a smile.

I gathered my courage, tried to think of a good opening line, and headed back inside.

I saw Lance chatting with two girls from his school. A couple of guys from the Super Duper were also in the living room. How did I miss them getting here? My Slattery friends were still in the same corner. I needed to check on them, but I couldn't now that Gwen was here.

I went out onto the back porch, grabbed a fresh plastic cup, and filled it up from the tap. I scanned the people for Gwen and saw her leaning against the rail talking to another girl. I walked over trying my best to be nonchalant.

"Hi," I said unable to think of anything suave.

"Hey, you. Glad you're back at the party. This is my friend Nancy."

"Hi, Nancy, enjoying our party?"

"This is your party? I thought it was Andy's?" she replied.

"No, we were paid by Mr. Sherman with the keg for painting one side of the house. This is the first keg. We are getting one each time we finish a side."

"So, three more keggers?" Gwen asked.

"Yes, if we can stay motivated to get the painting done."

"When do you leave for Virginia?" Gwen asked.

"Oh, um, I got into UVA but I didn't get the Army scholarship, but I'm a first alternate, so I haven't completely given up hope. It kind of looks like I'm staying here and going to St. Benedict's," I said.

Hearing those words made me feel more disappointed than I imagined.

"I'm sorry, but that's fine. If you left Genesee, you'd never come back. I can't be the only one stuck here," she said.

Nancy left to get a beer and I took her place up against the railing. I nursed the beer I had in my hand to make sure I was okay to keep going, especially now that Gwen and I were talking.

My Bishop Slattery friends came out onto the porch to refill their beers. I was glad they had stayed and were getting refills. I was even happier when they saw me talking to Gwen.

"I needed the scholarship to be able to go. I may try to save up and transfer later."

"I think you should try. If you're going to be a writer you need to go out and experience the world and believe me, Genesee is not the world."

"Have you travelled at all?"

"A little. Been to New York, Boston. Some other places with my parents when I was a kid. The best place was in Florida. We went to Clearwater Beach on one of our family vacations. It's on the west coast of Florida, so we got to see these amazing sunsets. In the middle of a Genesee winter or even in the middle of a cold rainy, summer day here, I think about moving there."

"You look like you would make a good beach girl."

"Are you kidding me?" She laughed. "Look at this red hair and pale skin. I would have to wrap up like a mummy to not get burnt to a crisp."

"Not everyone can be lucky enough to be Italian. Look at this tan I have from being outside painting all day,"

I lifted my shirt a little to show my tanned stomach. Too bold a move, but luckily, she laughed.

"You asked me the last time you were here if I had a girlfriend. Do you have a boyfriend," I prepared for the gut shot of an affirmative answer, but I had to ask.

"No boyfriend," she said with a far-off look.

"Great," I said. "It seems impossible, but I like that answer."

We talked for what seemed like hours. The rest of the party faded into a blur. I was afraid to leave to go to the bathroom, fearing she wouldn't be there when I returned, but I could not hold it any longer. I ran up the stairs and pushed three guys out of the line saying I was going to puke.

"False alarm," I said when I finished and ran back downstairs.

She was still there.

"I didn't think you were going to come back," she said when I took my place.

"You thought I wouldn't come back, are you kidding me?"

We talked about her college classes and my mother after I told her about her passing away. She held my hand when I told her about how Mom died of cancer. We laughed together at the funny stories. It felt so natural, and I wanted to hang onto the feeling of a connection to a girl so beautiful for the rest of my life. The gaping hole in my heart was being filled with her laugh and the way she looked at me when we talked. It all made me dizzy. I wanted to kiss her and tell her I would be her boyfriend.

"You are so sweet. Why couldn't I have met you five years ago?"

"Other than the fact I was twelve, I really do wish we met."

She put her hand on my cheek and kept it there for a second while she looked me in the eye, before taking her hand away.

"What's wrong?" I asked.

"Nothing at all. What were we talking about?"

We continued to talk about a myriad of topics. She smiled and laughed, which made me feel giddy, until I saw her expression change as she looked down at her watch.

"Well Joe, this party has been great but I'm afraid I'm going to have to bail again. I'm sorry."

"You can't stay?"

"No." She looked at her watch again. "I have to get home to the babysitter."

"The—" I couldn't finish.

"Yes, I have a two-year-old daughter. Her name is Holly because *Breakfast at Tiffany's* is my favorite movie."

"I love Audrey Hepburn too." I couldn't think of anything else to say.

"Hey, look, you're a great guy and you'll make a great catch for some very lucky girl someday. But I have to go before I do something crazy and like I said I told the babysitter I would be home by one. Good luck with everything Joe, maybe we'll meet again someday."

She leaned into me and lightly kissed me on the lips, then turned and walked away.

Life outside the shell made it easy to get hurt.

CHAPTER 34
IN THE DUMPS

"And then she walked away," I said with a little catch in my voice.

"Man, that stinks, she was really pretty," Marty said.

"She was gorgeous, long red hair, blue eyes, you saw her. But what I liked the most was that she was so smart, and it seemed she knew me. It just wasn't talking to a girl, it was more. Does that make sense?"

"Yep."

"Not that there's a lot to know about me," I said. "She's right, I'm just a kid, I haven't done anything yet. I haven't really even kissed a girl, just some meaningless make out sessions that barely amounted to playing a game of spin the bottle."

"I know, there's a girl out there for you. I wish I could tell you how I got Anne, but it just kind of happened," Marty said.

"I'm happy for you. Marty going to the prom with Anne Begley, you're a lucky guy. Sorry, about the whining. Thanks for letting me tell someone. I can't believe I'm heading to college without ever having a real girlfriend. I'm going to look like an idiot."

"I'm sure you won't be the only one."

"What about the prom? Do you think I should go?" I asked.

"Do you have anyone in mind?"

"No, not really. I can't see asking someone just to go. I don't want to go that bad. If I don't like the girl, it seems pretty meaningless," I said as I pictured Gwen kissing me.

"Just imagine if you had showed up at the prom with Gwen, you'd have been a hero. Every guy in our group at the back of the gym during the dances would've made you king, me included."

"Thanks, but that's not going to happen. Not a lot of prom dates have to hire a babysitter. I really need to stop thinking about her, but I can't."

"Things will turn your way."

"But add Gwen to my list of disappointments. Jeez, I've worked so hard, paying for school, getting the grades, and trying to get myself out there and not being so shy. Why do I try so hard?"

"It'll pay off eventually, I'm sure," Marty said. "Sometimes I feel as though my love for life can be unrequited, so I know how you feel."

"Where did you come up with that?"

"I saw it somewhere and liked it. Hopefully someday I'll really know what it means."

I laughed. Marty always knew how to make me feel better.

"You're going all the way to California for school, Stanford, I'm very jealous. What are you and Anne going to do?"

"She's going to Bowdoin College in Maine. I don't think we could have been farther apart if we tried. But we talked about it, and we are both going to write and keep in touch. We'll probably see each other over the summers. But we agreed that we wouldn't let us being apart take away from having fun at college. Now that I know chicks dig me, I'm sure I'll meet someone at Stanford."

"Very adult of you," I said.

"I try, even though I'm just starting this adult thing."

"Well, something needs to happen. Maybe I'll go light a candle at the church and ask for divine help."

"Go for it," Marty said.

"Thanks, pal. I hope Anne has a boyfriend before the end of freshman orientation," I said.

"I'm sure she will," Marty said. "I'm sure she will."

CHAPTER 35
DEATH DEFYING ACT

After weeks of painting the front of the house, we had established an efficient system. We scraped the windows and trim first. When the windows were done, two guys worked on reglazing the glass while the other one started scraping the siding. Both jobs took about the same time.

The daunting task of painting the peak of the dormers still loomed. We didn't have a ladder tall enough to reach the top. We threw out ideas of tying a rope around Colin and having him climb out of the window where he could stand on the sill and paint the dormer. Colin was willing, but in a dry run on a first floor window, he was unable to reach the top by just a few feet.

"We'll have to get your father to rent a bigger ladder," Colin said.

"I think it's the only way we're going to reach the top," I said.

Lance sat on the hood of his father's car staring at the dormer.

"Lance, you there? Earth to Lance," I said, waving my hand in front of his face.

"Yeah, yeah, I'll tell him. We may need to leave it to the end because I don't know if he has the money," Lance said.

"Well, I don't want him to use it as an excuse to say we didn't finish the side and not get the next keg," Colin said.

"Would he do that?" I asked Lance.

"Yeah, he would, especially if he was in a bad mood, which is all the time now it seems."

"What about Hugh Seeley?" Colin asked. "His dad has all kinds of tools. Lance, give him a call to see if they have a bigger ladder. And while you're at it, ask him to come down and help us paint."

Lance went inside to call Hugh while Colin and I took Lance's spot on the hood of his dad's car. We stared up at the dormer and hoped for inspiration.

"Water balloon filled with paint?" Colin suggested.

"Wouldn't that make it a paint balloon? Besides, I don't think that would work."

"You're a smartass. How about we start a small fire in the kitchen, you know we can't make the kitchen any worse. When the fire department gets here, we ask them to hoist me up in the bucket with a can of paint and a brush."

"Very creative, Colin, but I think they wouldn't appreciate that."

"Come up from the other side with ropes and kind of rappel our way down?"

"Again, good thinking but too dangerous. I know you'd do a lot for a keg party, but I don't want to add dying to the list."

Lance returned from calling Hugh. He was drinking a

Coke and finishing off the last crumbs of chips from the bag.

"Last Coke, I bet," I said. Lance finished the bottle and then added a huge belch.

"Yep."

"Any luck with Hugh?" Colin asked.

"Yeah, actually, they have the ladder we need, but he has to ask his dad and we have to get it here."

"Do you think it's too big to fit onto the top of the station wagon?" I asked. "It has a rack we can tie it to."

"If I can drive the Battle Wagon in reverse across five miles of the city, we can get the ladder here a quarter mile from Hugh's house," Colin said with confidence.

"Well, stay on Hugh about an answer," I said. "Lance, make sure he asks his father. Earth to Lance again."

This time Lance was staring at his father's car.

"Yeah, I'll call him every day," Lance finally responded.

"And get him down here to help paint. If he's part of the job, his father will be more likely to loan us the ladder," I said.

We painted until dinner and made good progress, but the specter of the unpainted dormer hung over our heads and threatened our chances for the next keg party.

"I'll be up tomorrow after church," I told the guys as we washed out the brushes.

"If Joe isn't going to be here until later, I'm sleeping in," Lance said.

"Fine, I'll be here after lunch too then," Colin said,

The next day, I stopped at Colin's, because there was a good chance he was still at home and not at Lance's working. I stood prepared to yell at him until he got dressed. I knocked on the door and heard Colin say, "Come in".

"Let's go," I said to Colin, who sat at the dining room table reading the back of the cereal box he had just emptied into a bowl his mother used for the family's mashed potatoes.

Mrs. Foley looked over her glasses at me and raised her eyebrows.

"I'm very sorry, Mrs. Foley."

I walked out of the dining room, waited a few seconds, and then went back in.

"Good morning, Mrs. Foley, how are you this fine morning? And Mr. Foley, I hope he is well, too," I said with exaggerated graciousness.

"Much better, Mr. Di Capra. Thank you. My husband and I are quite well. Please say hello to your father for us," she said in a level even haughtier than my attempt at social graces.

She smiled at me for effect, then turned to her son. "Finish your breakfast, get dressed, and get to work."

Colin shook the box into the bowl to make sure he hadn't missed a stray flake, shoveled the remaining cereal into his mouth, then slurped the milk for good measure.

"And I'm the one in need of etiquette lessons?" I asked Mrs. Foley after Colin went upstairs to get dressed.

She gave me another look and went back to her romance novel and coffee.

We turned the corner and saw that Lance's driveway was empty.

"Mr. Sherman not make it home from the Mohawk last night?" I asked.

"Wouldn't be the first time," Colin answered.

When we got to the house we went inside and called for Lance.

"Where is he?" Colin asked after a few minutes of searching.

"Don't know," I said. "Let's get started."

We walked outside and turned into the driveway. We both stopped dead in our tracks.

"Are you seeing what I'm seeing?" Colin asked.

"Oh God."

Mr. Sherman's car was in the driveway. It was parked under the dormer. On top of the station wagon, tied to the roof rack, was the biggest extension ladder we had. Dave Taylor was standing on top of the car. He was holding the ladder and looking up at Lance, who stood on the top rungs, painting the dormer.

"I don't believe it," I said, holding in my desire to scream at Lance.

"At least he's getting it done," Colin said.

Dave saw us.

"What's up boys?" he asked.

"Heard Lance was going to die, and we just wanted to check out the rumor to see if it was true," I said.

"Whose idea was this?" Colin asked Dave. He turned to me. "Even I'm not this stupid."

"Lance's," Dave replied. "He called me last night and asked me to come over and help him."

As we continued our questioning, Lance finished the dormer and started to climb down.

"Lance, I can't…" unable to find any words to describe the events I just witnessed.

"At least he got it done," Colin said.

Lance walked over to us, smiling, and wiping his hands on his old t-shirt.

"I thought of this last night and wanted to get it done before my father woke up," he said.

"You got it done, great job," Colin said, giving Lance a high five.

"Just let it go," I said to myself. I forced a smile.

It took all four of us to get the ladder down from the top of the station wagon. Once Lance moved the car back into its usual spot, we all got inside and pushed up with our shoulders to get rid of the big depression in the roof caused by the weight of Lance and the ladder. We eradicated most of the evidence.

"I don't know why I went to church this morning," I said, "because God was here in the driveway making sure Lance didn't die."

CHAPTER 36
INVITATIONS

With the end of school only weeks away, homeroom was optional for the seniors. All you had to do was tell your homeroom teacher you were there and then you could go down to the lunchroom that doubled as the Senior Class Lounge.

I sat at a table by myself trying to get my homework done even though it didn't matter because grades were already posted, and everyone already knew what colleges they had gotten into. Patti DiPietro surprised me and sat down next to me at the table while I was working out my last math problem.

"You don't have a date to the prom, do you?" she asked.

She had a notebook with a page divided down the middle with boys' names on one side and the girls' names on the other. There were lines connecting one guy to a girl, like a matching test. My name didn't have a partner.

"We are trying to get dates for everyone," she said. "The girls without a line are available. Who do you want to go with?"

"Patti, I appreciate the help, but I don't know if I want to go to the prom, especially with someone I don't like. Wait, it's more accurate to say with someone that doesn't like me."

"But you have to go; it's the prom."

"I don't know, it's expensive," I said. "Besides, I don't have a car. Thanks Patti but I think I'll have to pass on this."

"I don't understand, I thought you were trying to put yourself out there."

I wanted to tell her all about the crazy stunts I did with Colin and Lance. I wanted to tell her about how Gwen broke my heart, and I wouldn't be able to go to the prom with anyone without thinking about her the entire time.

"I have been doing a lot. I even seriously considered your offer about the prom. You heard I had a keg party?"

I purposely didn't invite Patti because I thought she wouldn't believe me.

"You did? Why didn't you invite me?"

"It's a long story but I'll tell you about the next one. We are going to have a couple more. I'm painting a house with some other guys, and we are getting paid with a keg per side, pretty cool, right?"

"Joe Di Capra had a keg party. Huh, now I've heard everything. Well consider the list, look Carrie McNeil is available."

"I'll especially pass taking a girl named Carrie to the prom." We both laughed. Patti had a nice laugh – not too loud and always with a big smile.

I thought about telling her about Gwen but decided it would be tough to explain what happened without sounding crazy.

"Okay, let me know if you change your mind," Patti said, getting up from the table.

"Thanks again Patti, I appreciate you being nice to me by the way. I just wanted to say that while I had the chance. Did Sister Mary put you up to it?"

It was a question I wanted to ask since the first time she talked to me in homeroom.

"No, why would you think that?"

"Never mind. Thanks again," I said.

I resisted the urge to call her back and ask her why she had talked to me, but she was already at another table with her list. It was the first good news I'd had in a while, and I couldn't help but smile.

CHAPTER 37
GRADUATION

Our graduation ceremony took place at the St. Benedict's College Field House, which seemed appropriate since so many kids from Bishop Slattery were taking the short trip to the east side of Genesee for their college experience. Including me at this point unfortunately. I almost asked my father if I could skip but he had invited the entire family. I tried to buoy my spirits with the thoughts of the graduation cards filled with cash.

I was exhausted from all the activity and emotion of the final week of school, cleaning out my locker, getting people to sign my yearbook and saying goodbye to the school that had helped me reach a potential I wouldn't have met if I had gone to the neighborhood public high school.

Since St. Benedict's was right on the edge of my neighborhood, it didn't feel like a college to me. The campus was nice, but it didn't have the grandeur or age of the bigger schools I had seen in pictures in the catalogs in the Guidance Office. Other than a handful of trips to Seneca

University for football games and my scholarship interview, I had not been on any other college campus.

I was in a daze that I could not shake. I didn't know if it was from being exhausted or just the shock of having my world about to change. If I went up the street to St. Benedict's, would it really change though? I knew I needed to get away. I needed ivy covered buildings over a hundred years old. I needed to sit in classrooms where famous people, maybe presidents, had learned as eager young people.

I remember my name being called and walking across the stage. At the end I handed in my cap and gown and met my big family in the back of the field house. I bounced from aunt to aunt and tried my best to act cheerful while I accepted the cards and kisses. My father said how proud he was, but I felt as though I hadn't achieved very much. My Aunt Eva couldn't believe I didn't want a party.

"Maybe will have a cake in a couple weeks at Fourth of July," I said.

"Not as good as a party," she said shaking her head.

I told my friends I would meet them at Franklin's house for the first party later and told my father I wanted to walk back to the house. I needed to be alone for just a little while so I could think about my future. I hoped the walk wasn't a rehearsal for the trip to St. Benedict's for classes in the fall, but I resigned myself to the fact that my future was set.

I tried to get motivated for the graduation parties. I was going to wear my Virginia t-shirt, but there was no point now. I put on a regular t-shirt, my best one, and the only pair of Levi's I owned and headed to Franklin's.

Franklin's party had great food but no beer, at least for

the graduates. I ate an amazing catered sandwich and started to feel better. Marty was talking to Anne and holding her hand. I was happy for my friend, I hoped I would find the right girl – sometime.

The next stop was Patti DiPietro's party. When we got to her house there was a huge tub of beer in the backyard. She gave me a big hug and introduced me to her parents.

"Your daughter was very kind to me throughout school," I said. "You should be very proud."

I had a couple beers and made it a point to try to appear positive about college and my future.

By the time we got to our third party I was out of gas and wanted to go home. I told my friends I was heading out and left without looking back. It was a two-mile walk home across the city and all I could think about was college and what lay ahead for me.

The next morning, I knew I needed to lose myself in doing nothing at Lance's house since I hadn't been there in a couple weeks. I showered, put on my painting clothes, and headed over. My mission was to work on the house and not think. Not think about college, scholarships, or anything else than the banter between my friends and painting the house.

My future was out there and for today, I was going to leave it there. High school was done and what was next was still up in the air and, for the moment, I was good with it.

CHAPTER 38
THE NEW ARRIVAL

Big Jim Foley was not only involved in sponsoring Irish immigrants, he was also one of the main organizers of Project Children that brought kids from Belfast and Derry in Northern Ireland to the United States for the summer, so they could have a few months of peace away from the sectarian violence. He sponsored his first kid in 1975. This year he expected a young man named Liam Keoghan, age sixteen from the Falls Road section of Belfast, one of the most violent areas of the city.

The first two participants had been much younger according to Colin, so we were looking forward to a kid closer to our age, someone who could hang out with us and lend some character to our group. I hoped he wasn't a good-looking guy because if he was and with his accent, I wouldn't have a chance with any girls that came to one of our parties. We also saw him as an extra hand in painting the house, which we desperately needed because the three of us faced quite a bit of work to get the house finished, even with sporadic help from Dave and Hugh.

We waited at the Foley house for Big Jim to return from the airport with Liam. They were throwing a party for his arrival with all the Genesee Irish in attendance and tons of food and beer. It seemed like the party was taking place somewhere in the Emerald Isle with all the accents and the Chieftains on the stereo. I tried my best to fit in.

By eight, the talk turned to why was Big Jim late. The flight must have been delayed. By nine, everyone was worried, but the worry was tamped down by the beer and the food. Soon after, people started to leave. At ten, Big Jim called from the airport saying there were several flight delays and a couple of mix ups on which kids were supposed to go where. From what he said, it was a complete mess at JFK. Everyone was welcome to stay but he didn't think he would be home anytime soon. The last flight from JFK was scheduled to arrive at eleven. He thought he'd come in sometime after midnight.

The crowd waned. Eventually it was just Mrs. Foley, Colin, me, and a few others who helped clean up. I was gathering paper plates and left-over beer bottles in the back yard when I saw Big Jim's car pull into the driveway. I looked at my watch. It was twenty past midnight. If the guest of honor was in the car, he had missed a great party.

I put the trash in the can by the back door and walked out to the car to say hello to Liam. Colin was on the front porch and Mrs. Foley was at the door wiping her hands on her apron. Big Jim got out of the car and opened the trunk.

"Where's our guest?" Mrs. Foley asked.

"Asleep in the front seat," Big Jim replied. "What a mess. The poor kid has been up for over twenty-four hours waiting for everything to be sorted out. I'll wake her up in a second."

"Her?" Colin and I said at the same time.

"Yeah, like I said, it was all screwed up. Liam ended up in Rochester with the Hanna family. We have a girl."

The front door of the car opened, and I saw our female summer guest emerge. She stepped out, stretched and yawned.

"I'm so sorry," she said in an Irish accent. My heart melted.

"Everyone, meet Ailis O'Fallon. She's seventeen from Derry. Ailis, this is Mrs. Foley, my son Colin, and his friend, Joe Di Capra."

I was mesmerized. She was beautiful. She was nearly as tall as me. She towered over Colin. Long reddish-brown hair shimmered in the dim streetlights. It was hard to tell anything about the rest of her because she was wrapped up in Big Jim's Post Office jacket that fell mid-shin.

"Nice to meet everyone, cheers," she said.

I was in love.

"Get your chin off the driveway," Big Jim said as he handed me the biggest suitcase. I carried it inside, all the while trying to catch a glimpse of our visitor. I put down the suitcase at the foot of the stairs to the second floor and joined everyone in the dining room.

"Ailis, are you hungry? What can I get you?" Mrs. Foley asked.

"Nothing really, I'm too tired," Ailis replied. She smiled at Mrs. Foley then looked over at me as I stood in the dining room door. She smiled again and I felt my knees go weak.

Mrs. Foley pushed past me and got busy pulling food out of the refrigerator and piling it in front of Big Jim who had taken his seat at the head of the table.

"Joe, go get some beer for everyone," she said.

I came back into the dining room with an arm-full of beers, opening one and putting it in front of Big Jim. He looked at me over his glasses.

I opened one for myself and then one for Colin. I thought of offering one to Ailis but that seemed way too daring. I took the chair across the table from our new arrival who smiled even though she looked like she could fall asleep at any moment.

"What happened," Mrs. Foley asked when she took her seat.

"Just a big mix up, they got the plane tickets wrong, about six kids got switched around," Big Jim said. He took a bite of his sandwich.

"So, Ailis, welcome to Genesee," Mrs. Foley said taking her usual seat. "How do you spell Ailis?"

"A-I-L-I-S, pronounced A-lish. Everyone wants to put an H at the end but there isn't one," she said. I drank in every lilt of every word.

"So pretty," Mrs. Foley said. "Are you sure I can't get you something to eat?"

"Just a wee cup of tea right now would be grand if it isn't too much trouble, please," Ailis said.

"I'll put on a kettle," Mrs. Foley said. She got up from the table.

Colin and I exchanged glances. I raised a Belushi-like eyebrow; Colin smiled. Mrs. Foley returned with a plate of cookies and put them in front of Ailis. I was glad Ailis was the center of attention because otherwise it would be obvious that I stared. I had to force myself to turn my head when someone else spoke.

"I'm exhausted," Big Jim said as he finished his second

sandwich and third beer. "I'm, going to hit the hay. You boys take the luggage up to Colin's room."

I saw Colin brighten. So did Big Jim.

"And Colin," he said," "you get all the sheets and blankets off the rollaway bed in your room and bring them down to the couch. Make it comfortable because you'll be there for the rest of the summer."

Colin's smile disappeared as he and I got up to do as Big Jim told us.

"Holy cow," Colin said once we got out of earshot of the dining room.

"I can't believe our luck; I'll take her over some dude named Liam any day." I replied.

When we got back to the dining room Ailis was drinking her tea. She'd taken off Big Jim's jacket. I didn't think I could be more surprised but what had been hidden under the jacket was even better than I had imagined. This time I drew the Foleys' attention.

"Well, this is going to be an interesting summer," Big Jim said. He got up to go to bed.

"I'll take care of things here. I'll get on the phone first thing in the morning and start finding things for Ailis to do other than hang out with our delinquents," Mrs. Foley said.

"Good idea," Big Jim said. He snorted. He kissed his wife on top of the head as he left the room. Mrs. Foley went to finish putting the food away in the kitchen, leaving Colin and me alone with Ailis.

"So Ailis, how was the flight?" Colin asked.

"It was cracker, I mean amazing," she said. "It was my first time on a plane. I saw icebergs out in the ocean, and we got a great view of New York City when we landed. I couldn't believe how big it is, the skyscrapers, I was shocked. Then once we were in New York, that's when everything got mixed up. The tickets weren't right and then the planes got delayed. I thought I'd never get here."

"I'm sorry you had to go through all that, but I'm glad you're here now," I said. "So, we had all kinds of things planned for Liam, but that's all out the window. What do you like to do?"

"I like hanging out with my friends and listening to music. I also love to read. I read all the time. Is there a library close by?" she asked.

"There's a public library right up the street. I can take you there," I said before Colin had a chance. "Colin hasn't been in a library in his life."

"I'd object if that wasn't true," Colin said.

"Whenever you want to go, just let me know. We can use my library card, something else Colin's never had."

"Joe is our egg-head friend, Mr. Catholic School," Colin said trying to insult me, but Ailis smiled.

"Okay, that's enough for tonight, gentlemen," Mrs. Foley said. "Ailis, follow me and I'll show you your room and the bathroom. Say good night boys."

"Goodnight, Ailis, it was very nice to meet you, see you tomorrow," I said with too much enthusiasm.

"Goodnight, Ailis," Colin said, giving me a dirty look.

When Mrs. Foley and Ailis were safely upstairs, I motioned to Colin and we went outside, grabbing two more beers on our way through the kitchen. We sat down in the chairs in the backyard.

"Well, that was the best surprise I have had in a long time," I said.

"Surprise? She's the prettiest girl I've ever seen, and her accent makes me warm in all the right places."

"I know, this is shaping up to be a great summer. Do you think your mother will let her go over to Lance's house? I wouldn't be surprised if she didn't."

"I don't know. But if every guy in the neighborhood is chasing her, my mom will be on the porch with a shotgun."

'Yeah, I wouldn't blame her," I said. "Your dad is a bigwig with the summer program and I'm sure he doesn't want anything to happen. If she comes over to Lance's, we need to make sure nothing happens too. We can't let her get drunk like the rest of us and she absolutely can't come with us if we are stealing something."

"I hate to agree with you, but I do," Colin said.

Colin and I finished our beers. I headed home around 2:00 AM.

"I'll call you in the morning," I said.

I floated down the hill with Ailis's voice carrying me the entire way home. I knew in my heart that everything I had done since the start of my senior year allowed me to talk to Ailis and to look at her as I did. A year ago, I would have eased myself to the doorway, pushed by Ailis's presence, and melted into the scenery.

"She is cracker," I said.

CHAPTER 39
INTRODUCTIONS

I was the first to Lance's to start the day's painting even though I didn't get home from the welcome party until very late. I grabbed a ladder and started to scrape the eaves on the corner of the house facing in the direction of Colin's house. My spot gave me the perfect vantage point to see when Colin turned the corner and if he brought Ailis. I'd called and gotten him up earlier in the morning to make sure she came along. He said "yes" and hung up. Knowing Colin, he would probably have no recollection of the call. I also knew that Ailis could sleep all day after the ordeal of her flight and might not be up to coming over to Lance's. I also worried Mrs. Foley would be busy making phone calls, trying to re-build an itinerary for a young lady who was supposed to be a guy spending most of his time hanging out with us.

I had been working for a few hours when I looked down the street to the corner. I'd been scraping the same bare spot over and over. I saw her auburn hair over the bushes. They turned the corner, and I began my descent, timing it so I jumped off the last rung just as they got to the front yard.

Lance came out the front door, not noticing Ailis until he saw me standing up straight and trying to look as manly as possible with my paint splotched t-shirt and frayed jean shorts.

Colin introduced Ailis to Lance since he hadn't stayed to the end of the party. Lance was stunned to have a good-looking girl in our company when there wasn't free beer to be had. He looked at me with a big question on his face.

"Is she real?" he whispered.

I nodded and whispered back. "Not a mirage."

"So, are you going to stay and work?" I asked Colin, knowing that if he stayed Ailis would stay also.

"Yeah, my mother said I have to take good care of Ailis and make sure none of you animals do anything out of line. Don't get any paint on her and if she gets bored, I have to walk her back right away."

"Ailis, do you want to help out or we could do something else?" I asked.

"Um, I guess I can work. Something easy. I've never done any painting or any work like this."

"Well, we're not painting yet, we are still scraping off the old paint on the driveway side of the house," Lance said.

"Yeah, almost all the priming is done, and Lance figured out a suicidal way to paint the dormers," I said pointing to the top of the house.

I could see that Ailis was trying to take this all in as she stood in a new country with a bunch of guys she barely knew.

Ailis as I showed her what to do. The guys just stood and watched for a few minutes before they finally got back to work.

While we worked, I asked Ailis questions about herself and what it was like in Northern Ireland. I could tell she was still tired, but she smiled when she answered my questions, and we maintained eye contact. I was too new talking to girls to know whether something was "there" between us, but I knew I had fallen in love when I first saw her.

By the time we took our first break around three o'clock most of the siding on the right of the house had been painted. Colin was working on the second-floor trim. If we were all trying to impress Ailis I thought we had succeeded because we had accomplished more than any previous day. We stood and admired our work.

"I better tell my dad that he'll be getting that keg really soon," Lance said.

"I think we can set a date for the kegger; we are almost done," I said. "Start telling people about next Saturday guys. I'll do the same. Lance, go in and get your dad so we can show him."

"We better get back to the house," Colin said to Ailis.

"I'll go with you," I said. We walked to the corner. I looked at the vision on my right. "I hope you didn't mind scraping paint today, Ailis."

"No, it was fun," she replied.

"You don't have to be polite around us," Colin said.

"I'm sure Mrs. Foley will have a lot more interesting things for you to do soon," I said.

"Later," Colin said. They turned towards his house. I

searched for something witty to say. All I got was "See you later."

Ailis turned and waved. My heart soared.

CHAPTER 40
THE SECOND KEG

We finished the second side of the house, which we owed in large part to Lance's death-defying painting of the peaks and the fact it was the easiest one. It only took us half a week after Ailis arrived, even though we lost a few days to weather. The siding had fared better on the other side because it was partially sheltered by the neighbor's house. We didn't have the same level of scraping. We had the back and the south side of the house left. The back was going to be tricky because of the porch and all the angles. The fourth and last side presented us with daunting challenges.

The last side had the sun porch – almost all windows. It would take forever to scrape, reglaze, and paint those. The other problem was that the ground sloped away towards the Castleman's house, so it would be very tricky to set up the ladders. I made Lance promise not to put any ladders on top of the car again.

We surveyed each side trying to figure out which one to do next or whether we should divide our forces and take on both. The last time Dave and Hugh helped us they suggested we do both so we could have a party with two kegs.

I gave an impassioned speech about one side at a time because I wanted to ensure we had another party before Ailis went back to Ireland. My argument won the day.

"We have a more important decision to discuss," I said once we had settled on a side.

"The next keg," Colin said with a growing smile.

"Yes, the keg. It's a good thing it's next Saturday. We can take advantage of the momentum from the first kegger. A lot of people were talking about the first party before school ended. I think we might have a bigger crowd this time," Lance said.

"Well, I don't think we'll need your brother's guy friends this time," I replied.

"Done. I already told him he can be there but only the girls he knows can come."

I thought of Gwen and figured with the way she left that I wouldn't see her. But I had Ailis to think of now. Whether I had any chance was a different story.

"I'll invite the guys from Bishop Slattery. I told a bunch of people at graduation that we would be having a couple keg parties this summer, so I'll make some calls. That leaves more room for kids from your school," I said.

"I'll start spreading the word," Colin said.

"School is over," I said. "My graduation is over. We can say it's an end of school party. We should plan on the third keg for the end of July and the last one right before school starts again. If we pick dates for the rest of the parties, we can tell people at the second keg party."

"Good idea," Lance said.

"But if we pick the dates, we have to make sure the painting is done," Colin said.

I couldn't believe that Colin was the voice of reason.

"We'll have to make it happen, maybe enlist a few more guys to paint," I said,

"Yes, we'll have to," Lance said.

"What about your friends Dave and Hugh? Can they commit to everyday?" I asked.

"I think they'll be up for it," Lance replied. "They helped us a bunch so far and were here for the first keg. I think we can get them here every day."

"I'll call them," Colin said.

Colin being the voice of reason and taking charge all in the space of ten minutes, an amazing turn of events.

"Okay, we have a plan, but are you going to be able to get the word out now that school is over?" I asked.

"I knew we'd be having more keggers, so I got phone numbers before school finished," Lance said. "Plus, when people asked me about the next party, I put their phone numbers in a notebook."

"Lance, you're amazing," I said. "Great job thinking ahead. I'm impressed."

"This guy will go to great lengths to get laid," Colin said. He grabbed Lance's shoulder.

"It's a great motivator," I said.

"I'll start making the calls. Who's going to tell my father to get us another keg?"

"You are," Colin and I said at the same time.

§§

We were prepared this time for how much the keg

weighed. We asked Dave and Hugh to help out, since they agreed to be part of the painting work crew.

Colin, Lance, Dave, Hugh, and I were all jammed into the car. We lifted the keg into the rear of the station wagon and back out with ease. We placed it in the tub of ice with the gentleness of putting a newborn to bed.

I asked Ailis the day before if they had keg parties in Derry and she said they had parties, in the back room of the pubs and that there was nearly a pub on every corner. Everyone had their favorite "local," the pub they went to regularly.

"What are keg parties like here?" she asked.

"Well, I've seen kegs at First Communion parties here in Genesee," I said.

"I don't think the priests in the Bogside would like that." She smiled with her eyes, bright and intense, and I knew I would do anything for her.

"Well, the last one we had right before you got here. I drank too much too fast and almost passed out before it really got started. I won't make that mistake again."

"But you are going to have a wee drink?"

"If wee means like a fish, yes. But a much more responsible fish that wants to make it to the end of the party."

"I can't wait to see all the guys looking like eejits," she said.

E-jits? I thought, afraid to ask her what it meant.

"It'll be buzzing so?" she asked when I hesitated.

"Buzzing, yes, a lot of buzzing. But I hope we get a decent crowd. We are starting to get a good reputation with our parties. We've tried different things, but nothing worked better than having a keg. A keg means it's a serious party. A keg means we want everyone to have a good time.

No one will be talking about a bring your own beer party for the rest of the summer."

'I'll be there, no bother. But I need to take it easy too. I know the Foleys don't care, but the older kids were told by the organizers in Ireland that we weren't supposed to drink in the States."

"Asking Irish people not to drink, isn't that a sin?"

"Aye, it is." She smiled again. "It surely is."

§§

The people started showing up right on time and within thirty minutes it was obvious we would have a good crowd. We tapped the keg right at eight and it poured true with no foam. I delivered a beer to Ailis who was busy making friends. I tried to play it cool by going from group to group, asking if they were having a good time and making sure they knew where the keg was and to make sure to save their cups. All the while, I watched out for Ailis.

Patti DiPietro arrived with six other girls from our class.

"Thanks, Patti," I said. I told her and the other girls that the keg was on the back porch.

"I had to show up just so I could see if you were telling the truth. This looks like a great party so far."

"Well enjoy yourself. If you or any of the girls need anything, just come find me. And that guy over there with the crazy hair is my friend Colin. If he comes up to you run away."

My hopes for a great party grew with the crowd. I nursed my first few beers then took up a normal pace once the party really got going. We had a solid music strategy and Dave did a great job as the DJ. I promised him I would bring him beer all night if he promised to play something slow if he saw me dancing two songs in a row with Ailis. Two songs then a slow one. That was the deal.

Ailis looked over at me, raised her cup, and smiled, my cue to walk over.

"Having fun?"

"Yes, this is cracker. My first keg party and I have to say it's a lot of fun."

"How's your beer, need a refill?"

"No, I'm good. Thanks anyways."

Dave earned his beers just then. He played *Rubberband Man* by the Spinners.

"Ailis, would you like to dance?" I asked as people moved to the living room dance floor.

"Sure."

We made our way out into the middle of the living room, and I tried my best to make it look like I knew how to dance. As the floor got more crowded and with less room to move, I didn't have to try as hard, much to my relief. I looked at Ailis and she smiled.

The next song was just as good, *Twist and Shout* by the Beatles. I didn't have to ask Ailis to keep dancing, which was a great sign. Dave did just as he had agreed. He played *Sometimes When We Touch* by Dan Hill.

I looked at Ailis and offered my hand. She nodded yes. I pulled her closer and we started to slow dance.

She felt wonderful. I wanted to put my head on her shoulder and pull her even closer, but I knew I'd be overplaying my hand. The song lasted forever, and we danced to the very last note. When the song finished, I moved away far enough to talk.

"Ready for that beer now or would you like to keep dancing?"

"Beer. We can dance some more later then?"

"Absolutely."

We went out onto the porch, and I poured the beers. We moved to the rail, the same spot where Gwen said goodbye to me. I didn't know if that was a bad sign, but I didn't want to break the moment.

"How are you doing Ailis, homesick at all?" I asked.

"Aye, I'm a little homesick but I'm having a good time. It's nice not to worry about all that is going on back home."

"I can't imagine what that's like. I complain about how rough this neighborhood has gotten in the last ten years but thinking about where you live, I have no reason to gripe."

"There were twenty-four bombings this past March alone."

"It must be awful. I've seen the news, but you're living in the middle of all of that."

"We're second-class citizens in a lot of ways. It's all from hundreds of years of problems. I pass by the Brits and their guns everywhere I go. They arrested my neighbor before I left. Broke down his door and dragged him away. I don't see anyway it'll ever change, but I can hope."

"There are parts of America where Catholics aren't wanted, but nothing to that extent."

"Well, I'm glad I'm having this experience. It'll be something I can think of for the rest of my life. I'm lucky. So few of my friends will ever be able to do something like this."

"Is there anything you really want to do now that you're here?" I asked.

"I did want to go to New York City, there are some things I really want to see there."

"You could ask Mrs. Foley; she is trying to find things for you to do other than hang out with all the guys."

"Aye, she made a list of things for me. She has all kinds of things set up for me, you know girl things, not scraping and painting."

"Well make sure you save time for us; we are a lot of fun. I can take you to the library and anything else you would like to do," I said.

"You're sweet, I'll take you up on that."

My heart did summersaults. I tried to play it cool, but I knew she could tell I was head over heels for her. She had me wrapped like every other girl I had fallen for. But the others were from afar. Ailis was right in front of me.

Dave proved to be a savant at playing the right music to keep the dance floor full.

"Would you like to dance again?" I asked when Dave started the soundtrack from *Animal House.*

"Sure," she replied.

I offered my hand without thinking and felt relief when she took it. I led her through the crowd to the living room. We danced on and off for hours. The house was empty, everyone else had melted into the walls and furniture. I only saw Ailis.

The keg ran out just before 2:00 AM, the time Colin had to make sure to get Ailis home. I told Colin I would take her back. He readily accepted because he had spent most of the evening talking to a cute brunette from Armatas.

I didn't want Ailis to be late, so we had to walk a lot faster than I would have wanted to. When we got to the

Foleys', Mrs. Foley sat on the front porch. At first, I could have sworn she had a shotgun in her lap, but it was just my mind playing tricks on me.

"So, Joe, you're bringing Ailis home. How interesting," Mrs. Foley said with a raised eyebrow.

"Yes Mrs. Foley, Colin was fully prepared, but he was busy leading a Bible study at Lance's house, so I volunteered," I said.

"Hah. Good try, young man. Thank you for bringing the girl home, say goodnight."

Mrs. Foley went inside and left me on the steps with Ailis.

"Well, thanks, I had a great time. Remember, whatever you want to do, I'm here," I said.

"Thank you. It was great craic, especially all the dancing. Goodnight Joe," Ailis said, turning to go inside.

My heart sank. I hoped for at least a hug.

"Joe," she said turning back. "Can we go to the library tomorrow; can you collect me after lunch?"

"Of course, I'll be here at one?"

"Sounds great."

Ailis took a step forward. She kissed me on the cheek. We stood looking at each other.

"Well, goodnight, Joe, I'll see you tomorrow."

"I'm looking forward to it," I said.

I watched her go inside, resisting the urge to follow her. I finally left, walking a block toward my house before realizing I needed to go back to Lance's.

CHAPTER 41
AILIS AND THE FAERIES

Our trip to the library was better than I expected. I showed her the titles by some of my favorite authors. She checked out *The Complete Works of Robert Frost* and *A Brave New World* by Aldous Huxley based on my recommendations.

She showed me an anthology of the work by W.B. Yeats and although I hadn't read much poetry other than Frost, I was mesmerized when she read me *The Stolen Child* with her whispered Irish lilt.

"For the world's more full of weeping than he can understand." Her voice grieved at the end of each stanza.

When she finished, I could not speak. She blinked away a tear.

"We should head back," I said, looking at my watch.

We held hands on the walk back. Much to my disappointment, Mrs. Foley was sitting on the front porch so I couldn't try to kiss Ailis goodbye. I knew I needed to be alone with her to see if what I was feeling, an avalanche of what I could only say was love, was real and reciprocated.

"See you tonight?" she asked.

"Of course, can't wait."

§§

Lance and Colin told me they really pushed to get the painting done on the section above the porch and finished all the scraping on the back of the house. I was impressed with the progress they made. The addition of Dave and Hugh made a big difference. I didn't need to be there to keep them on track.

"It's really nice outside, do you guys want to sit on the porch?" I asked as I handed out beers. I crossed my fingers and waited for their answers. I hoped no one would notice my nervousness.

"Naw, we're about to watch *Taxi*," Lance replied.

"I'll come out with you," Ailis said to my delight.

We sat at the rail and looked out into the dark backyard.

"So, is there anything that you want to do? Maybe the library again or see a movie?"

"Any of those would be grand. My aunt doesn't want me to go to the pictures at home because it isn't really safe to be in a place with so many people. It's a target and there always seems to be a bomb scare."

"Target? Wow, I never thought of that. How do you deal with that every day?"

"It's been the same since I was a wee girl. There was always the separation between the Catholics and the Protestants, but the violence now is the scary part. And the Brits, the patrols, and the helicopters, it can be overwhelming. That's why I'm here, to have a summer of peace, which is great, but no matter what, I'll have to go back."

I didn't know what to say. I took her hand and we sat without talking. It was difficult to fathom her life and I admired how graceful she seemed in the face of the violence.

"Look," I said. I pointed out into the backyard. Fireflies had begun to light up the grass by the fence. "They're fireflies, do you have those in Ireland?"

"No, what are they?" Ailis asked. She stood to get a closer look.

"They're bugs. A chemical reaction in their abdomens causes them to light up."

"They are wonderous," she said. "Amazing."

"Do you want to see one?"

"Aye."

I went out into the backyard and gently caught one in my cupped hands and brought it back to Ailis.

"Is it hot?" she asked.

"No, look," I said.

Ailis peered into the small opening I made with my fingers. The firefly lit up my hands.

"It's a faerie," she whispered.

"A what?"

"When I was a wee girl, I wanted to go live with the faeries," she said.

"Really?"

"Aye, Irish faeries, the little people, they are magical. To this day people still believe in them. You'll see circles of trees in a farmer's field he won't cut them down because that is where the faeries live and if he did, they would take their revenge out on him. The next time we're at the library I'll show you *Irish Fairy Tales and Folklore*. Yeats wrote more than poetry."

"Yes please. It's kind of like *Midsummer Night's*."

"Shakespeare?"

"Yes, the play, *A Midsummer Night's Dream*, it's about magic and fairies."

"That sounds class," she replied.

"It does? Do you like Shakespeare?"

"I haven't read anything by him or been to one of his plays, but I'm sure with all the people that love his work, it would be worth going to see one."

"That's good to know," I said. I knew there was going to be a student production of *A Midsummer Night's Dream* at St. Benedict's the following week. I had been thinking about asking her to the play and now I had the perfect opening to do so.

"Do you still believe that faeries are real?"

She looked up at the sky and took a deep breath.

"Yes, they are real. And I'm one of them. In some way, I just need to know how to find a wee bit of magic."

I wanted to ask her more, but she seemed lost in thought.

I let the firefly go and it floated between us on the porch. I looked at her to see if she was joking but she looked out into the darkness. Her eyes were moist, and I knew she was thinking of something else. I squeezed her hand and then rubbed her arm. I wanted to lean across and kiss her temple but couldn't find the nerve. She put her head on my shoulder, which gave me the courage to put my arm around her. If she tried to find magic for herself, I wished I could share all the enchantment she had given to me.

"So if you could find the magic. what would you be able to do?"

"Oh my, I would be able to do so much. I would get my family back; I would stop all the hate. Listen to me, that's not going to happen. I must sound like an eejit."

There's that word again, eejit, I thought, *I need to ask her what it means.*

"I don't think so, anything is possible. What happened to your family if you don't mind my asking?"

"Well, I think I'll save that for some other time, Joe. Can we just watch the fireflies?"

"Of course."

CHAPTER 42
MIDSUMMER NIGHT'S DREAM

I dialed Colin's phone number but stopped before the last number and hung up. I picked up the phone, dialed again and then hung up again.

"You're a coward," I said out loud.

I picked up the phone and dialed all the numbers. I took a deep breath as it started to ring.

Mrs. Foley answered. *Crap* I thought.

"Hi, Mrs. Foley, it's Joe. Is Ailis in?"

"Still pining over her?"

"Who said I was pining?"

"Everyone."

"Well, thanks for letting me know. Is she there?"

"Yes, just a minute," I heard the phone hit the counter and Mrs. Foley call for Ailis. I paced in a circle tethered by the cord.

"Hello."

"Hi, Ailis, it's me, Joe. How are you?"

"Grand."

"Well, umm, I was wondering. There is a play up at St.

Benedict's College, Saturday night. I have been to a bunch of the plays up there and they're always great. I was wondering if you would like to go with me?"

"Are you asking me on a date?"

"Well, not technically a date, but kind of a date. We would be going together, and I'll buy your ticket, but I just thought you would really enjoy it. In fact, I know you will like it."

"Aye, that sounds like fun. Do I have to get all dressed up or anything? You aren't going to show up looking to pin a corsage on my dress?"

"No, nothing like that. It's a college play. The students will be wearing jeans. It's very casual. I went to my first play when I was in fifth grade, I was hooked. This particular play…ah…you'll really like it, I promise."

"What's the play?"

"I want it to be a surprise if that's okay."

"I'll trust you this time, but just this once," she said.

I laughed too hard at her joke and kicked the telephone table for my mistake.

"Okay, I'll check with you on Friday to make sure everything's still on. I'll see you before then too." I said, regaining my composure.

"Thanks for asking me. This is something different. I've never been to an upper-level college."

"The guys that hang out at Lance's can say the same thing for a completely different reason."

CHAPTER 43
IF WE BE FRIENDS

I knocked on the Foleys' door even though everyone else just walked in. Ailis walked out onto the steps. She wore a simple dress with blue and yellow flowers. It was the first time I had seen her in anything other than jeans. I think I let out a slight gasp and coughed to try to cover it up.

"You look great," I said, summoning the courage to continue to look at her.

I had dressed up a little with the pants I wore to school and a button-down shirt.

"You don't look a mess," she said.

"Shall we?" I asked. I pointed up the street in the direction of the college. "It's a nice night for a walk," she said.

I found myself especially vigilant because I had Ailis with me. I couldn't envision asking her to run with me through backyards if I saw any potential trouble. We walked and chatted about little things while I scanned the streets.

My plan if there was any trouble was for us to walk up to the nearest house and ring the doorbell. If someone answered, I'd make up an excuse about having the wrong house and even if no one answered, we would be less vulnerable on someone's front steps.

"So, what is the play? Can you tell me now?"

"You'll see in a few minutes," I said not giving in to her curiosity.

She stepped off the curb when we crossed the street and lost her balance. I grabbed her arm and steadied her. I looked into her green eyes and wanted to kiss her.

"How much farther?" she asked diffusing the moment. Was there a moment for her? "Mary and Joseph didn't have to walk this far to get to Egypt."

"It's right there," I said. I pointed to the bell tower of the administration building at the center of the small campus.

"Oh, I was imagining a much bigger school," Ailis said.

"It's just a small Catholic college, nothing like some of the huge universities we have here in the US. I can show you Seneca University. It's probably the kind of school you were thinking about."

We walked into the lobby of the Administration building where the theatre was located. It was one of the original buildings on campus, having been built shortly after the school was opened at the end of the Civil War.

"This school was founded by Father Niall Halligan, an Irish immigrant. He fought in the Civil War. At the Battle of Gettysburg he promised God that if he survived the war, he would become a priest and build a Catholic college. Gettysburg was an especially bloody battle. Almost every man in his unit was either killed or wounded. He felt that God saved him."

"Really," Ailis said, "that's impressive."

"So, here we are," I said as we got to the ticket counter.

"*A Midsummer Night's Dream*? Shakespeare? Is this why you wouldn't tell me?"

"You'll really love it. I promise. You're in it."

"What?" She grabbed my hand.

"Faeries, remember from the back porch?" I said and handed her the program.

"Aye, that's grand." She smiled.

We took our seats. Ailis looked around at the crowd and the beautiful architecture of the theatre. She seemed to radiate the buzz and anticipation of the evening. She flipped through the program, looked up, and smiled at me.

"This is truly class, Joe, thank you so much."

I smiled and patted her hand. I wanted to say I would do anything for her.

"You're welcome. I can't believe you like this better than scraping paint," I said.

The lights dimmed and the curtains opened.

"Well, that remains to be seen," she said.

§§

As the play went on, I snuck glances over at Ailis. She was enthralled. Each time I looked she seemed to be leaning just a little bit closer to the stage as if she wanted to be there with the actors, floating with the faeries, being sprinkled with dust.

At the intermission we went out into the lobby, and I bought cokes. We found a corner, out of the way of the crowd.

"So what do you think so far?" I asked.

"You are right, it's magical. I hope the rest of the play is just as good so."

"I think it's better, but you can be the judge of that."

We finished our drinks and returned to our seats just as the lights were turned down again.

The second half of the play was much better. The dialogue lifted me high above the audience. The words combined with the joy I saw on the face of the beautiful girl at my side. I never imagined the happiness that warmed my heart and sent shivers through my soul was possible. I didn't want the night to end – ever.

As Puck gave his farewell speech, I saw a single tear fall down her cheek and without thinking, I wiped it off. She grabbed my hand and squeezed until we stood with the crowd and cheered and clapped for the players.

We lingered, letting the crowd disperse until it was easy to leave. As we walked out into the evening, I saw that she still smiled, blissfully immersed in the words of Mr. Shakespeare.

"Joe, that was completely captivating. I've never seen anything like that in my life. It was beautiful. Thank you, thank you, thank you."

"I thought you would enjoy the play."

She took my hand, and we headed outside.

"They have a summer festival where they do some one act plays. Last year it was a lot of fun. I went with some of my friends from high school."

"Oh, I can't wait. I thought I wouldn't like Shakespeare, that I'd be bored to death, but I was hanging on every word. We have to go to the next one."

"We can, I'll find out when they put out the schedule. I was hooked when I saw my first play. I want to be a writer, but I don't think I could ever get the nerve to get up there on the stage. Maybe I'll write a play someday."

"You'll have to send me your first novel or whatever you get published," she said.

"Of course, I will. Do you need to get back right now?"

"No, why?"

"I want to show you something else," I said taking her hand.

We walked to the center of campus and sat on a bench and watched a few students walk by. They were headed to the library or their dorms, walking casually in this oasis on the edge of my neighborhood.

"This is a whole other world. I'm going to go to school here. All my plans fell through because I didn't get the scholarship I applied for. I'm a first alternate, so I guess there's still a chance I'm leaving, but most likely not," I said imagining myself as one of the students walking by.

"What school did you want to attend?" she asked.

"The University of Virginia."

"When would you leave if you do get the scholarship?"

"Well, that's still up in the air, if there is a miracle and I get it, I'll leave right after you go back to Derry. If I have to go here, the same, I'll start right after you leave. Do you want to go back?"

"Aye, I miss my friends. I miss my family. I don't miss the Troubles. I don't miss the soldiers. I don't miss everything that is going on. You think you have it bad sometimes in the neighborhood, and you do, I see it, but it's nothing compared to what I live in."

"I'm sorry, I can't imagine. I know we have it very lucky here in most ways. The neighborhood here isn't too bad if you're smart. And if you know where you can go and where you can't go."

"Hah, that's just like Derry."

"Having all my friends helps. Colin is fearless and he knows a ton of people, which has gotten us out of some jams. I don't like walking to my house after leaving Lance's at night, so a lot of times I just sleep over."

"Are you going to miss it if you go off to college?"

"No, I don't think so, but I probably will. I won't know anybody. I'm a little scared about being there by myself but I'm also very excited. But right now, I have to resolve myself to the thought that I'll be going here. I've worked so hard for college, and I can't stand the thought of just walking up the street here to St. Benedict's. Don't get me wrong, it's a great school and I love the campus, but I want more, I know that sounds selfish and I should be happy I even have the chance to go to school."

"No, I understand. You need to see the world, to experience everything you can," she replied even though she seemed to be saying it to herself and not to me.

"My job at the grocery store let me pay for the tuition at Bishop Slattery. I would have to keep working there or maybe get a job someplace else if I go here. It all seems the same. Between work and school, I wouldn't be able to do much else. I wanted to join a fraternity and attend lectures, and of course as many plays as I can. I can do most of that here but there aren't any fraternities."

"You paid for your own school?"

"Yes, it wasn't easy, but I made just enough. And for college there's still a chance that I'll get the Army ROTC scholarship. But like I said, I have no idea what kind of chance there is for me to get it."

"What's ROTC?"

"Reserve Officer Training Corps. The Army pays for college and then I have to serve for four years after, But I'll be an officer. If not, I'll have to do the same with jobs and financial aid. My father doesn't have much money, so that means I get more aid. But I went over the numbers with my guidance counselor and if I go to UVA, I'll still have about seven thousand dollars to pay for myself."

"That seems like a lot of money, I wouldn't have guessed you were poor."

"I guess we are in a way. We definitely are compared to the kids I go to Bishop Slattery with. They have cars and great clothes. I have to buy my own clothes or wait for Christmas presents from my aunts. I also get hand me downs from my older cousins, which helps. Enough about boring me, tell me about you, about Northern Ireland, are you done with high school or whatever it is called in Derry?"

"I have one year left at St. Bernadette's Convent School, it's all girls, but I really like it there. I'm like you. What did Colin call you, Mr. Catholic School? I have done well and if I keep up my work I should be able to get the required grades on my A Level exams. That'll mean I could go to Queens University in Belfast or stay in Derry and go to the University of Ulster."

"I'm very impressed. I'm sure you'll do great. What do you want to be?"

"Well, there aren't a lot of options for girls other than being a teacher. I couldn't imagine myself being back at St. Bernadette's teaching maths or science."

"Yeah, I say I want to be a writer but I really don't know. It seems so far away but I know I don't want to work in a department store like my father. What about your family? I know you didn't want to talk about them before."

"I've already told you a little, but…" She cleared her throat.

"But what?"

"I told you I live with my Aunt Bridget but not why."

"It's okay, I won't say anything."

Ailis looked up to the night sky, she looked like she was trying not to cry and started to talk without looking at me.

"My parents split up when I was young. My father left Derry. My mom couldn't deal with that and me, so she left too, went to England to work. That's how I ended up with my aunt."

"I'm sorry," I said. I took her hand and gently pulled her closer. She put her head on my shoulder. We held hands and didn't speak for a few minutes; it felt both sad and exciting. The newness of this intimacy thrilled me. I didn't want to leave.

"We better get back, so Mrs. Foley doesn't worry," I forced myself to say.

"Joe?"

"Yes, Ailis."

She smiled then gave me a hug. I waited until I felt her start to pull away. When she did, I pulled her back for another hug.

We held hands all the way back to the Foleys' house. Mrs. Foley wasn't waiting for us on the porch. I tried to see if she was spying through the curtains. I looked at Ailis and smiled. I pushed her hair behind her ear.

"You know you can give me a wee kiss," she said.

I kissed her lightly on the lips, once, then again.

CHAPTER 44
INQUISITION

"Have a seat and stop pacing around," Mrs. Foley said while I waited for Ailis to finish getting ready.

We were going over to Franklin's house so Ailis could meet my high school friends. To this point they didn't believe I had met a girl especially since I told them she was pretty and from Northern Ireland.

"You could have made up a better lie, like she was from Ohio or even pushed it to Canada," Chuck said when I first told them.

It was a regular poker night, so I thought I would bring Ailis over to meet them before the game started. After an hour of hearing the guys make fun of me and telling Ailis she could do so much better than Joe Di Capra, we could head over to Lance's where I had already been through that crucible after I took Ailis to the play at St. Benedict's.

Ailis came down into the dining room where Mrs. Foley had finally succeeded in getting me to sit down. I stood up out of habit.

She had on a light green blouse and jeans, her hair tied

back with a matching green ribbon. She looked simply amazing; she was going to make my friends speechless.

"Have a seat," Mrs. Foley said to Ailis, sounding as pleasant as if she were extending an invitation to afternoon tea. She then glared at me. I knew better than to chance her wrath again, so I took the chair beside Ailis.

"So, what's the plan for this evening?" she asked. She sipped from her eternal cup of coffee.

"We're going over to Franklin Adams's house so Ailis can meet the guys from Bishop Slattery," I replied.

"They don't believe she's real, do they?" Mrs. Foley asked.

"Of course not, and they're in for a big surprise," I said, smiling at Ailis.

"What's this all about then?" Ailis asked.

"Seeing your young friend here, Mr. Di Capra, with a girl, was a rare sight before you showed up." Mrs. Foley laughed.

I felt myself turning red and tried to laugh with her.

"They will be as shocked as I was when they first see her," I said while I tried to regain some dignity.

Ailis gave me a quizzical look. I refocused on Mrs. Foley.

"Youse kids have fun and Joe…"

"Yes, Mrs. Foley?"

"You be a gentleman and make sure Ailis has a good time."

"As always Mrs. Foley," I replied.

I held Ailis's hand for the short walk over to Franklin's house.

"You were shocked when you first saw me so?" she asked.

"Shocked in a good way. Shocked in the best way," I said.

"Hmmm, I don't know about that," she said.

"Believe me, it was the best way."

I changed the subject because I didn't want to tell her that I was in love as soon as I saw her. Instead, I went over the roster of my friends while we walked down the street.

"It's Franklin Adams's house, his father is a doctor, he's going to the University of Pennsylvania. Then Chuck Lucas, his father works for New York State. He's going up the street to St. Benedict's. Marty Reilly, his father is a professor. Marty's been my close friend since we were in kindergarten. He's going to Stanford, in California. There might be some other guys there, and I'll introduce you if they show up."

"Should I be nervous about meeting them?" Ailis asked.

"Not at all, they are going to stare at first because you're so pretty." I laughed. "But they're really good guys, very different from Colin and Lance, you'll see."

Ailis gave me a smile and squeezed my hand.

"It'll be easy," I said. I knocked on Franklin's door.

I heard Franklin yell "come in" from the basement where we always hung out. I took a deep breath and led Ailis down the stairs. I said a quick prayer in the hope the guys wouldn't start telling stories about my geeky past, which would be entirely possible given my geeky present.

Entering the room was like walking into a board of inquiry. All conversation stopped and everyone in the room stared, frozen.

Not only were my core friends there as I expected, but every one of my Bishop Slattery friends, even some that didn't live in our neighborhood. I guessed they expected me to show up alone and no one wanted to miss the chance to pummel me for lying.

"Hi, I'm Ailis, I'm real," she said waving to the stunned group.

"You guys really didn't believe me," I said.

I introduced each of my friends, resisting the temptation to say that this guy wet his pants in first grade and this one brought his cousin to the Junior Prom. Once I finished, I was invisible. The guys peppered Ailis with questions.

"So, where are you from?"

"That's a great accent, can you say leprechaun?"

"You're an idiot, don't ask her something like that. Ailis, how long are you here for?"

"How did you end up with Joe? Well, everybody is thinking it, I'm the only one that asked."

"Ailis, do you have a sister or any cousins here in Genesee?"

"Where is Derry in relation to Dublin?"

"Like you know where Dublin is, you couldn't even find Albany on a map."

"No, really, how did you end up with Joe?"

Ailis handled the barrage with the skill of a seasoned politician talking to the press. She was polite and clever. She charmed the pants off my friends, which created a different set of problems as I became more invisible.

"Ailis, would you like a Coke?" Franklin asked.

"Aye, that would be grand," she replied.

Three guys fought with each other to run upstairs to the kitchen. Chuck won the race and when he went to hand Ailis the can, I grabbed it and opened it under his chin just in case it produced a geyser from being manhandled on the trip downstairs.

"Why don't you have a seat?" Franklin said, getting up from his chair and offering it to Ailis.

I was relegated to the standing room only crowd.

"So do any of you have a girlfriend?" Ailis asked.

All heads bowed except Marty's.

"I do!" Marty sounded like he had just filled his Bingo card.

"Lovely," Ailis said.

"Her name is Anne, she's going to college in Maine, and I'm going to California, but we are going to remain friends and I took her to the prom," Marty said in one breath.

"Lovely," Ailis said again, this time turning to look at me. I could see she held in a laugh.

The questions continued to fly, and Ailis handled them with ease. I envied her poise and quick wit. I made eye contact with her and motioned with my head toward the door. She shook her head a little and continued with her conversations.

I pulled Marty aside, but I never took my eyes off Ailis.

"Really, no one believed me? Not even a little? I need to find new friends."

"Well, some of us believed you, but we also thought there was no way she was pretty. Then you show up with a real girl and she's beautiful. Chuck was willing to bet she would be some cashier from the Super Duper trying to fake an Irish accent."

"I can see how you guys could think that," I said with added sarcasm.

"If I didn't have Anne, I wouldn't have believed you either," Marty said.

"It was nice of your parents to let you stay in Genesee by yourself so you could spend the summer with her."

"Looks like you'll be having a good summer too," Marty said.

"There's only one thing for both of us to do then," I said.

"Don't screw it up," Marty said.

We ended up ordering pizza and staying until it was time for me to take her back to the Foleys'. My friends fawned over her every step, and my insecurity forced me to throw in gentle reminders throughout the night that she was with me.

Ailis cleaned up at the poker table. If they let her win, they deserved to lose all their money for the interrogation she received when we arrived.

Once back at the Foleys', we went into the dining room to let Mrs. Foley know we were back.

"Youse kids have a good time?" she asked.

"It was cracker," Ailis said, "Joe's friends were total gentlemen. They were quite different from the lot that hang around Colin and Lance."

"Well Colin and Lance are…" Mrs. Foley searched for the right word.

"I think we can settle for different," I said.

"You're too nice," Mrs. Foley said. She snickered. "There's beer in the fridge. Make sure you save some for Big Jim, I'm heading to bed."

Mrs. Foley gave Ailis a hug and pointed her finger at me for a few seconds to make sure I understood the long list of things she didn't want me to do.

CHAPTER 45
MARY'S FOURTH APPEARANCE

My father and I learned about the next miraculous appearance of the Virgin Mother on the six o'clock news.

"The statue of Mary showed up at Butch's Cycle Shop and Tattoo Parlor. Mary was perched on the handlebars of a 1971 Harley-Davidson FX Super Glide. She was looking into the window of the tattoo parlor," the news anchor said.

They cut to footage of the scene on the west side of town and the recipient of the heavenly visitor.

"Probably looking for a religious tattoo," Butch Snyder, owner of the shop joked to the reporter. "I thought the highlight of my day was going to be the engine rebuild on a flathead, but I found Mary waiting for me instead. I put her on the shelf behind the cash register."

"And do you consider this a miracle?" the reporter asked.

"Maybe, if more people come down for tattoos or to buy a bike, I might believe. A tattoo of Mary is half off today, so come on down to Butch's."

"There you have it, Genesee, the fourth statue appearing out of nowhere. The Diocese of Genesee has assured us here at Channel Nine that there is no need for any investigation and the chance of any involvement from the Almighty is impossible. This is Frank Fink for Channel Nine News."

There were two dozen old women in veils standing outside the tattoo shop praying the rosary. The camera showed buses of the faithful pulling into the parking lot. I looked to see if Chuck was anywhere to be seen selling rosaries.

"I don't think those ladies are getting tattoos," I said.

"Just tell me this isn't you and your friends," my father said.

"Sorry Dad, not us." I walked into the kitchen then called back to my father, "but I wish I had thought of it."

CHAPTER 46
AILIS AT THE SUPER DUPER

I was in the back room of the Super Duper goofing off with my friends Brian and Jeff. We put a box with the bottom cut out on top of the stock shelves and we were playing basketball with a roll of toilet paper we had secured in plastic wrap. The game interrupted when the intercom squawked.

"Special cleanup aisle five."

It was the code to let all the male employees know that a beautiful girl was in the store and we should all take a look. I grabbed a bale of paper bags and put it up on my shoulder, a very manly and impressive look I thought, and headed to the cash registers via aisle five.

As I passed the deli, Brian sprinted past me.

"Aisle five is super-hot, hurry and check her out," he said.

I turned the corner to the aisle and looked, it took me a second to recognize her.

"Ailis, what are you doing here?" I said when I was about twenty feet away. She turned and smiled.

"Hi, Joe, I had to come see the famous Super Duper that you are always talking about."

"Well, this is it. Let me take this up to the front and I'll be right back to give you the grand tour."

"You know her?" George asked when I passed the office.

"Yeah, she's a friend of mine. She's from Northern Ireland; she's here for the summer."

I threw the bale of bags in the storage area and ran back to where Ailis waited before any of the other stock boys could hijack her.

"Okay, ready to be amazed?" I asked as I caught my breath.

"Amaze me."

We walked over to the deli, and I showed her all the different Jewish favorites. She thought the whole smoked whitefish and lox looked appetizing.

"I'm more of a corned beef and pastrami guy myself. Are you hungry? I can make you a sandwich."

"No thanks. Mrs. Foley is making pot roast for dinner. I'm hoping to get a potato and a carrot before the feeding frenzy ends," she said.

"Yeah, keep your hands away from Colin when he's eating," I said. I thought about Belushi and the cafeteria scene in *Animal House*.

I showed her the kosher food section. She was just as disgusted by the gefilte fish as I was, especially the ones packed in jelly.

We wound through the store, with me giving her fun facts about each section. We went into the back room where all the guys were waiting. I was glad to have had the experience at Franklin's house, so I wasn't worried about what the stock boys could throw at me.

"Guys this is Ailis, she is from Derry in Northern Ireland. She's here for the summer and staying with my friend Colin's parents. Ailis this is Brian and Jeff, they're stock boys like me. The old guy is George, he's the manager."

"Pleased to meet you," Ailis said with a big smile.

"Wow, that's a great accent," Brian said.

"What are you doing hanging around with Joe?" George asked.

"That's a good question," Jeff said.

"Joe's done a great job of making me feel welcome in Genesee. He's told me all about each of you and I'm surprised because you guys don't appear nearly as bad as Joe has made you out to be," Ailis said. She gave me a small wink.

"Hey," Brian said giving me a dirty look.

"I told her you guys are the best crew to work with, that we have a great time after the bosses leave, and that I wouldn't want to work anywhere else even though they probably treat you better at Price Chopper. And probably pay you better too," I said in my defense.

I showed Ailis all the fun things in the back room, including the monster oven we used to burn boxes and garbage. I apologized for not having anything to burn for a demonstration.

I walked her to the front and introduced her to the cashiers. There weren't any customers, so they were sitting on the end of the conveyor belt where we would bag the groceries, drinking Cokes and looking very bored.

"You're his friend?" Laurie asked.

"That's exactly the same question the guys in the back asked me. Isn't that funny," Ailis said. She gave me a nudge.

"I love your accent, where are you from?" Peggy asked.

"Thanks, I've had it all my life. I'm from the Bogside, Derry," Ailis said.

I cut in. "Okay, that was all of the Super Duper. I hope you were genuinely impressed."

"It was cracker, can't wait to come back. Nice meeting you," she said to the cashiers.

I walked Ailis to the end of the parking lot.

'Well, thank you, that was a pleasant surprise. Are you going to be at Lance's tonight? I can bring some beer."

"Sure, I'll be there, no bother."

"Thanks again for coming to see me."

"Why did they all look so surprised? Didn't you tell anyone about me? Or do you have a deep, dark secret past you haven't told me about?" she asked with a sly grin.

"I told everyone about you. They got mad because I wouldn't stop talking about you. But none of them believed me, just like my high school friends. They did say you might be real but there was no way you were beautiful and if you were, there was no way you were hanging out with me," I said. "And I don't have a past, just a regular quiet guy. Very quiet and shy, that's why everyone and I do mean everyone, is acting so surprised. Hopefully that's everyone so we won't have to go through this again."

"That's really funny. Well tell them it was nice to meet them."

"And next time you come in, mention that I didn't pay you to come visit."

"I promise."

CHAPTER 47
THE FOURTH OF JULY DI CAPRA FAMILY PICNIC

Other than Christmas and the Feast of the Seven Fishes, the Fourth of July was the biggest Di Capra family event. Our huge clan included my father's eight sisters, their husbands, and kids. Many of my nearly fifty first cousins were married and had kids of their own. We took up almost half of the county park where we held the picnic each year.

I hesitated to invite Ailis to the celebration because I worried it would be overwhelming. In addition, I wasn't sure that we were officially a couple. I was taking a chance with inviting her to meet my family.

After her trials by fire with my high school friends and at the Super Duper I knew she could handle the onslaught of the Di Capra family. One thing I wasn't worried about was that any of my cousins would ask her what she was doing with me. They knew I was a Di Capra. My aunts would love her right away and try to make her eat, because they made everyone eat.

The picnic lasted all day, from breakfast to dinner, with

lunch and snacking in between. The county park was about ten miles outside of Genesee. The area was beautiful with big rolling hills and a picturesque creek running through the picnic area.

Ailis joined my father and me for our trip to the grocery store the night before the Fourth. We went to the Price Chopper because the Super Duper only had the kosher deli. We went up and down the aisles loading the cart with food and snacks.

Bacon, eggs, Italian bread, sausage, roasted red peppers and that was just part of breakfast.

"Is all of this just for us?" Ailis asked.

"You're right, we need to get some potatoes," my father responded.

"What's for lunch then?" she asked.

"Well, we're heading to the deli next," I told her.

Ham, capicola, mortadella, salami, pepperoni, more roasted red peppers, mozzarella, provolone, rolls and roast beef.

"What'd we forget this time?" Ailis was laughing.

"Well, my sister Eva brings a bathtub of potato salad," my father said.

When we were done, the cart was overflowing. We filled the back of the station wagon to the brim with bags.

"We'll be by at seven to pick you up tomorrow," I said when we dropped Ailis off at the Foleys' house. "It's supposed to be chilly in the morning, then get hot. And of course, its Genesee, so be prepared for rain."

"I'll try." She waved goodbye.

We arrived right at seven after I made my father drive around the block three times so we wouldn't be ten minutes early. We were the first ones to get to the park as planned.

My father and I began our annual task of moving the tables into the area with the good grills and firepits. Ailis volunteered to start unloading the food and had the station wagon emptied even though I kept telling her she was our guest and didn't need to help.

My father started three fires in different grills using wood he had been gathering from our backyard for the past month and charcoal we bought at the store the previous night. By the time the first of my aunts arrived with her family, we already had a tray of bacon ready, another tray of potatoes my father cooked in the bacon grease, and the Italian sausage was nearly done.

Ailis and I helped my Aunt Eva and Uncle Dominic unload their car after I made quick introductions.

This pattern continued for the next half-hour. Those who were there helped the new arrivals. It was the same ballet we performed every year; we were a well-oiled family. We moved with the efficiency of a military organization. Aunts and uncles everywhere shouted orders to gaggles of their children, while simultaneously bringing up memories of the year Uncle Tony forgot the hamburgers in the freezer and the years it rained so hard we had to cook and eat from the tailgates of each family's station wagon. There was a mix of laughter, relatives yelling in Italian, and advice being thrown around about how to cook something properly or the only place in Genesee to buy real Italian sausage. It was grand chaos, family style.

Thankfully my father made us sit down and eat once he had the eggs cooked and had toasted the bread next to the fire. When the tumult of the set up finished and everyone had eaten breakfast, I exhaled and looked at Ailis.

"Are you ready for all the formal introductions?" I asked.

"The first introductions weren't good?"

"Unfortunately, not. My aunts didn't get a chance to put you through their old Italian tests to make sure you don't have the evil eye."

"Me evil? Go and catch yourself on."

"Well, if they go to the 'you're not Italian' route, say something really Catholic. That should work."

I expected her to look like a deer in headlights in all the activity, but she was calm, composed, and most importantly, radiant.

I started with my Aunt Eva and worked my way counterclockwise through the tables. There were non-stop, "You're so pretty" and "What a lovely accent" comments from my aunts. My uncles were less subtle with "che bella ragazza" and "Joey, you're batting outta your league."

Ailis was brilliant, handling each new introduction skillfully even when a couple of my uncles tried to put an arm around her.

"What does che bella ragazza mean?" she asked on our way back to the table.

"They were saying that you are beautiful."

There were so many aunts to introduce Ailis to that lunch was ready by the time we finished with the last one. The platters of deli meats and rolls were spread out on several tables.

My sisters finally arrived while lunch was being served, allowing my father to join my uncles at the poker game that would run until it was time for dinner.

"Are you hungry?" I asked Ailis. She was surveying all the food.

"Barely," she replied.

After lunch we took a walk along the creek.

"What do you think about my big crazy family?" I asked.

"They are wonderful, no bother at all. I especially like when they are speaking Italian."

"Well, half of the Italian you're hearing are swear words, so be glad you can't understand them."

"Why are you so quiet when your family is so…" She hesitated to finish her sentence.

"Loud? You can say it, they are loud. It's because I can't get a word in edgewise, you saw them. No really, I think it's because I lost my mom when I was so young. I don't know. But I enjoy listening to all of them. I'm sure they'll show up somewhere in a novel if I ever write one."

"Aye, there are some interesting characters."

"Is your family loud like this?" I asked. "The party you missed the day you arrived with all the Genesee Irish was pretty loud, especially as the night went on."

"Aye, we have a lot of characters in my family too."

"I'd like to meet them someday."

I saw Ailis's expression change for just a second. I was afraid I'd crossed a line.

"Did I say something wrong?" I asked, my fear rising.

"No, no, don't worry. I just thought about my family. I get waves of homesickness when I do. Don't worry. I enjoy your company."

"That's good, because I don't have much experience with girls and I'm sure I'm making tons of mistakes. I'm sorry if I'm moving too fast, again because of my inexperience and the fact that the end of the summer…" I trailed off, unable to finish talking about her leaving.

"I know, Joe, please don't take this the wrong way, but me and you, this is happening fast as you said."

I held my breath and prepared for Ailis to tell me we should not be spending so much time together.

"But, I've never felt this way with anyone. It just feels right to me, and I don't think about the end of the summer because I just want to be with you, here and now."

"Ailis," I said, holding back the thought of telling her I loved her.

Ailis looked at me and tilted her head.

"I feel exactly the same way and if this is the part where you tell me it's okay to kiss you, let me know, cause that's my favorite part." My joke broke the tension.

She laughed so I gave her a small kiss. We looked at each other, I was afraid to ask her what she thought. I didn't know what to do next, so I used the best fallback position Italians have, food.

"Well, we better get back, it's almost time for pre-dinner, but make sure you save room for the real thing," I said.

"I don't know how you are so thin Joe, with all this food."

"My body is just storing all the potential fat. At forty, I'll balloon up like my Uncle Gennaro. But I promise I won't add the Bermuda shorts and knee-high black socks."

Ailis's laugh filled my heart with helium and made it soar. It was quickly becoming my favorite sound in the entire world.

When we got back to the picnic area, my Aunt Eva waved us over to where she sat alone. She pointed to the lawn chairs next to her. She leaned forward in the chair. Her toes barely touched the ground. She was just over five feet tall but as the oldest of the aunts, she could control the entire family with just a stare over her glasses.

"Vieni qui e siediti. C'mon sit down."

I sat next to her and pulled a chair in close for Ailis.

"So youse kids, I have a feeling about youse two. It's a firma dall'alto, a sign. I can always tell. Go ask Aunt Vicky. I always know."

"And what's the sign, Aunt Eva," I asked even though I knew I'd be embarrassed by her answer. I looked at Ailis and she smiled, so I took her hand.

"Joey, your mother, God bless her soul, would be so happy to see the man you are. And now with this girl, Ailis, such a nice girl and so, so pretty and smart. She's smiling from heaven."

I had to look away to hide my tears. Ailis squeezed my hand.

"Thank you," Ailis said. She got up and gave my Aunt Eva a hug.

"See, Joey, I knew, this is a good girl, don't let her go," Aunt Eva said, putting her hands on Ailis's cheeks. "All she needs to do is learn how to cook, but your aunts and I will take care of that, non e niente."

"She is special Aunt Eva," I said, glad I found my voice. "But we just started dating and she has to go back to Ireland at the end of the summer."

"Che non importa, I know, it don't matter, she is special."

"Thank you, Mrs.,—"

"You call me Aunt Eva honey, don't even think about calling me anything else."

"So, we have you're blessing?" I asked.

"Ailis, tell Joey that if he doesn't bring you to my house for dinner, he won't be my favorite nephew anymore."

"When did I become the favorite? I heard you call Stevie your favorite just this morning."

Aunt Eva waved away my question.

"Youse kids get something to eat. Are you hungry?"

"I'm good, thank you," Ailis said.

"Me too," I said.

"Well, when you come to my house, I'll make something good for you."

I stood up and gave my aunt a kiss on the cheek. Ailis gave her another hug.

"Are you okay?" Ailis asked on the way back to our table.

"Yes, thanks, I wasn't expecting her to talk about my mom."

Ailis hugged me and then held my hand.

"I guess we have a dinner date then. I would recommend not eating for a couple of days before we go," I told her. We walked back to where my father played poker with my uncles.

"That was nice," Ailis said, "you're lucky to have her."

"She didn't embarrass you, did she?"

"Not at all, who knows she may be right," Ailis said with a wink.

CHAPTER 48
MR. SHERMAN'S DATE

Mr. Sherman talked a lot about all his girlfriends, bragged would be a better word. We never saw any of these women, but there were plenty of times where he was gone for a couple of days then he'd come back home long enough to grab a few things and leave again. Lance suspected those absences were attributable to his having a new girlfriend, but Lance also said the relationships never lasted very long, mostly because the women got tired of giving him money.

Mr. Sherman made a pitcher of whiskey sours when he got up in the morning. After dinnertime, he went to the same bar, the Mohawk Tavern, where he spent the rest of the night until closing with his drinking buddies. There were times I had to help Lance carry him inside, especially in the winter, so he wouldn't freeze to death. How he drove home the 1.4 miles from the Mohawk Tavern that drunk without crashing, killing someone, or getting arrested was always a mystery. It was before there was a crackdown on drunk driving, but I was sure some of the times he was gone for more than a day, he was a guest of the Dewitt or Genesee Police Departments.

After we finished painting for the day, the three of us were watching television in the living room when the door opened. An older woman walked in. She wore a tawdry yellow polyester outfit; a cigarette dangled from her gaudily painted lips. She looked like she was dressed for an episode of the *Love Boat* with a paisley scarf and white shoes. We all turned and stared.

Finally, Lance spoke.

"Can I help you?"

"Just waiting for your father to get the bags out of the car, hon," she said with a smoker's voice.

Before Lance could ask another question, his father banged through the front door with his arms full of bags from the Price Chopper.

"I'm going to cook you guys a real dinner tonight," she said.

She was lucky that the kitchen was relatively tidy. The house was a little cleaner than usual because Lance's brother had done some cleaning the day before. Maybe his father had told him to get the house ready for a "real dinner," but I was sure he didn't give the news with as much flair as Mr. Sherman's latest girlfriend.

Mr. Sherman excused himself. "I'm going upstairs to take a shower, be down in a jiff."

I looked at Lance. "Jiff?"

Lance shrugged.

Within minutes the kitchen was full of the sounds of cooking. Pans banging, cabinets being opened and closed and the occasional, "Where do you keep?" shouted through the open door.

I was very curious and wanted to go look but knew that wasn't polite. Lance didn't have any reservations, especially since she kept hollering at him.

I leaned out of my chair toward the kitchen so I could clearly hear the discussion.

"What ya making?" Lance asked.

"Steaks, baked potatoes, fresh green beans, and a salad, hon. You're really going to enjoy it."

Since Lance did almost all his own cooking, I agreed with that statement.

"Can you do me a favor, hon? And go tell your father to hurry up and get out of the shower. He said he was going to make drinks, and I'm definitely ready for one."

Lance ran up the stairs.

Since Lance had broken the ice, I motioned to Colin that we should go into the kitchen. We walked to the doorway from the living room and watched until we finally caught her attention.

"Hi guys, sorry, but we didn't buy enough for Lance's friends."

"That's okay," I said, "I have to go home for dinner anyway and so does Colin. I'm Joe by the way."

"Oh hi, I'm Carol. I'm Walt's friend."

She held her cigarette aloft in her right hand and with her other hand she held her elbow. She blew her smoke in the air after taking long drags from her cigarette.

"Hey, do you guys know where they keep the tin foil?"

I opened the cabinet over the stove and handed the roll to her.

"Thanks, hon."

Colin and I stood and watched as she washed, then wrapped the potatoes in foil and stuck them in the oven.

She put her cigarette in her mouth so she could check her watch. She grabbed a huge package wrapped in butcher paper from one of the grocery bags. She opened it and took out the biggest steaks I had ever seen. There were four of them, all bigger than the single piece of meat my mother used to cook for our family of seven when all my sisters still lived at home.

I looked at Colin. He also stared at the pile of beef like it was the best Christmas present he'd ever seen. It looked like a cow starter kit.

"Five bucks says that's Toby the goat," I whispered.

"No, Mr. Sherman took him back to the farm after the party. The police made him."

"Why didn't you tell me?" I asked.

Colin was more interested in the food than giving me an answer.

"How are you going to cook those?" Colin asked, pointing to the steaks.

"Oh, lots of salt and pepper then I'll sear them in a pan and finish them in the oven. I hope they like medium rare. Anything past medium rare is a waste of a fine steak."

She sounded like the polyester version of Julia Child with a smoker's rasp instead of the *French Chef's* shrill voice. I had no idea what sear or medium rare meant but it all seemed wonderful. The few times we had steak at my house it was always a cheap cut and cooked to leather in the broiler by my father.

Lance came running down the stairs with fresh clothes and wet hair. He wanted a shower to be worthy of the meal. Mr. Sherman finally appeared. He wore a button-down shirt. His hair was slicked back, and he had on so much Brut cologne that I worried he would explode if he lit up a cigarette.

"There you are hon, make drinks," Carol said when Mr. Sherman made it into the kitchen.

"Your wish is my command," Mr. Sherman said in a flirty voice I had never heard him use.

Mr. Sherman washed out his whiskey sour pitcher, a step he skipped when he made them for himself, and mixed the drinks. He got clean glasses out of the strainer, poured a glass for Carol, and handed it to her before he poured one for himself.

"Aliens have abducted Mr. Sherman and replaced him with this guy," I whispered to Colin.

"I can't look away; it's like watching *Leave it to Beaver*, but with drunks," Colin said.

Mr. Sherman went back to being himself when he looked at the three of us standing in the kitchen.

"You two clowns, get out," he said. "Lance, get four plates out of the china cabinet."

"We have a china cabinet?" Lance asked.

"It's in the dining room, you idiot."

"Now, hon, be nice, he's just a boy," Carol said. She tickled Mr. Sherman under his chin.

Colin couldn't confirm my claim, but I was sure I heard Mr. Sherman giggle. I wished Ailis was here to witness this because she was never going to believe the story.

Soon, better smells than anything that had ever come out of the Sherman kitchen were filling the house.

Colin and I walked out together. We wanted to stay for the show but had to get home. It was time for my dinner, the one I would burn myself on when I peeled back the foil.

"Carol is definitely a keeper," Colin said.

"She is different, but look at the way she tamed Mr. Sherman," I said.

We asked Lance about the dinner the next day.

"I ate the entire steak, and it was the best thing I've ever eaten. I had to lay down on the couch as soon as I was finished, and I passed out as soon as I did. Carol washed all the dishes and left the kitchen cleaner than it was when she got there. The only bad thing about the dinner is that the steak clogged me up and I haven't taken a dump since yesterday."

Colin shook his head. "Only you could ruin the story about a steak dinner."

CHAPTER 49
GOING SWIMMING

It had been an especially hot week and the guys were tired of scraping and priming the back of the house where the paint was markedly worn and peeling. I had been working without my shirt on, but only when Ailis wasn't there and because we were working on the back of the house where no one could see me from the street.

When we couldn't take any more of the heat, we took down the ladders. I turned on the hose on the side of the house and soaked my head. The guys followed suit.

"We need a day off, go to Green Lakes, and go swimming," I said.

"How are we going to get there?" Colin asked.

"Ask your mom if you can borrow the car," I said.

Lance laughed. "Might as well ask her to buy us beer."

"Colin isn't going to ask her," I said. But an idea popped into my head. I started laughing.

"What?" Colin and Lance said at the same time.

"Let's get cleaned up and go over to Colin's."

The guys complied and we walked to Colin's and into

the dining room where his mom sat at the table drinking coffee and smoking a cigarette. She was reading an old romance paperback and actively ignoring the ironing board and basket of clothes in the corner. I said hello to Mrs. Foley and kept walking to the living room. Colin and Lance sat down at the dining room table with Mrs. Foley.

Ailis was in the living room on the couch. She was reading my copy of *The Dead*. She and Mrs. Foley had spent the morning at the regional farmer's market and were planning on making preserves but changed their plans because of the heat. I put my finger to my lips to shush her and motioned to the front porch. She arched one eyebrow, a trait we shared.

She looked amazing in white shorts and a sleeveless t-shirt. She had her hair piled on top of her head. I immediately wanted to nuzzle her long neck and blow in her ear but that was only in my dreams.

When we were safely on the porch and out of earshot of the dining room and Mrs. Foley, I looked at Ailis and completely forgot what I was going to say.

"You alright?"

"Yes, sorry, I need a favor. See, we want to go swimming out at Green Lakes but if Colin asks for the car his mom will say no. But if you say you want to go swimming and that you heard people, not us by the way, some of the girls Mrs. Foley introduced you to, talking about Green Lakes, she'll make Colin take you there."

"Catch yourself on." She laughed. "You said all of that on one breath."

"Do you understand what I'm asking though?"

"Not a word."

I started to repeat what I had just said when Ailis put her hand in front of my face.

"Watch yourself. I understood. Now tell me more about what I should do. I want to see this Green Lakes place now, is it really that nice then?"

I wanted to say that any place where she is standing is nice, but I just said "Yes."

"It would be cracker to go swimming, especially in this heat. Do you think it'll work?"

"I know you can do it. Make sure you say how much the heat is killing you because it never gets this hot in Northern Ireland. Talk about the girls you met the other day bragging about Green Lakes and how it is such a fun place to go. But wait about an hour after we leave so you asking doesn't seem too obvious."

"And what do I get for all this espionage?"

"You get to go to Green Lakes. The place is amazing."

Ailis smirked and pushed me out of the way as she went back into the house.

§§

Ailis wouldn't tell me what she said to Mrs. Foley, but it worked like a charm. That night at dinner, Mrs. Foley told Colin that he could have the car tomorrow if he took Ailis to Green Lakes. Colin had a terrible poker face. He stared at his plate and said, "Sure."

"It's supposed to be hot as all get out tomorrow," Mrs. Foley said. "Ailis says she's never been swimming because the Brits closed all the beaches back home."

Colin shared the success of our plan with Lance and me.

"Don't tell the other guys that we are going," I said. "If you do, we'll have your mother's station wagon loaded with everyone we know, all staring at Ailis in her bathing suit," I said,

'Right, you'll do enough staring for a whole station wagon full of guys," Colin said.

I couldn't argue with the truth. "Exactly."

We agreed to meet at Colin's at eleven. It took all I could to make Colin and Lance swear they wouldn't tell anyone else. I promised each of them a six-pack for their silence. They quickly accepted. Stupid. I would have gone higher.

I was ready to go at nine and tried to keep myself occupied for the next two hours. I wasn't very successful and started to walk to Colin's at 10:15. I had on my Adidas shirt that I was saving for college. I also had my best jean cut-off shorts, frayed and faded to perfection.

I was very thankful I had acquired a solid tan for the first time in my life. Getting tanned in one of the rainiest cities in America was quite an achievement. I knew both Lance and Colin had a weak farmer's tan, at best, and Colin's junior beer belly would be almost fish white.

I walked very slowly up the street so I wouldn't be embarrassingly early. I did my best to look out for anyone that might see me carrying a beach towel, because I knew they would ask where I was going and would want to tag along. I still made it to Colin's before 10:30. I looked into the living room hoping to see Ailis, but it was empty. I yelled "hello" from the front doorway.

"In here," Mrs. Foley called from the dining room.

She sat in her regular chair that no one else dared sit in, alone at the table, drinking coffee and smoking a cigarette.

"So, Ailis heard all these wonderful things about Green Lakes, huh?" she asked.

"She did? Well, it has been crazy hot and a day at the beach will be a perfect relief, so I'm not surprised." My smile was weak and unconvincing.

She looked at me and raised an eyebrow. I knew she knew we told Ailis to ask her, but for some reason she was still letting us go.

"You make sure things don't get out of hand. You make sure nothing happens to Ailis. You make sure she has a good time but not too good of a time. You got money to buy her drinks?"

"Of course," I said.

"I knew you would. I gave Colin five dollars, but he'll blow it or lose it by the time she needs a drink."

At the mention of his name, we heard what could only be Colin stomping down the stairs.

"Speak of the devil," Mrs. Foley said of her son. "You remember what I said."

"Yes, Mrs. Foley. You know I'll take care of her."

She gave me another look that I interpreted as "take care of her but keep your hands off."

Colin continued his stomping into the dining room and asked his mother where his shorts were, then where his Led Zeppelin shirt was and where a beach towel was. Mrs. Foley looked at me and rolled her eyes after each request. Colin ducked into the bathroom to change.

When he emerged, Mrs. Foley called Colin into the dining room.

"No speeding, park the car in the shade, be a gentleman with Ailis, don't get in any fights unless it is to protect Ailis. There's a full tank of gas and if that car comes home empty, you'll never drive it again. So, no joyriding around the city to try to impress Ailis. Besides, if you show her Genesee, she won't be impressed. Go straight to Green Lakes and then come back home."

Colin grunted agreement.

Lance showed up and asked to borrow a beach towel. Mrs. Foley already had one ready for him.

"Did you eat?" she asked Lance.

Lance didn't respond right away.

"Go make a bowl of cereal."

"What time do you want us back?" I asked.

Lance walked past me with a huge bowl of cereal. I got another eye roll from Mrs. Foley.

"Before dinner."

"I'll make sure we're here."

I felt a hand on my shoulder as Ailis went past me in a blur. I turned quickly and saw that she had on a beach wrap. Mrs. Foley had splurged at the mall to get her ready for the day.

I gave Lance a look of "hurry up and eat that cereal," which he amazingly understood because he started to shovel in the corn flakes.

Somehow, Colin managed to be ready on time, and we piled into the station wagon. Lance called shotgun, which he didn't need to do because I was going to sit in the back with Ailis anyway.

"Seatbelts," I told everyone.

"Yes, Dad," Colin said.

"Hey, we have to do this right, or we won't have any chance of doing this again," I said.

He shrugged. He knew I was right.

"You did a great job. Whatever you said to Mrs. Foley worked," I told Ailis on the way out of the driveway.

"It was easy, but I think she knew what I was trying to do."

"She did, but here we are, on our way. So, you've really never been swimming before?" I asked.

"Not really, so you better be prepared to jump in and save me if I begin to drown."

"I don't think there's a spot in the lake that'll be over your head, so no need to worry. Since it's a Tuesday, I'm hoping it's not too crowded. If we went on a Saturday on a day this hot, we wouldn't be able to move."

"So, do we spend all of our time in the water splashing around like a bunch of fools?" she asked.

"Well, we go in when we get too hot, then we get out and lie on our towels until we get too hot again."

"Sounds complicated."

"I have faith you'll catch on," I said.

That earned me a punch in the arm.

We found a great parking spot in the shade as Mrs. Foley had instructed. My favorite spot on the edge of the sand with a little bit of shade from the trees was open and we grabbed it without any hesitation.

Colin and Lance dropped their towels, ripped off their shirts and shoes, and sprinted to the water. I laid out my towel and Ailis did the same next to mine. I sat down and pretended to look off in the distance as I waited for her to take off the beach wrap.

Ailis looked around and then untied the belt on the wrap and placed it on top of her matching beach bag. I casually looked over to her as she began to sit down on the towel. She had on a green bikini. It wasn't too showy, but it still was a bikini. Her skin was pale but not a sickly pale. It looked lustrous and to me, perfect.

"What do you think?" I asked.

"This is really nice. I can't believe Mrs. Foley bought me this bathing costume. I hope I don't look out of place."

"You look great," I said staring a bit too long.

She kept my gaze, almost daring me to keep looking at her.

"Well then," I said changing the subject and looking away. "We'll have to come back a few more times to make sure it doesn't go to waste. We do need to be careful that you don't get a sunburn though. That'll make you never want to come back."

"Let me know if I'm getting red then."

"I'll keep my eye on you," I dared to say with a little inflection, this time staring on purpose.

Thankfully, Ailis laughed.

I took off my shirt and put it on the towel. I propped up on my elbows like Ailis.

"How'd you get so tan?" she asked.

"One of the many benefits of being Italian. Plus, all the painting we've done. I take off my shirt for a while to get some sun."

"I don't think I could ever get that dark; I've never had a tan in my life."

"As I said, you need to ease into it. A sunburn is not fun."

We chatted about different things until Ailis finally said she was ready to go in the water.

"Do you want to run in or just walk in and get used to it?" I asked.

"Let's run," she said. She stood up and took off to the water.

Ailis hit the water and when it was up to her thighs, dove in and went under. I was right behind her, diving in, but I popped up right away so I would be there when she came up. A few seconds later she surfaced right next to me. She wrapped her arms around me. While by brain and my fantasies were saying, "She's hugging me," she planted her foot on the bottom and pushed me over.

I came back up immediately to find her laughing hysterically.

"You're going to pay for that," I said. I swished towards her.

I caught up, picked her up under her arm and leg, and threw her forward with all my strength. She went under with a big splash.

She jumped up and flung her hair back and with her first breath she began laughing again. She moved towards me but this time I was ready. When she tried to trip me, I stood firm and unmoving. She tried another move, but I had my feet dug into the sand. She stopped and again hugged me, looking into my eyes and tilted her head. As soon as my concentration melted, she moved to the side and tripped me again.

I grabbed her in a bear hug but when I looked at her, I stayed focused – no melting. I moved her wet hair out of her eyes and pulled her close. I kissed her in front of God and everybody. When we parted, she looked at me and smiled, then pursed her lips to kiss me again. I closed my eyes, but instead of feeling her lips, I felt her hands pushing me under. I grabbed her arm just in time and pulled her under with me.

When we came up, Colin was there laughing like a maniac. He began to splash us. Lance soon joined until all four of us were moving half the lake at each other.

Exhausted, we headed back to the towels. Reluctantly I told Ailis that she needed to put her beach wrap on.

"You're getting a little pink. Do you want to get a Coke?" I asked.

"Aye."

We walked over to the snack bar holding hands. As we waited in line, I kissed her again.

Someone behind me spoke. "So, it's all smoochy, smoochy now, is it?"

Colin was three people behind us, with Lance running from our spot to join in.

"You came all the way from Ireland, and this was what you settled for?" Colin asked Ailis while pointing at me.

"He's dead on and a gentleman," Ailis responded.

I couldn't tell if she was serious or just giving it back to Colin.

"Right now, he's the one with cash and he's buying the drinks," Lance said after joining the line.

When we got back to the towels, Ailis reached into her bag and got out some suntan lotion.

"Mrs. Foley said this is new and it's supposed to help you from getting sunburned," she said as she read the label.

"Well, it can't hurt, you should put some on."

She took off her beach wrap and sidled up next to me.

"Can you put some on my back?" she asked. She turned, handed me the bottle, and lifted her hair. "Go ahead."

I squeezed a little on my hand and rubbed it into her shoulder.

"Oh."

"Does it hurt?" I asked.

"No, it's cold."

I put some more in my hand and did her other shoulder before moving to her back. I didn't know who invented this lotion, but I was going to write them a letter of thanks when I got home. I took my time because she felt wonderful.

"That feels grand," she said.

I almost passed out.

"All done?" she asked.

"Almost, let me check if I missed a spot."

This time I could not resist her bare neck and kissed it softly. The lotion tasted terrible, but it was worth it.

"I didn't see that part in the directions," Ailis said.

"It should be."

"Good, I'll call Colin over so you can put some on him." Her eyes sparkled with mirth.

I turned her around and kissed her softly. Colin and Lance, who seemed to be professionals at showing up at the worst time, came back to our spot just as I was about to kiss her again.

"I listened very carefully to my mom's instructions," Colin said, "I don't remember the part where she said that Joe was supposed to grope Ailis in public."

"She told me when we were at the mall," Ailis said. "She specifically told me to have a good time, and this has been really a good time."

"Yeah, for Joe," Lance said.

"Well, I think he's been class," she said.

Colin and Lance laughed together. I didn't care because the word "class" was all I could hear.

We spent the rest of the time either in the water or in the shade and I pointed out to Ailis the part of the instructions on the bottle of lotion that said, "reapply often."

"You just like putting it on me," she said.

"Yes, yes I do. I do very much."

CHAPTER 50
TRIP TO LIBERTY HILL

My relationship with Ailis had reached a point that when I called and asked her if she wanted to go somewhere she always accepted. She knew we would have a good time. I was incredibly happy to achieve this level in such a short time, because the calendar was not our friend. The plan I had for today was risky, not because it was dangerous but because we were both only seventeen and since she was a visitor to the country, I wasn't sure if she'd want to take a chance on getting in trouble.

When I got to Colin's house she was dressed in jeans and a white blouse. Her hair was pulled back, and I could see she had a little make-up on. She was lovely as always.

"This is going to be an adventure, I hope at least," I said.

"I hope so, because I'm getting tired of how boring you usually are," she teased.

After a half a block, I stopped at the corner.

"This is it, the corner?" she asked.

"This is a special corner."

She looked around trying to ascertain what could make it special.

"Okay, I give up, what makes this wee corner special?"

I laughed and pointed down the street at an approaching city bus. It stopped to pick us up. I paid the fare for both of us and asked for transfers. We took a seat behind the driver and headed downtown. Once we got there, we walked a block to the main bus stop and waited.

"A fancy bus stop sounds like a lot of fun," she said. She perused the once great center of the city.

"No, one more bus and we'll be there." I smiled.

"Okay, I almost trust you, but this better be cracker," she said.

"It will be."

"What's happening here," she asked pointing to a beautiful brick building that was boarded up and covered in graffiti.

"The city has seen better days. When I was little, downtown was a special place, especially at Christmas. It is a shame what is happening now," I said. I saw our bus and cut short the reminiscing. "This is us."

"Liberty Hill? That's the Irish section, right?"

"Yep, it is. Try not to stand out. You know, blend in, don't embarrass me."

That comment earned me a punch in the arm. We got on the bus, and I handed the driver the transfers.

The bus wound out of downtown and past the rail yards where my grandfather worked as an immigrant right off the boat from Italy. It chugged up the hill to the stop light at the heart of Liberty Hill.

"So, we can go over there to the Irish gift store, supposedly all the merchandise is from Ireland, so it's probably stuff you've never seen. Or we can go over to Quinn's. It is the most famous bar on Liberty Hill. Everyone goes there on St. Patrick's Day, and we can get a pint or two."

"Do you think they'll serve us?" she asked with a smile.

"Of course, you're my secret weapon. Try to look old when we walk in but don't do anything to all you're beautiful."

I saw her blush. She'd regained her composure by the time I opened the door. I took a deep breath that my plan would work.

Quinn's was nothing like the smaller corner bars on the northside that I had visited with my father when he went to get his football parley. The bar was made of a dark, polished wood with brass fixtures. It didn't reek of cigarettes, only the soothing smell of a man in a cap smoking a pipe at the corner of the bar. I recognized the Chieftains reel playing from the parties at the Foleys' house.

Quinn's had an impact on Ailis; I could see her eyes welling with tears. I grabbed her hand, and she squeezed it before turning to me.

"This place is class." The words caught a little in her throat.

"I'm glad you like it; let's sit at the bar," I said.

"Wow, this place almost looks real. Not bad, I'm impressed for a bunch of Americans," she said.

As we were about to sit down, I whispered in her ear. She nodded and smiled. The bartender came over and skillfully threw down two coasters in front of us. It was time for Ailis to put my plan into action.

"Yes, it'd be class if you could pour two pints of the black stuff for me and my fella," she said and leaned into the bar.

"So, you're from the north. What brings ya here?" The bartender had a slightly different accent.

"Joe here. He brought me over. After all the Troubles, I decided to start over in America," she replied with a hint of sadness.

"Aye, I know. Welcome to Quinn's" he said.

He poured two pints. I put a ten-dollar bill on the bar, and he nodded.

"You were amazing, I knew it would work," I said. We clinked glasses.

She did most of the talking, opening up more about living in Derry and what it was like with the soldiers and the bombings as a part of everyday existence in the city. She tried her best to live a normal life, but the threats of violence at any given moment frayed her nerves at times.

"How can I be so homesick and not want to leave here at the same time?" she asked.

"I don't know, I've never been away from Genesee for more than a week. I don't think I've ever been more than fifty miles. I put my dreams into a college that I've never been to and have only seen pictures. It's five hundred miles away. Tell me that isn't crazy. So, I was scared to death about leaving, but more excited about going than I've ever been about anything in my life. But I don't need to worry about that now unless the scholarship comes through."

"I felt the same way coming here. I wanted to see America, even if it is only Genesee, but it is a completely different way of life. No Brits, no worrying about the bus we were just on blowing up. And this," she said holding up her pint, "tastes almost as good as it does back home then."

"Well, I'm very happy you're here," I said. I wiped my mouth. "I don't even want to think about when you leave.

It'll be a lot at once, you're leaving, then me starting college right after."

"You are very different than Colin and the other guys. Why do you hang out with them?"

"They're fun," I said. "They don't care that I have different ambitions. I think I started going to Lance's house because it was a challenge to break out of my small circle of friends and be more adventurous. Plus, I wouldn't have met you. I would have seen you in church and wouldn't have had any courage to go talk to the beautiful new girl."

Ailis smiled.

"Were you raging you guys got me instead of the guy to help you paint the house?"

"Don't be crazy. I couldn't be happier that we got you. How about you, where were you supposed to go originally?"

"I don't want to say, it'll upset you."

"No, really, I want to know. But don't tell me if it was someplace that would have been amazing."

"I'm just kidding. I was going to Scranton, Pennsylvania."

"Then you definitely did better. You got Genesee…and me of course."

"Ha, that's pretty bold to include being with you as an improvement."

"I'm too bold, 'tis not to me she speaks."

"What?"

"It's Shakespeare, *Romeo and Juliet*, the balcony scene."

"You're quite a slabber".

"Jeez, I hope that's good."

"It means you're showing off, quoting Shakespeare, trying to impress me or something."

"Well, you enjoyed *Midsummer Night's Dream* so much, I thought—"

She cut me off. "I had you going, didn't I?"

I tried my best to smile and hoped I wasn't sweating.

"They're putting *Romeo and Juliet* on at Central Stage; would you like to go?"

Ailis sat stone faced and then smiled. "Aye, I would love to go see *Romeo and Juliet*. Do you know anyone I could go with?"

"Ah...me?"

She laughed again.

"I knew you were joking, so is that a yes?" I asked.

"Yes, it's a yes, you eejit."

"I keep meaning to ask you, what's an eejit? I know it doesn't sound good, but how bad is it?"

She jerked a thumb to her right. "Ask the barman."

I called the bartender over because we were ready for another pint anyway.

"Two more pints, and a question. What's an eejit?"

He looked at me and then at Ailis.

"I saw the way you're looking at this wee girl. Have you told her you love her yet?"

I couldn't help but blush and look down.

"I'll take that as a no. Then you're an eejit," the bartender said. He left to pour the pints.

"Idiot, it means idiot," she said putting her hand on my arm.

I stared at Ailis; she was so beautiful. Her hair mimicked the color of the autumn leaves and her green eyes had flecks of gold. She wore perfume for the first time, the smell more intoxicating than the Guinness. I wanted to take her in my arms and hold her. I wanted to smell her hair, trace the line of her neck with my lips and kiss her, a real passionate kiss. I wanted to tell her that I loved her because I knew I did. I didn't want to be an eejit anymore. We didn't have time.

She smiled and held my gaze. The pints came but we just stared at each other. I finally handed a pint to her. I raised my glass.

"What should we toast to?" I asked.

"To now and not thinking about the end of the summer," she said.

"I can drink to that, but I'll add a thank you for coming across the ocean to be here with me. I've never been happier than I am right here and right now. To Ailis."

We clinked glasses and took a drink.

"Joe, thanks for bringing me here. I really needed this, thank you."

"Absolutely, I've heard so much about Quinn's, it's an institution in the city."

She started, "But, Joe…"

"Ailis, what is it?"

"Nothing, just thank you. I'm very happy sharing a pint in this American version of a pub, with this American version of Guinness."

"You looked like you wanted to say something," I said hoping she would suddenly blurt out that she loved me.

"Well, there was another reason I wanted to come over for the summer. I told you that my mother left when I was young and my father left before her."

"Yes, I remember. My mother died when I was young, I know how that feels."

"Well, my father left and came here to America. He is living in New York City, in the Bronx."

I was shocked.

"Do you want to go see him?"

"Yes and no. I haven't seen him since I was six, when he came back to visit. I have an address and my aunt thinks that it's current. He's supposedly remarried and has kids. I overheard my aunt and uncle talking one night."

"We can take the Greyhound to New York City. We could get down there and back before anyone knows we're gone if we played it right."

"You think we could then?"

"We can stop at the bus station downtown on the way back home and get a schedule. I think if we say something like we're going camping out at Green Lakes. I don't know, we can figure it out, something that will buy us enough time."

"Really?"

"We can find a way; I promise."

She stood and hugged me, kissed me lightly on the lips. I was too stunned to do anything but hug her back and wait for another kiss. I didn't have to wait long. It was sweet and wet, the room blurred, and I felt dizzy.

"Glad to see you're no longer an eejit," the bartender said. He put down two more pints. "On the house."

CHAPTER 51
COLLEGE SURPRISE

The summer wore on, I resigned myself to going to St. Benedict's College and living at home, at least for the first year. I had my time with Ailis, the most pleasant distraction from these thoughts, even though I knew it wasn't going to last. I tried to enjoy every moment we were together.

I got home from painting and saw the mail on the table. I had stopped rushing to the mailbox because I wasn't expecting anything. A big envelope stood out in the stack. My curiosity piqued, I flipped through it. The envelope was addressed to me from the Army, TRADOC in Virginia, whatever that stood for. The Virginia address made me cringe a little.

I opened the envelope and started to read the letter:

Dear Mr. Di Capra,

Congratulations....

My hands began to shake.

Congratulations we are happy to offer you a full Army ROTC scholarship to the University of Virginia. We have enclosed a set of forms for you to complete and return to the ROTC office at UVA.

I got it. I danced around the living room and screamed at the top of my lungs. I ran to the phone and called the admissions office at UVA and confirmed that my spot was still available. I danced and screamed some more. I had to tell Ailis.

I grabbed the letter and ran up the street to Colin's house. I banged on the door and went in for the first time without waiting for someone to open it. Mrs. Foley poked her head around the corner from the dining room.

"Ailis?" I asked completely out of breath.

"She went to the store with Colin. I sent them to get some things for dinner. They should be back any minute. What's wrong with you?"

Mrs. Foley ended up being the first person who heard the good news.

"I got it, I can't believe it, I got the Army ROTC scholarship to the University of Virginia. A full ride, everything paid for, I can't believe it."

"Well congratulations, you worked very hard for that, and you deserve it. We'll have to have a party."

"Yes. Okay, thanks, I'd appreciate that."

We looked at each other. I didn't know what else to say.

"I'm going to wait outside for them to get back."

I looked up and down the street. I didn't know where they'd gone for sure, but I'd never seen Mrs. Foley at the Super Duper, so I knew not to look in that direction.

I spied the green station wagon coming from the direction of Erie Boulevard, the Price Chopper of course. I flagged them down. Colin pulled into the driveway and put the car in park but floored the accelerator a few times for show. Ailis jumped out of the car.

"What's wrong?" she asked.

I went over to tell her, but I couldn't speak, so I just shook the letter in front of her for a second.

"What?" she asked again.

"I got it…I got it! I'm going to Virginia I got the scholarship!"

It took her a second to understand what I said.

"You got it?"

"Yes." I held up the letter again as proof.

She jumped and clapped then gave me a hug and spoke in my ear.

"You did it. I'm so proud of you."

Colin finally got out of the car and walked over and gave me a hug.

"Congrats, man. I'm going to miss you. But we're coming down for the party as soon as you join a fraternity."

"Of course, you can come to a fraternity party. I'm going to go home for dinner and then go get a case of beer so we can celebrate at Lance's. See you guys there in a bit."

I ate my dinner standing up and then showered and changed. I pulled out the brand-new University of Virginia t-shirt that I'd purchased when I was accepted but put away when I got the letter about not getting the scholarship. I went to the Super Duper and bought a case of Heineken; this was definitely a reason to splurge.

"What's with you, did you win the lottery?" George asked when he saw me bouncing through the store, smiling, carrying the case of beer.

"Yes," I replied.

"You what?"

"Not the lottery lottery, but the college lottery. I got the letter today. I have a full ride to the University of Virginia. I got the ROTC scholarship."

"Congrats, that's great. When are you quitting?" he asked.

All I could say was, "Soon."

I carried the case on my shoulder over to Lance's, buoyed by the day's news and the thought of the night of celebration.

When I got to Lance's, I told him the great news and he gave me a congratulations high five. He helped me load the beer into the fridge, putting a six pack in the freezer to chill while we waited on Colin and Ailis. I knew they couldn't leave until family dinner was over. Colin wouldn't leave while there was still food on the table.

I had to fight Lance to keep him away from the freezer because he didn't want to wait for the others. When they finally walked in the front door, I gave Lance the nod and he returned with four open Heineken's with just a sliver of ice inside the neck of each bottle.

I held up my bottle and the others followed suit.

"I hate to sound conceited, so I won't toast to me or to my future. That's a hint for one of you to do it. I want to toast the United States Army for finally seeing the light that I would make a great officer and for paying for my college. And to the University of Virginia, for realizing that all my hard work should be rewarded. Cheers."

"Cheers," they repeated and we clinked bottles.

"I have a toast," Lance said after his long chug. "To Joe, he is a real pain in the ass sometimes, but he brings me lots of beer and he is a good guy most of the time. You really deserve the scholarship although you'll probably lose it after you join a frat house. Cheers."

We clinked bottles again.

"Thanks, Lance, that was almost heartwarming," I said.

Ailis was next. When she hesitated, I saw a tear form in the corner of her eye. She excused herself and went out to the back porch. I followed her.

"What's wrong?"

"Nothing. I'm just an eejit. I was just thinking about your future, you leaving for school. I'm here, away from Derry. I have already been thinking about leaving at the end of the summer and going back home to an uncertain future. I love being here, but it is going to be so hard to leave even though at times I'm so homesick my heart hurts."

I waited to be sure she was finished. "I'm happy that I got my scholarship," I said. "I'm going to my dream school, but part of me dreads the thought of getting on the bus and leaving Genesee. And I won't let myself think about you leaving. It's just too much. I can't believe you had the courage to get on a plane and fly across the world."

"Well look at what I left behind. Bombings, soldiers, occupation. The things you worry about in this neighborhood are nothing compared to that."

I laughed because it was better than crying. I wanted to hug her more than I had wanted to do anything in my life. I put down my beer and pulled her into me. I looked at her and wiped her tear from her cheek and hugged her tighter. It felt like I was embracing a dream. She was warm and her hair smelled like Herbal Essence shampoo.

"His heart checked upon her movement like a cork

upon a tide," I said, surprised my voice didn't crack with emotion.

"Are you trying to impress me by quoting Joyce?"

"Absolutely, did it work?"

She leaned in and kissed me – a real kiss with passion.

I wanted to be with her, in this moment, for the rest of my life, but Lance and Colin came out onto the porch with more beers. We sat on one of those beautiful upstate New York summer nights where it was almost cool enough to have to wear a jacket and a breeze kept the mosquitos away but didn't stop the fireflies from lighting up the backyard. We sipped our Heineken's and talked about everything other than leaving, moving on, and things changing.

CHAPTER 52
NOAH'S ARK WEEK

The forecast foretold unrelenting showers for the next week. I thought it was some of the best news of the summer. It meant a week of no obligations, even work because I had Mr. O take me off the schedule.

My mood after finding out about the scholarship soared, and now that I'd be heading to Charlottesville, the weight of pressing decisions had been lifted. The rain meant we couldn't paint, and it also gave me the chance to spend almost all day with Ailis. We could venture farther outside the neighborhood and do more as we huddled beneath umbrellas, taking the city bus to the different parts of Genesee.

The first day of spending time with Ailis, the rain wasn't that bad, just spotty showers, so we headed up to the zoo since there were also indoor exhibits. The rain made some of the parts of the zoo smell especially pungent but we didn't mind and we jumped the puddles on the paths between the animal cages.

"Aren't you going to excuse yourself," I asked Ailis as we approached the elephant exhibit.

"Pardon?"

"That wasn't you?" I asked. I sniffed the air.

Ailis realized what I said and gave me a roundhouse to the shoulder. I was laughing too hard to try to block.

An old lady with two wet, unhappy children in tow gave Ailis a dirty look.

"It's okay, Miss, he's my boyfriend."

"Boyfriend?" I asked.

"Well not if you think I smell like an elephant you dose."

"You are the farthest thing from an elephant. Now those baboons over there, well."

That earned me another round of swats.

"Okay, enough of the smells of the zoo. Let's go inside and get something to drink and then we can look in the gift shop," I said in an act of contrition.

"Don't start me again. Smell like an elephant. The nerve of you."

"Sorry, but let me check," I said. I nuzzled her neck.

She pushed me away but held my hand on the way inside.

I bought her a stuffed tiger at the gift shop, and all was forgiven.

The next day of the rain we took the bus to Seneca University. I had a new love for this school because of the interview that led to my scholarship, and I wanted to show Ailis a real American university.

It was old and beautiful with ivy covered buildings, the grounds seeped knowledge. The Quad was the calm, welcoming heart of the school. I loved going to football and basketball games there, but knew it wasn't the school for me. We walked around campus and went into the different buildings. It was mostly empty because it was summer but there were a few students walking around.

"UVA is even older. It was founded and designed by Thomas Jefferson," I said when I could see she was impressed by the Seneca campus.

We went into one of the campus bars on Marshall Street and tried to get a beer, but the bartender took one look at us and asked for ID. I bought Ailis a Seneca University t-shirt in one of the bookstores and we had lunch at Bob Barker's Hot Dogs where Ailis introduced me to vinegar "chips."

Day three of the rain meant we went to the mall. Malls were new to Genesee. Ours wasn't huge, just a converted strip mall where they kept adding stores onto the original building. But we didn't have to worry about downpours or getting splashed while we walked.

We had lunch at the food court and window shopped. She was enthralled with the record shop and especially with the bookstore. I bought her a copy of the *Complete Works of Shakespeare*. I was also considering buying her some Joyce, but she gave me a look when I approached her with a stack of books.

"I have to carry all of this back to Derry you know," she said.

"I'll carry it for you. How do you think I'd fit in over there?"

"You wouldn't last a day."

"C'mon, I'm worldly. I'm from the mean streets of the east side of Genesee, New York. I'm Italian, incredibly good looking and the smartest person I know."

This caused her to laugh again.

"Mean streets? You have no idea," she said.

I knew not to press it.

We got ice cream at Baskin Robbins and walked around until it was time to get the bus back to the neighborhood. She leaned her head on my shoulder and we watched the rain-streaked neighborhoods of Genesee pass by.

On the fourth day of rain, we visited the old Italian side of town.

We went to Lombardi's Italian Grocery for our first stop. Ailis was floored by the incredible smells of the Italian specialties as soon as we walked in the door. I played tour guide and showed her the different foods that I knew from all the family feasts from the holidays, weddings and the "Uncle Pete parole parties." Ailis was amazed.

"We don't have anything like this in Derry. There's one Italian restaurant but I think its run by Indians."

"You have Indians in Ireland?" I thought of American Indians.

"Aye, Indians from India, not cowboys and Indians, you…American."

We sampled different meats from the deli: prosciutto, a couple of different salamis, capicola, and pepperoni. I got some provolone, roasted red peppers, and a small loaf of Italian bread. It was still warm. We went outside to one of the patio tables. I spread out the deli paper and tried my best to slice the bread with a plastic knife. I arranged the meats and showed her the different combinations.

"Jeezus this is fabulous," Ailis said while she munched on one of the slices I had prepared.

"Pretty good huh? This is a big step up from the deli at the grocery store where we got the food for Fourth of July."

"I was going to joke that a cheese and "tayto" sandwich was better, but it's not even close. I'm lured, this is much better than the food at the Fourth party," she said. She had more of the prosciutto.

"Yeah, we don't get this really good stuff for the Fourth because we'd have cousins descend on our picnic table like a swarm of locusts. They'd even eat the tablecloth."

We polished off all the food in no time.

"Hungry?" I asked her.

"What?"

"Well, the next stop was going to be Caroma's for lunch, but I think we might need to walk around a little to build up our appetites."

I showed Ailis the rail yards where my grandfather worked when he came over from Italy. We walked past the old shoe factory where so many in my family had worked. I was especially proud of St. Joseph's Church. It always amazed me considering it was built by poor Italians who weren't welcome in the German and Irish churches. I added this fact for historical accuracy.

"Believe me, I know about how religion can divide people," she said.

We went inside and blessed ourselves in the holy water.

"I want to show you something," I said motioning to the right side of the pews.

We walked up and stopped at a stained-glass window of Saint Barbara. I pointed to the small brass dedication plaque.

Ailis read aloud. "Dedicated to the Di Capra Family."

She ran her fingers over the engraving. "That's really special."

"I know. My father and his sisters did this for my grandparents. Whenever we come over here for Mass, we have to sit here under Saint Barbara. She is the patron saint of Davoli, the town in Calabria my grandparents came from."

We walked out of the church down the center aisle. I held her hand and envisioned Ailis in a wedding gown, the church full of flowers. I had to stop myself. I was just increasing the hurt I was going to feel when she left.

"Ready to eat?" I asked when we got outside.

"I'll try but I can't promise anything."

We walked over to Caroma's, a very unassuming Italian restaurant, but the best in the city.

"We have to have the baked ziti; it is better than my Aunt Vicky's, which is saying a lot. We can get one order and some chicken parmigiana. I know it's what you see on the menu of every Italian restaurant but the way they do it here is different, really special. We can share if you don't mind. It's exceptionally good, I promise."

"I believe you and that sounds cracker," she said.

I ordered when the waitress came over.

"So, what do you think of the Italian section so far?"

"It's grand. Why don't you live here then?"

"I don't know. I think after World War Two, moving out of the neighborhood meant that you had gained some success. There was also what was called redlining before the war. Italians couldn't buy in certain neighborhoods. I've never asked my father questions about all the details, but I should. Only a few of my relatives still live in this neighborhood but we are the only ones that moved to the east side."

"You don't have much choice in Derry. Some people have gone to the south since they have family, but in Derry there is the Catholic section, the Bogside, and the Protestant section, the Waterside, which is called Londonderry. There is no interaction, and you wouldn't have the choice of where to live."

"I can't imagine."

"Well, when the Troubles started it got really bad. I can tell you all about that, but I don't want to ruin the day."

I looked at her and tried to imagine the depth of the impact of the conditions Ailis endured every day. How did she remain so sweet and cheerful?

Our antipasti came as a welcome distraction.

Just the first dish was enough to feed four people and when the waitress brought the main courses we ordered, we both sat wide eyed at the amount of food.

Ailis tried both entrees, her eyes fluttering with each new bite, but we hardly put a dent in any of the dishes.

"Oh, my goodness again, that was so amazing. I think if I lived here, I'd be as big as a wee bus because I'd have to eat here all the time."

"Well, I watch my aunts cook, so I think with a little practice I could make some of these dishes."

"If you can cook like this, you are going to be very successful with the ladies." She winked.

I wanted to say she'd be the only lady I would want to be with, but I just thanked her. We waddled back to the bus stop and made it back to the neighborhood in time for dinner. We walked into the Foley's with two bags of leftovers, ready to lie down and recover.

"Dinner is ready, sweetie," Mrs. Foley said when she saw Ailis and me come in.

"No thank you, Mrs. Foley. I need to rest a bit."

"What did Joe Di Capra do to you?"

I smiled and tried to act innocent.

"He just showed me how Italians eat. I'm so stuffed, I can't move."

§§

On the last day of rain we were pretty worn out from all our travels but I saved the best destination for the end.

We went back to Quinn's and listened to an Irish trio. Ailis got misty during some of the tunes and hummed along with some of the others. There was a good crowd. They probably wanted to get out of the rain too. We enjoyed our pints and talked about what kinds of stories I wanted to write.

I grabbed a napkin and asked the waitress for a pen.

"We're going to write a novel right now," I said.

"What? Is this a wee joke?"

"No, I'll start, and I'll write down the highlights of the plot and then someday I'll write the book. It'll be yours too because it'll be your ideas along with mine. I'll start and make it easy. Once upon a time there was a skinny kid from Genesee that met this beautiful girl from far away."

"Ah, go on then." She blushed.

"What comes next?"

"The skinny guy doesn't deserve the beautiful girl, but he tries very hard to prove he is worthy of her hand so," she said.

"Okay, this is fiction remember so we don't have to hit too close to the truth," I said,

"You asked for a story and I'm the beautiful girl," she said.

"Okay, the skinny guy romances her and tries to convince her that she should stay in Genesee and not go back to the land far away," I said.

"But as hard as he tried and as much as she began to see that the skinny guy was almost amazing—"

I interrupted. "He is amazing isn't he."

"I said 'almost' amazing. Anyway, she had to go back to her family. She had to go back to her life because Genesee was just a wee dream and it was not real life, at least for now, even though a part of her wanted to stay. But not necessarily with the skinny guy." Her smile made me feel a little better.

I feigned a wound to the heart.

"And the skinny guy leaves," she said, "to go to a great university and he learns all that he can learn, and he falls in love with every college girl he meets."

"But the skinny guy ignores all the college girls because none of them can compare to her. He knows he would lay down his life for her, that she had changed him, made him see that there was a world outside of Genesee. She helped him see he was meant to go out and explore. He knows fate brought them together and fate will make sure they meet again."

"This is getting pretty mushy, so it is, but it's not bad so far. At least you haven't thrown in any kissing."

"No kissing yet, but some would be nice," I said. "Keep going, add some action and don't forget that kissing is action."

"The beautiful girl from far away had to say goodbye, she didn't have a choice. But she thought of him every day and looked for him from time to time when she saw someone walking towards her down the lane."

"And the skinny guy kept a corner of his broken heart only for her and never let anyone near it because it was hers," I said. I held her gaze and kissed her gently.

The waitress came over with two new pints and broke the moment.

"It'll be a best seller," she whispered to me.

"But how does it end? Will it be a happy ending or the type of ending where the reader weeps with joy and goes through an entire box of Kleenex?" I asked.

Her eyes were glazed and wistful. "I don't know. I wish I did."

CHAPTER 53
MOVIE NIGHT

Planning an entire party without Colin finding out was a lot tougher than I imagined. I had to enlist Mrs. Foley to give Colin chores so we could meet at Lance's while he was busy. Somehow, we got it all done without his spoiling anything. Of course, we could have told him there was going to be a party, but I thought the night would be a lot better if it was a surprise.

When Colin showed up at Lance's for what he thought was a regular night of a couple beers on the back porch, he found Lance's house full of his friends, a film projector in the living room with a makeshift bedsheet screen hanging over the fireplace.

"What's this?" Colin asked. "Dirty movies? That would be awesome."

"Nothing that good," Lance said.

I jumped in to change the subject. "No this is a surprise for you, we arranged everything." I handed Colin a beer and led him to one of the overstuffed chairs we had placed in the middle of the room with the best view of the screen.

I yelled above the din. "Everybody get a drink. Movie time in five minutes."

"What the hell is this?" Colin asked again.

"Well, you're partially right about dirty movies. Your mother lent me her home movies. One of your first haircut, your first birthday and of course you bare-assed in the bathtub." I couldn't drink my beer because I was laughing so hard.

Ailis hit my arm. "You're too cruel, Joe."

"Shh, don't ruin it," I smiled. "That's what makes it fun."

Everyone took their places, the lights were turned out and I started the projector.

After a few seconds of fuzzy frames, the image came into focus. It was Euclid Hill.

"NO WAY! Is this really THE FILM? Tell me it is," Colin said.

I pointed to the screen. "Watch and see."

Colin jumped out of the chair, threw his arms into the air signaling victory, and screamed. He danced around before retaking his seat, sitting on the edge of the chair, and leaning toward the screen.

There was a pan up and down the street, then the camera focused on the top of the hill. When the Battle Wagon appeared at the top of the hill, the room cheered. The camera followed the car as it hit the flat spot and went airborne. Joel Fleischman skillfully focused on the car until its frame crunching impact and fishtailing, skidding stop.

Colin danced around the room again, receiving and giving high fives. He dropped to his knees with his hands folded as if in prayer. "Again. Again."

I lost count how many times we reshowed the jump,

but it never lost its magnitude. It was, to my mind, the greatest two minutes of film ever shown on the east side of Genesee.

"How did you do it?" Colin asked as he released me from a gigantic bearhug.

"I went over to Fleischman's grandparents' and got his address in Brooklyn; it took a lot of wrangling, but he had a copy made and sent it to me."

"That was amazing," Colin said. "Thank you, thank you, thank you."

"I had to make sure the legend of the Battle Wagon didn't die. Maybe we can find a way to charge admission for showings so you can get the money to have her fixed," I said.

"That's a great idea, we can show it every Friday."

"Well, if you really want to make money, maybe you should go back to your original guess and show real racy movies," I said.

"I just might do that." I could see the wheels inside his head turning.

The night ended with Colin sprawled out on the hood of the Battle Wagon, kissing the windshield and whispering his undying love to the rusted metal and cracked frame.

CHAPTER 54
AFTER JULIET

Ailis and I attended the matinee performance of the Center Stage production of *Romeo and Juliet* held in the palatial, refurbished opera theatre in downtown Genesee. The community had banded together to save this local treasure from the wrecking ball. To me, it was a sign that there was still hope for Genesee.

The performance was mesmerizing. The young lady playing Juliet had an English accent and looked a little like Ailis.

"Juliet looks like she could be your sister," I said.

"No, she's English. And Romeo looks nothing like you," she replied.

She left me hanging in wonder. At the end of the scene, I tapped her shoulder. She giggled because she knew that I stewed over her statement the entire time.

"You are much better looking than him and I hope you don't own a pair of tights like that, because I don't think I can see you again if you do."

By the time Romeo and Juliet were married, she held

my hand. We both were holding back tears. When Juliet ended her life, we both gave up and let the tears flow.

After the Prince gave his closing speech, the crowd stood and applauded, and the applause grew as each actor came forward.

When all the clamor finished, we sat in our chairs not wanting to leave. Outside sat the real world where we would be separated, an ocean apart. Here in our seats, we lived in an imaginary realm where love's power was unstoppable.

Finally getting up to leave, we stood in the lobby in that slight state of confusion when you transition from the fantasy world of the stage to the reality of life. Having been immersed in the tale of young lovers, we weren't sure if we wanted to leave their orbit. I knew I wanted so badly for my reality to include this beautiful girl who was next to me, holding my hand. She had stolen my heart.

Ailis positively gushed. "I don't know which one was better, *Midsummer Night's* or *Romeo and Juliet*. It was so sad and so beautiful."

"I really enjoyed the live performance, I didn't think I could love the play more after we saw the movie in ninth grade but after this, I know it's my favorite. After we saw the movie, I memorized parts of the play because I was so taken with the story," I said.

"Are we star-crossed?" Ailis asked.

"No, not at all. I couldn't be happier that we are together, even if it's for a short time. But I promise you, I haven't thought once of visiting an apothecary."

"I don't own any daggers," she said.

"That's good to know."

"Eyes, look your last. Arms, take your last embrace,"

she said. "Why don't you ever say anything like that to me?"

"You're just lucky I don't stammer like an eejit every time I see you. I can't believe how good some of the things I say to you are. I need to write them down. You let me open up; that's never happened before."

"Well, I like romance, so keep it coming. I like that you don't talk about football scores and what you and your friends did at the pub."

"If the Joe Di Capra from last year was watching the Joe Di Capra of today, he wouldn't recognize him. He'd say how did you get so cool and how did you get such a beautiful girl?"

I took her hand in a "holy palmers' kiss."

"We have the rest of the day, what would you like to do?" I asked.

"What would Romeo and Juliet do?"

"You mean if they hadn't killed themselves?"

"Don't ruin the moment," she said.

"We could sneak up to Our Lady of Sorrows and ask Monsignor McCarthy to marry us," I said. I watched her face for a reaction.

She smiled.

"Way too fast, Mr. Di Capra," she said. She changed the moment with a laugh, this one genuine.

"Right, there's a jewelry store down the block. We could look at engagement rings."

"Slower still so," she replied.

"Quinn's for a pint?"

She took my hand. "Now you're not being an eejit, let's go," she said.

CHAPTER 55
MARY APPEARS TO ME

Ailis and I watched a re-run of *Saturday Night Live* on the Foleys' couch laughing and eating popcorn. I didn't feel like sharing her attention with everyone all the time at Lance's, so we started to do more things on our own. We could both feel the end of the summer looming like a darkness on the horizon, too close to ignore. After the show ended, I helped her clean up and we made plans to meet at church in the morning and then go to Lance's.

"Be careful going home," she said. I kissed her goodbye on the Foley's front steps.

"I will. I'm a pro at making the trip. But if you're really worried, I could sneak upstairs with you" I replied, kissing her one more time.

"And do what?" she asked. She tried to look indignant.

I stammered and searched for a reply.

"Good night then," she said. She kissed me one more time, with passion, leaving me dizzy. We watched each other until we were out of sight.

As I walked through the parking lot at Our Lady of Sorrows school, a car pulled into the lot and screeched to a halt in front of me. I was just about to run when I heard Calvin Upton yell out of the window.

"Get in, I need some help."

I knew he didn't need help lifting something heavy or because he had a trunk full of food he wanted to deliver to starving orphans. I had a feeling the help he needed might eventually involve running from the police.

"C'mon, it won't take long," he said.

Against my better judgment and every fiber in my body telling me to go home, I jumped in the front seat of his father's BMW. I marveled at how nice the car appeared. I was used to rusted out Detroit behemoths that propagated the neighborhood. This car was polished and there wasn't an empty beer can or candy wrapper to be seen. Calvin put the car into gear and squealed out onto Salt Springs Road.

"Where are we going?" I asked.

"Just down to Erie Boulevard, a short trip., I have something to drop off. Like I said, it'll only take a minute."

We turned onto a side street and wound our way through the neighborhood down to Erie Boulevard. Calvin pulled into the parking lot of the Great Wall Restaurant and Tea House. He took an unlit spot close to the building and left the car running.

"Watch the entrance to the parking lot and yell if anyone comes."

"What have you gotten me into Calvin?"

"Don't worry, it's nothing illegal, I think. It's just a lot funnier than I ever thought."

He opened the back door, reached down, and took the

blanket off something on the floor. He turned to me and smiled. In his hand was a statue of the Virgin Mary.

"You? You're the one who started all this craziness? You know this is a national story. People are coming from all over the country to see the statues."

"Yeah" Calvin said. "I really didn't expect that to happen and almost stopped because it was so nuts. I was bored one night, and had a couple statues that I took from the old garden shed behind the church. I was going to leave a few in a couple of funny places. After the second one, it turned into the big circus; so I had to keep going."

"You are a genius."

"I know," Calvin said. He ran up to the decorative fountain and placed Mary in a strategic place where she was illuminated by the floodlights that lit up the streams of water and the front of the building in a rainbow of colors.

We jumped into the car and headed back to our neighborhood.

"How many more of these are you going to do?" I asked.

"That's the last one. I'm leaving this week to go to Boston. My father wants to get me settled in and registered for classes. There's a pre-freshman program I have to attend. I can't wait to be on my own. There's so much I have planned for my release. I'm gonna try to join the Harvard Lampoon, if they'll have me."

"Is that anything like National Lampoon? They created the greatest movie ever, *Animal House*."

"The guys that started National Lampoon were all at the Harvard Lampoon." He beamed.

"Well if you tell them about starting a national religious movement with a prank, you are a shoo-in."

'Yeah, I was thinking about leaving one in front of my parents' house before I go, but it's too risky."

"You're not a genius; you're an evil genius."

"Thanks, that's quite a compliment."

"You haven't been around, so I haven't been able to tell you. I got a full ride to the University of Virginia. I'm leaving at the end of August. I plan on joining a fraternity if they have one close to the Delta House."

"Congratulations," Calvin said. "I hope our little excursion has prepared you in some way for college and the higher educational goals of pledging a fraternity."

"It has. I'm going to miss you, Calvin. Make sure you come up to Lance's if you're back in town."

He smiled in a way that said he might not be back.

"Do you want to go in?" he asked when we got close to Lance's house.

"No thanks, I have to get home."

I saw Jennifer's Olds in the driveway, *Why isn't she at work?* I imagined a new black eye and cringed.

"Do you have any more statues? I mean, you might not want to let the greatest prank I've ever seen die."

"Sure, there are about five more in the shed if you want one. The window facing my backyard doesn't lock. I'll keep an eye on the news to see what you do. Live long and prosper, grasshopper."

"Thanks Calvin, *Star Kung Fu Trek*, my favorite show." I laughed. "Good luck in Boston, stay in touch."

He let me out in front of my house, and I waved as he pulled away.

I turned on the midday news the next day just to see the response to Calvin's last Mary statue. Since it was a Sunday, there were busloads of faithful headed to Erie

Boulevard right after church, crowding the parking lot. The police had Mary blocked off with yellow tape. People knelt and prayed. The Great Wall Restaurant added a makeshift food stand by the front door, serving fried rice and egg rolls to the multitude in lieu of the loaves and fishes.

CHAPTER 56
MOVING ON

I had let the Super Duper know I planned to quit. I didn't need the money and I wanted to spend every hour with Ailis. I also stopped showing up to paint. I thought Colin and Lance would give me endless grief about it, but they knew why I wasn't there. Besides, they had Dave Taylor and Hugh Seely working full time.

In addition, because of my decision to spend all my time with Ailis, I was never home and rarely saw my father. I was up and out of the house before my father rose and when I did come home, he'd long since gone to bed. We passed each other on the way to one thing or another and exchanged pleasantries. My guilt about leaving him alone for dinner grew to the point where I called my oldest sister to ask her to help out. She told me not to worry, which I found strange because my sisters could win Olympic medals in worrying about my father. I said, "Okay" and trusted she was right.

A rainy Sunday morning revealed why my sister told me not to worry. I went to church with my father for the first time in months. It was the first Sunday I hadn't worked in as long as I could remember. I thought my father would be happy that I was able to go with him, but he seemed nervous and kept looking around the church as we walked to our regular seats.

"Dad, I'm going to go to the main entrance and wait for Ailis."

My father nodded.

I looked at him again, trying to figure out what was going on, but I didn't want to miss Ailis in case she wanted to sit with me instead of the Foleys. I saw her walking down the hill towards the church by herself, I could tell it was her from two blocks away even with her face completely obscured by the hood of her raincoat. When she waved, I hoped I'd never lose the feeling that ran through me.

Since she was alone, she readily accepted my offer to sit with us for mass. When we headed up the aisle, I saw someone sitting to the right of my father, I slid in next to him with Ailis on my side.

"Good morning Mr. Di Capra," Ailis said.

It was then I realized that the lady in the pew wasn't sitting next to my father, she was sitting *with* my father.

"Good morning, Ailis, this is Mrs. Dembrowski," my father said. He leaned back. Mrs. Dembrowski leaned forward so Ailis could see her.

"That's a beautiful accent, where are you from?" Mrs. Dembrowski asked.

"Derry, Northern Ireland, I'm here for the summer, staying with the Foleys up the street," Ailis said.

I looked at my father while the two ladies exchanged

pleasantries and furrowed my brow hoping my father would get the question I was trying to ask.

He mouthed an answer. "After mass.,"

We were saved from any more questions when Monsignor McCarthy came out from the sacristy to begin the service.

§§

I walked Ailis to the Foleys' house after mass. We sat on the front porch talking and watching the rain.

"What was going on with your Da?" she asked.

"I'm not sure. I haven't been home very much lately, and my mom has been gone for over ten years. I think he has a girlfriend."

"You Di Capra men are quite popular with the ladies." She gave me a sideways glance. "How do you feel about that?"

I stopped and thought. "I don't know yet. On one level, I'm happy for him because I was very worried about him being all alone with me going to college. On the other hand, I didn't think he would ever go there after my mother. They had been together since he got back from the war."

"They look like a nice couple so," Ailis said.

"I don't know yet, but for now I give them my permission to court."

"Court? What century do you think this is?"

I laughed. "I'll be over around two so we can head over to Lance's?"

"Well, there's this wee fellow I met, that Mr. Foley introduced me to last week. He's supposed to come over and watch the tele with me. He's also Irish," she said. She looked at me over as if to remind me of my heritage.

"Then I'll be there too, sitting between you two and making sure he doesn't spend a second alone with you."

"And what gives you the right to do that, Mr. Di Capra?"

"I have the right because we are courting."

Ailis laughed and gave me a hug.

"Tell your Da I think it's great that he has a girlfriend."

"Well at least there is one Di Capra man with a girlfriend," I said trying to sound hurt.

"I don't know about that," she said with a slight smile. She kissed me on the cheek and went inside.

§§

I ran down the hill to my house. Dad was pulling into the driveway.

"Did you go somewhere after church?" I asked.

"Millie and I went to get some coffee," he said. He watched for my reaction.

"I take it Millie is Mrs. Dembrowski. Dad, I'm happy that you have a friend. Is she a girlfriend?"

"I know it sounds funny for someone at my age to have a girlfriend, but you could say that. You know I've been helping Monsignor with chores at the church. I met Millie setting up for a fundraiser," he said.

"Are you guys serious?" I asked and then realized a part of me didn't want the answer.

"Yes, we are. We are going to get married. There's no reason to wait. We are both sure."

"No way," I said because I couldn't think of anything else to say at the moment.

"Yes, I'm afraid so," my father replied.

"And all my sisters already know all of this?"

"Yeah, I told them already. You haven't been around much and since you are still at home I was worried about your reaction."

"Don't worry, Dad. Mazel tov."

"You've been working at the kosher store too long." He laughed.

"I don't know how to say congratulations in Italian, but really, it's great."

"Well, what do you think about being my best man?" he asked. "It isn't going to be a big ceremony, just family. Millie doesn't have any kids, so it'll be just her two sisters, her brother, and their kids. Our side on the other hand is tough to boil down to fit the definition of small."

"Best man, so I'll have to give a speech and all that?"

"You can if you want. And invite the 'pretty Irish girl' as Millie called Ailis. She could tell you really like her."

"I do," I said. I was a little too loud.

"That's my line," he said.

CHAPTER 57
NOT ENOUGH MAKEUP

Ailis and I were walking to Lance's house after going out to lunch with Mr. and Mrs. Foley. They made up some excuse to take us out, but I got the feeling they were making sure that we didn't do anything crazy like elope.

"Do you really think so?" Ailis asked.

"I think so, but…"

I didn't finish my sentence because I saw Jennifer getting out of her car and struggling with two bags of groceries. I rushed ahead to help her. One of the bags tore and the contents fell to the ground. "Thank you," she said. She wouldn't look at me. It sounded like she was crying.

"Jennifer? Are you okay?" I asked.

By then Ailis had caught up and helped collect the groceries from the ground.

Jennifer finally turned to face us. She had fresh bruises and a split lip that she had tried to cover with heavy makeup. I looked at Ailis and I could see by her expression that she saw the same thing.

"Jennifer, are you okay? I asked again in a softer voice.

"Yes, Joe, I'm okay. I just need to get inside. I appreciate your help."

Ailis moved quickly from my side and hugged Jennifer. Jennifer quietly sobbed into her shoulder. Ailis looked at me with pleading eyes.

"Joe, can you do something?" she said.

I shook my head. I didn't know what to do.

We helped Jennifer inside and I put the groceries on the floor by the front door. Her boyfriend came into the room as Ailis, and I were about to leave. I glared at him.

"What? What are you going to do tough guy? I'll beat your ass. C'mon if you think you're tough."

Ailis stepped behind me and grabbed my hand. I stood my ground and kept looking at him.

"C'mon, Joe, let's go,' Ailis said. I could hear the panic in her voice.

We walked out but I kept staring at him. And he continued to threaten me.

Once outside, Ailis hugged me and started to cry.

"Is there anything you can do?" she asked.

"I don't know, I'll talk to the guys. I can't do much alone, you saw the size of that guy."

"I don't want you to get hurt but we have to help her."

"We will," I said. "We just have to figure out a way."

CHAPTER 58
THE OFFER

My father and I never really had any heart-to-heart talks. There was a lot that was unsaid but understood. I knew what his expectations were of me, and I did my best to exceed them at every turn. I never gave him any reason to worry about me, on purpose that is, and what he didn't know about my new life outside the shell was probably a good thing.

The announcement of his impending nuptials added to all the changes that were taking place at the end of the summer. The closer I got to leaving for Virginia and Ailis's return to Northern Ireland, the more overwhelmed I felt. I tried as hard as I could not to think about life without her but our increasing feelings for each other was making what was once a difficult event seem insurmountable.

Sundays before church became the only time that my father and I could catch up on all the changes going on in both our lives.

"Joe, we need to talk."

My father looked serious and I scrolled through all the possible topics.

"I wanted to tell you about our house."

I wondered about what the living arrangements would be after my father got married. Mrs. Dembrowski lived in one of the huge, old Victorian houses on Genesee Street, built when it was the main highway between all the upstate cities bordering the Erie Canal. It was a beauty with a brick façade and columns and even though I'd never been inside I guessed we could probably fit our entire house in the living room.

"There is no reason to have two houses," my father said. "I know this is the only house that you've known, but it doesn't make sense for us to live here when Millie's house is practically a mansion."

I didn't want to tell my father that this was also the house where my mother got sick, wasted away, and eventually died. Those were memories I could leave behind and I really had no allegiance to this house.

"I understand, Dad. It's the right choice, an easy choice."

"The for-sale sign goes up tomorrow, I really don't know how long it'll take to sell but there's no mortgage, so I think we'll be okay."

My father still looked concerned.

"I understand, don't worry about it. What is it?"

"Well," he said, "I talked it over with your sisters and they all agree with my decision, so that's good. I told them I want to give the money from the sale of the house to you. That way you could pay for Virginia without having to take the ROTC Scholarship. You won't owe the Army four years after graduation. I just wish I could have known this a lot earlier, so you didn't have to go through all that worry."

I stood there blinking at the news.

"I...I don't know. I've already accepted the Army scholarship. I want to be an officer But the Army doesn't pay for my room and board. I have to find the money for that."

"I can pay for it," Dad said.

"That means I won't have to get a part-time job, which would be great. I can concentrate on school."

"Consider it done, I'm glad to help, especially since you had to pay for high school yourself. But in a way I'm glad you did. I feel bad for not being able to do it myself, but look how it made you grow up, take responsibility. You may not see it now, but it will go a long way for you in your life."

"I know, Dad, thanks. While you're feeling guilty can we talk about a car? They don't let freshman have cars on campus, but maybe next year?"

"We'll look into that when we see how much the house sells for," he said.

"Thanks, I appreciate the help. For the record, I never blamed you for not being able to pay for Bishop Slattery. You went through so much more than I did. Growing up in the Depression and then getting drafted into World War Two. Losing Mom. I've had it easy compared to you."

"Well, I'm very proud of all you've done. I'm glad I'll be in a position to help."

"Thanks, Dad."

CHAPTER 59
MARY'S COMMAND PERFORMANCE

My alarm went off at 5:00 AM. I jumped out of bed, got dressed, and grabbed the backpack I had sitting in my room. I left the house as quietly as I could and walked up to Lance's. The early Sunday morning streets were deserted.

I was filled with nervous energy because my plan had a lot of moving parts. If one of them failed, the entire plan would come crashing down. I took some deep breaths and tried to focus on my ultimate goal.

I saw a car coming down Salt Springs Road and ducked behind some bushes on the side of a driveway. When the car passed, I began walking again. I reached Lance's house and went inside without knocking. I took out the contents of the backpack and went back outside, taking a few more deep breaths so I would be ready to start. I looked up and down the street to see if there was anyone out or if there were any cars coming.

When I was sure everything was clear, I walked across the street and left what I carried on the front steps of Jennifer's house. I sprinted to the pay phone at the

Lebanese convenience store and called the WGEN news hotline.

"Good morning, WGEN," the person said much too cheerily for 5:25 AM.

"Yes, I want to report another Mary statue. It's at 223 Harwood Avenue." I said before hanging up.

I ran back to Lance's and made it inside just in time to see the WGEN News truck pull up to Jennifer's house. Within minutes a reporter arrived outside, and I saw the crew setting up a camera. The lights went on and the reporter talked for a few minutes before the lights shut off. The cameraman handed a tape to a young lady. She got into a car parked behind the news truck and zoomed away. I looked at my watch and silently cheered.

"I think they'll make the early news," I said to myself as I stood at the window to watch the commotion.

The noise of the evolving circus woke Lance. He came downstairs to find me looking out his living room window.

"What's going on? What are you doing here on a Sunday morning?"

"Another Mary statue across the street at Jennifer's house," I answered.

"Jennifer? Why Jennifer? How did you know about it? Has it been on the news already?"

"No, the TV news isn't on until noon. But I saw a couple radio station cars, so I'm sure they are already talking about it. It's just another miracle I guess," I replied.

By 10:00 AM there were more television reporters and carloads of the faithful. The police had arrived and were cordoning off the house with yellow tape to hold the crowd back. Colin and Ailis arrived while the police were blocking off the streets. That was when the first bus from St. Lucy's showed up.

In the middle of the chaos, I saw a policeman talking to Jennifer. He took her chin and closely inspected her face. I saw them walking to his car. Jennifer got into the front seat. She was crying.

"What's going on then," Ailis asked.

"Come with me," I said.

We moved to a window in the sun porch where we could still see everything. I told her the entire story.

"You? It's…been you?" she asked.

"No, just this one statue. The others were someone else., I'll tell you later. Look." I pointed to the police car.

The policeman that talked to Jennifer was out of the patrol car and talking to another officer. After a minute they went to Jennifer's front door. They knocked until Jennifer's boyfriend finally appeared.

The conversation seemed innocent at first but the boyfriend began to get more and more animated until the cops finally grabbed him, threw him to the ground, and cuffed him. They dragged him into a different patrol car while old women prayed the Rosary and made the sign of the cross. Jennifer's boyfriend spewed obscenities, all under Mary's watchful eye.

We rejoined Colin and Lance at the living room window.

"Can you believe it? A statue on my street?" Lance said.

"And Jennifer's asshole boyfriend in cuffs, it's awesome," Colin said.

I smiled the smile of the unsuspected. "It's a miracle," I said.

CHAPTER 60
THE WEDDING

My father's wedding was set for the first Saturday in August. Ailis looked forward to attending; she told me she loved weddings. I also invited Lance and the Foley family. My father wanted to keep it small but once his sisters were invited and their families with all my cousins, it grew to well over a hundred people just from our side of the family.

Mrs. Dembrowski, or Millie as she insisted I call her, her "two sisters, a brother and their kids" turned out to be over fifty people, so the "small" wedding became a large affair. My father secured the VFW hall since he was a member, and we used my cousin Stevie's restaurant to cater the food. Colin went with me to be fitted for my tuxedo. I prepared myself for the barrage of insults when I walked out of the dressing room, but he just smiled and said I looked good.

The big day arrived, and the church was filled with flowers. My Aunt Vicky owned a florist shop. I waited with my nervous father in the vestibule of the church.

"Feel like you are about to land on Utah Beach again?"

I asked him. He was peeking out of the cracked door at the growing crowd.

"Worse," he replied.

"C'mon, this is worse than Germans shooting at you?"

"I guess you're right. Thanks for being my best man."

"Of course, I'm happy that you are happy. Now I don't have to worry about you puttering around in an empty house. You'll be a newlywed, starting a family, babies, diapers, and all that."

My father laughed out loud, then realized he was probably too loud and returned to the door to see if there was any reaction in the crowd.

Monsignor McCarthy came up the back stairs from the rectory and went over to my father.

"Congratulations, Vince, I love doing weddings."

"Well, I'm sure the next time you thought you'd see me going down the aisle I'd be in a box, so I'm happy too," my father replied.

Monsignor chuckled and started putting on his garments. The two altar boys, kids from the grammar school I knew from serving midnight mass, were busy getting everything ready.

"Shall we, gentlemen?" Monsignor asked when he was dressed.

We went out and took our places at the altar. I looked through the crowd for Ailis. I was sure Mrs. Foley would take her shopping and that she would be gorgeous. I found her quickly. I did a double take because she and Mrs. Foley had gone all out. Her hair was up, and she had on a beautiful blue dress. I was frozen in place until my father elbowed me when Millie appeared at the back of the church.

The music started. Her brother escorted her down the aisle. I glanced over at Ailis and our eyes met. She smiled and my heart stopped beating for a second.

The ceremony was thankfully short. Throughout the entire service my father looked truly happy. I couldn't help myself, but I snuck glimpses of Ailis and I saw her get a little teary eyed during the vows. I couldn't wait to talk to her at the reception.

I stood in the receiving line at the VFW saying hello to people I already knew but there were new relations from Millie's side to meet. I saw the Foleys in the line finally and found myself getting nervous about what I would say to Ailis.

"You look amazing," I said when she got up to the wedding party.

"Thanks, and you in a tuxedo, pretty amazing yourself," she replied.

"Will you save space on your dance card for the best man?" I asked.

Colin joined the line with his parents. "Best man? That's a good one," he said.

"At least today I officially have the title," I said.

"I think he's grand," Ailis said.

"Grab a table and I'll see you guys when I'm done with this receiving line," I said.

I watched Ailis walk away, her dress swaying with each step. I was mesmerized, until Aunt Vera hugged me and kissed me on both cheeks. She told me how grown up and handsome I looked.

I thought she was right on target.

§§

The reception proved to be tame compared to a lot of the weddings I had been to but there was an open bar and since my cousin Anthony bartended, Colin and Lance took advantage of the lack of adherence to the New York State drinking age.

I tried to stay on an even keel since it was my father and new stepmother's big day. I didn't want a bunch of slaps to the back of my head if my aunts and sisters thought I had too much to drink. Ailis was on her fourth glass of champagne, which after her first taste she had declared to me was much better than stout or the beer we swilled at Lance's house.

The fact that Ailis was getting a little tipsy alerted Mrs. Foley and she gave me the evil eye when I walked to their table with a new bottle. I nodded my acknowledgement of the warning. If I gave any more champagne to Ailis, I was going to be in danger. I returned with a Coke and put it down in front of Ailis.

"Good job," Mrs. Foley said.

"You're no fun," Ailis said when she saw the Coke next to her empty champagne glass.

"Are you having a good time?" I asked.

She held up her empty flute. "Well, I was."

Mrs. Seeley from church came to the table to talk to the Foleys. Mrs. Seeley was the perfect cover for me since she had weeks of gossip to update Mrs. Foley on.

"Just a minute," I said. I grabbed her Coke and got up from the table while the Foleys were fully engaged in conversation. I returned less than a minute later and handed the glass to Ailis.

I motioned to her to take a sip and when she did, she tried to hold in a laugh.

"Shhh," I whispered.

She smiled.

I clinked my fresh beer with her fresh rum and coke. The DJ finally stopped playing one of the many polkas that encouraged only one couple from Millie's side to twirl around the dance floor and put on a nice slow song. I stood up from the table and offered my hand to Ailis.

"May I have this dance?"

"Of course, you can," she said. She practically fell into my arms.

"Okay, I think Mrs. Foley was right. We better not have anything more to drink."

"I don't know," she said. "At the rate we're going, you might just get lucky."

"Waiter, a round of drinks for the lady, please," I said.

"You're terrible so," she said.

I put my arms around Ailis, and we began to sway to the music. She felt as stunning as she looked. I pulled her closer. She put her head on my shoulder and I moved my hand up and down her back once. She began to shake ever so slightly.

"It's okay," I said.

"Yes, it is," she whispered back.

I wanted the moment to last forever. I tried not to let the thoughts of her leaving enter my mind, but I could not help it. I wanted to tell her I loved her and didn't want her to leave – or maybe that I would go to Northern Ireland to be with her. I thought I heard her say something.

"What?" I asked.

She pulled back a little so she could look at me.

"I don't want to leave."

"I want you to stay," I said. "You are the best thing that has ever happened to me. I want to be with you—"

I was about to say "I love you"– when Mrs. Foley tapped me on the shoulder.

"The song stopped a minute ago, Joe. They need you for the pictures of the cutting of the cake," she said.

I was surprised by how kind Mrs. Foley sounded, which confused me for a second. I held Ailis's hand and took her with me over to the cake.

The photographer took pictures of the wedding party around the cake. I motioned to him and pointed to Ailis and myself. He understood and took our picture. When he was done, I turned and faced Ailis. When she looked at me, my knees went weak and my throat was so dry I was afraid I wouldn't be able to speak.

"Ailis O'Fallon," I said. I squeezed her hand.

"Yes, Joseph Di Capra?"

"That's all I could think of saying because 'will you marry me' is way too crazy to say."

"Joe…we…you and me…"

"I know Ailis, I know."

CHAPTER 61
AFTER PARTY

My father and new stepmother were leaving right after the wedding for their honeymoon in the Berkshires. I had the house all to myself for the next four days. I invited Lance, Colin, and Ailis back to the house for a wedding after-party. What I really wanted to do was put on some comfortable clothes and get out of my tuxedo. But most of all, I wanted to continue the night with Ailis. I couldn't ask for her to come to the house alone because Mrs. Foley would have stopped that like the New York Giants' defensive line playing a high school team.

My cousin Anthony let me take a couple cases of beer and three bottles of champagne from the bar since my father had already paid for all the booze.

"Tell Uncle Vince I'll bring the rest of it up to Aunt Eva's for the next family party," Anthony said as he put the cases in my father's station wagon. My father was going to take us back to our house and then to Millie's for their drive east to Massachusetts.

I looked at Mrs. Foley. "We're leaving now. Colin,

Lance and Ailis are going with me and my father, back to the house."

"Okay, but youse kids be careful. I should make you help me get Big Jim into the car first. Just look at him."

She nodded in the direction of her husband who had a table of people surrounding him. They were hooting and laughing at his stories. Big Jim's tie was untied, his shirt unbuttoned halfway down. He was sweating from three rounds of the chicken dance, and he held a cold beer to his forehead.

The DJ announced that the bride and groom were leaving, and people gathered outside the door, a phalanx of rice throwers. I made sure to be well off to the side but close enough so I could cheer loudly for the couple.

My father took Millie over to her sister's car for her ride home. We piled into the station wagon for the short drive to my house. Dad shook rice out of every crack and crevice.

"That was a great wedding, Mr. Di Capra," Colin said in his polite, I'm talking to adults voice.

"It was so lovely," Ailis said.

We dropped Colin, Lance, and Ailis off so they could get changed.

"Do it fast and come straight to my house," I told Colin.

"Don't worry. What am I supposed to do again?" Colin laughed.

I got changed as quickly as I could and then I helped my father get ready. His suitcase was packed; I took it to the car while he put on some casual clothes that my sisters bought for him. I got the cases of beer and champagne out of the car and into the kitchen before he was finished.

"Here's fifty dollars if you need anything while I'm

gone. If you need more just call your sisters," my father said before he got in the car to go to his bride. I saw Lance, Colin and Ailis coming down the street.

"How do you like the For Sale sign?" I asked when they got to the front yard.

"At least you'll have Millie's mansion to come back to during school breaks," Lance said.

"Have you picked out a room?" Colin asked.

"I have. I'm going to take the attic."

"Hopefully it's haunted," Colin said.

"I feel so much better out of that monkey suit," I said.

"I liked you better all dressed up," Ailis said. "Now you're just plain Joe."

"Thank you. You looked great too." I smiled. "Let's go in and get some beers. Or would you like some champagne, Ailis?"

"Champagne of course," Ailis said in an accomplished French accent.

I laughed and took her hand. I turned to say something to Colin and Lance, but they had already gone inside and were in the kitchen opening beers.

"Well, come in. Make yourself at home," I said.

"Always do," Colin replied.

I opened the champagne. I filled a glass for Ailis and opened a beer for myself. Colin and Lance started a game of quarters at the kitchen table.

"We have to practice for the next keg party," Lance said.

Ailis and I went into the living room and sat on the couch.

"I can't believe my father got married, but it was a fun time and I'm glad you came to the wedding."

"It was so much fun. It was so romantic. You're a great dancer by the way," Ailis said.

"Beer. It loosens things up and I don't care if I look like an idiot."

Lance and Colin were engaged in a killer game of quarters. I could hear the coin hitting glass on every try and shouts of "Drink! Drink!" Ailis rolled her eyes toward the kitchen.

I poured her more champagne.

"Can I see your room?" Ailis asked. I almost spit out my beer.

"Sure, but there's not much to see," I said hoping she couldn't tell how nervous I was.

I led Ailis up the stairs to my room. I brought the bottle of champagne.

"This is it," I said, happy I had cleaned up because of the house being on the market.

Ailis walked around looking at the bookshelf, running her finger along the titles. I hurriedly took the crumbled tuxedo off the floor and laid it on a chair. She inspected the things I had on my desk.

"Looking for pictures of all my girlfriends?" I asked.

"Ha, those are probably in a wee album, sorted by how many times you kissed them."

"Sadly, no. Not a lot of kissing unfortunately."

"Well then, maybe I'll help you practice."

Ailis sat on my bed when she finished with her inspection of my room. I joined her.

"Did you read all those books?" she asked.

"I thought we were going to practice kissing?" I replied.

"Haul yourself a wee minute. What about the books?"

"Yes, I read almost all of them, even the encyclopedias. Pretty sad right?" I asked.

"Not at all," she said. She tilted her head and looked at me with a half-smile.

"What?"

She finished her champagne and put the glass on the nightstand, then looked at me again without saying anything. I was about to ask her what she thought when she leaned into me and kissed me. The level of passion increased quickly. Being so inexperienced, I had no idea what I was doing, so I just followed her lead.

Ailis grabbed my hand and put it under her shirt. I was amazed at the way she felt. Within seconds I understood every joke I had ever heard about how difficult it was to unhook a bra. There was nothing in the back. I fumbled around like a perfect idiot.

"It's in the front," she said while still trying to kiss me.

I moved to the front and still couldn't accomplish my mission with one hand. I waited to hear her start laughing at any second. She pulled back and I expected the worst.

Ailis took off her shirt and unhooked her bra. I stared in wonder. I pulled her to me, the passion rising to a level I had never experienced. We lay down on the bed. I took off my shirt.

I reached down and began to unbutton her jeans.

"Guys?" Colin called up the stairs.

I pretended I didn't hear anything and finished unbuttoning her jeans.

"Guys? Sorry? Ailis we have to go, I told my mom we would be back before two."

Ailis and I stopped. I looked at her and kissed her.

"Please stay," I said.

"Okay."

"Guys?" Colin said again. "If we don't get back soon, you know my mom. She'll be down here before you know it."

I found our clothes on the floor and handed Ailis hers. We both got dressed.

"Ailis, I don't know what to say. You are just wonderful; I wish you could stay."

"I've never done that before. I don't know what got into me other than the champagne, but I do want you and I don't know how far things would have gone but I know it was right and I didn't have any doubts."

I hugged her again. "You'd better go. You can't kiss me if Big Jim kills me."

"Goodnight Joe." she hesitated. "I…I …"

"I love you too," I said.

"Aye, I love you, Joe Di Capra." She gave me one long, final kiss, then she was gone.

CHAPTER 62
THE NYC PLAN

Ailis and I took every chance we could, without attracting too much attention, to talk through different plans on how we would get to New York City. We needed to find her father, then get back without anyone finding out we were gone or with the least amount of damage. The subject about what happened the night of the wedding didn't come up but the amount of kissing and physical contact had risen to an exciting level. I wanted to invite her over, but I thought it would be better if she brought it up first. I was sure I was an eejit for taking that strategy, but I didn't want to pressure her.

She came over to my house so we could be alone to plan the trip.

"If we use the camping with the guys as an excuse, then we have to bring everyone else in and they will really have to go camping," I said.

"Do we really want to bring Colin and Lance and maybe more into this? Won't that increase the chances of getting caught then?" Ailis asked.

"Yes, it will, it will greatly increase the chances. But how do we come up with a forty-eight-hour excuse? Mrs. Foley won't let you sleep over at Lance's or any girl's house from the neighborhood that we could recruit for the lie."

"We also have to go on a weekend. That increases the chances of finding my father at home. If we go during the week he could be working and that will add a lot more time," Ailis said.

"Let's look at the bus schedules again," I said. I spread them out on the table.

"I don't think we should take the 5:00 PM bus Friday night. It would get us to the Port Authority at 10:00 PM, and by the time we got to his house it would probably be close to midnight."

"Both the train and a taxi would get us there in an hour, but we don't want to go through the South Bronx. I don't think we'd want to do that even in the day," I said.

"Okay, if we take the midnight bus, we get to the Port Authority at 5:00 AM. Another hour to Woodlawn and we can be there for tea and scones." Ailis laughed and then she choked up and turned away.

I didn't think. I just put my arm around her, and she sunk her face into my shoulder.

"We're going to figure this out, don't worry," I said.

I felt her take a deep breath. She looked up at me and I knew I had to come through for her whatever the cost.

§§

It took several days and several different plans to decide on what we were going to do. In the end we had to bring in Colin and Lance because there was no way we were going to be able to pull this off by ourselves. We said we were going to a concert in Albany, and we would stay the night at my sister's house. That gave us almost three days to get to New York City and back to Genesee before anyone noticed.

My sister didn't agree right away, but when I told her the whole story about Ailis, she relented. Mrs. Foley was reticent, but she trusted that my sister would keep everyone straight. We said we were going to take the bus to Albany and back home, except Ailis and I were getting on a bus to New York while Colin and Lance were going to Albany. We walked through the scenario over and over. Everything was planned down to the minute, but we knew there still were a million things that could go wrong.

The day finally came. My father drove us to the bus station. We sat in the waiting room without talking. I held Ailis's hand and tried to imagine all of the emotions she was experiencing. I looked at my watch. We still had twenty minutes before our bus was due to leave. Lance and Colin were leaving thirty minutes after us.

I put my arm around Ailis.

"It'll be okay," I said.

She nuzzled into my shoulder. I looked up and saw a man walking over to us out of the corner of my eye. Big Jim.

He wasn't mad. He just wanted to know what was going on. I told him the truth as calmly as I could.

"It's all my fault, Mr. Foley," Ailis said. "I talked them into it. They are doing this for me. I don't know if I'll ever get another chance to see my father." She couldn't hold back the tears.

I squeezed her hand and looked up at Mr. Foley.

"How did you find out?" I asked.

He shook his head and put his hand on Ailis's shoulder.

"Ailis don't cry. Joe, take care of her," he said. "I'll be right back. Colin, Lance, go wait by the car."

He walked over to the bank of pay phones. He leaned on the wall with his back to us while he talked. I saw him nod a few times. He hung up and came back over to where we sat.

"Ok, Joe, take the tickets back and get a refund, we'll wait," he said. He rubbed his chin.

I did as he instructed and came back with my cash. We walked out to the car where Colin and Lance waited.

"Everybody in the car," he said.

The ride back to the Foley house was silent. Ailis had her head on my shoulder and held my hand. I stared out of the window. The ride was only ten minutes, but it felt like hours. We pulled into the Foleys' driveway, and I reached for the handle.

"Colin, Lance, hop out. Joe, Ailis, stay put," Big Jim said.

I waited for the lecture once Lance and Colin had closed the doors.

"Ailis, why don't you get up front. I'm not a chauffeur," Big Jim said.

"What?" I asked. "Why?"

Big Jim turned around and looked at us. "Because we have more than a three-hour drive to New York City."

My mouth hung open. Ailis looked at me as if she wanted me to confirm what we heard.

"C'mon, it's a long drive."

Ailis jumped out and got in the front seat. She leaned over and planted a huge kiss on Big Jim's cheek.

"Thank you, Mr. Foley, but I'm not going to kiss you," I said.

"Well thank God for that," Big Jim said. He backed out onto the street, then put the car in drive.

CHAPTER 63
FINDING DA

We headed toward Pennsylvania, then cut across on Route 17 and followed the New York – Pennsylvania border through the Catskill Mountains. We stopped for breakfast in Goshen, New York where we had bacon and egg sandwiches on hard rolls at the Patterson Diner. Perhaps it was the sense of adventure, but it was the best breakfast I had ever had in my life. Ailis smiled the entire time but kept quiet. I could see her apprehension grow as we got closer to the city.

I jumped in the front seat to hold the map and help navigate. Ailis sat in the back by herself. I looked at her every chance I could and put my hand over the seat so she could hold it. We crossed the Tappan Zee Bridge and looked down the Hudson at New York City.

"Are we going into New York?" I asked.

"Not the city itself. Ailis's father lives in the north part of the Bronx. Woodlawn is the Irish neighborhood. We'll head south right after the bridge."

§§

It was a quick trip down through Westchester on Interstate 87 to the Bronx. I looked out the window. The landscape became more urban, but it was nothing like I had seen on television and it definitely wasn't the Bronx I saw on the news. Woodlawn looked just like the older sections of Genesee with apartments and multi-family homes.

Mr. Foley had a mailman's sense of direction. I held up the map for him to glance at with a big red circle around Ailis's father's house. We turned on East 237th Street and I called off the building numbers as we got closer. I glanced into the back seat to see how Ailis was doing, I could tell she tried hard to hold herself together but she was wide-eyed and staring without saying anything.

We got to the house, a small, white single-family house with an emerald-green door. Mr. Foley found a spot, parallel parked, and turned off the car.

"Do you want us to come with you?" Mr. Foley asked Ailis.

She didn't respond; she just stared at the house.

I got out of the front seat and got in the back with her. I put my hand on her shoulder.

"I'll go with you," I said just above a whisper.

Ailis shook her head slowly. "No, I'll go then, by myself."

She took a deep breath and opened the car door. She walked up to the house and rang the doorbell. Mr. Foley and I both rolled down our windows so we could hear what was going on. She stood for a minute then rang the doorbell again. The door finally opened, and a man appeared.

"Da, it's me Ailis." Even from the street I could hear the emotion in her voice.

The man stood there blinking for a second.

"Ailis?"

"Yes, Da, it's me. I wanted to see you before I go back."

"Go back? How did you get here?"

Ailis told him the entire story. When she pointed to us in the car, we both waved. When she finished her story, he bent down and hugged her. They were both crying.

Ailis remained inside for about twenty minutes before she emerged smiling. She motioned to us.

"Don't sit out here all day, come inside," she said.

We followed her inside and were introduced to her father, his new wife, and two young boys. We shook hands. He thanked us for going through all the trouble of bringing Ailis to him.

His name was Michael O'Fallon. He worked construction and was illegal until he married his new wife, an American citizen. He said he made a good living, and that Woodlawn was a great neighborhood, a literal oasis in the Bronx. His wife brought out tea and we chatted. I watched Ailis; she smiled the entire time.

"Well, it's almost noon," Mr. O'Fallon said looking at his watch. "Why don't we head up to the Pub for lunch and maybe a pint to celebrate."

Mr. Foley and I nodded in agreement and within a few minutes we were walking down to McLean Avenue and into Rory Dolan's.

Rory's was a lot like Quinn's and Mr. O'Fallon was greeted by name as we came in. He introduced Ailis to a number of people and got hugs all around. We sat at a big corner table and ordered food and pints.

Once we got our drinks Mr. O'Fallon raised his glass and motioned to everyone at the table.

"To my wee daughter, Ailis. I thought I wouldn't see her again and then a miracle happened and here she is at my table. She has grown into a beautiful woman, and I'm so happy to raise my glass to her…to Ailis."

"To Ailis," we said in unison.

Ailis was smiling through her tears.

Lunch was served and after a few more pints Mr. O'Fallon asked Ailis if he could talk to her alone. They went over to another table. I tried not to stare but glanced over every time I thought I wouldn't be noticed. Ailis listened while her father did all the talking. She occasionally moved her head – "yes" or "no." When she came back to the table, she seemed deep in thought.

We finished lunch. Mr. Foley looked at me and then down at his watch. I understood that we had to go. I nodded in agreement.

"Well, I'm so happy we were able to reconnect Ailis with you, Michael, and I hate to be the bearer of bad news, but we have to get back on the road," Mr. Foley said.

Ailis got a pen and paper from the waitress and she and her father exchanged all their contact information. I could tell that Ailis tried very hard not to cry on the way back to the car. She held her father's hand and walked about three houses behind us.

There were many handshakes and hugs when we finally got into the car. I got in the back seat with Ailis. Mr. Foley didn't object. I held her hand while we drove away.

§§

No one spoke until we reached The Liberty Diner in Liberty, New York, where we stopped for a bathroom break and some food for the road. Big Jim ordered a huge meal, enough for all three of us but that was just for him. I ordered a grilled cheese. Ailis just wanted tea and toast. She stared out the window while we waited for our food. Big Jim looked and me and nodded his head toward Ailis.

"I'm going to hit the head, be right back," he said. He got up from the bench where we waited for the takeout. I took his cue and put my arm around Ailis's shoulder.

"How are you," I said, mad at myself for not having something better to say.

She kept looking out the window for a few seconds and then turned to me. There were tears in her eyes. I hugged her close. I could feel the soft convulsions of suppressed weeping.

I saw Big Jim out of the corner of my eye. He sat down at the counter and started to chat up the waitress.

"It's okay," I said, again wincing that I could not find the right words to comfort her.

I could feel her pulling away, so I let her go.

"My Da, he said he will sponsor me if I want to move here. I don't know what to think."

"That's great," I said a little too quickly. "I mean, if that's what you want to do at least you'll have the choice."

"I don't know what I want. It would be great to get away from all the trouble in Derry, but it would also mean leaving my friends and my family. I like it here in America, but I don't know if it's what I want permanently."

"I don't think you would have to make a decision right away," I said even though I was a little hurt by her indecision.

Her face brightened slightly, and I cheered myself for saying the right thing.

"You have time, don't you? He didn't say make up your mind by the end of the week or I won't sponsor you, did he?"

"No, not at all. We didn't talk about timing or anything like that. He hasn't seen me in eleven years, and he just blurted that out?"

"He's your dad; he loves you."

"Then why did he leave us?"

"Did you ask him?"

"No, I didn't have the guts. In a way I don't want to know why. But my mother is gone, and I know his leaving was the reason for her doing that."

I squeezed her hand and began to say something when the waitress showed up with our four bags of food. Big Jim was right behind her.

"Let's get on the road," Big Jim said taking the bags from the waitress and paying her.

"How long is the drive to Genesee from here?" I asked.

"About two hours," Big Jim replied.

"But with you driving, one and a half?"

"Of course," Big Jim replied. "You sit up front so you can hand me the food."

He looked at Ailis and reconsidered. He motioned for me to get in the backseat with her.

The drive back to Genesee passed by silently. Ailis fell asleep with her head resting on my shoulder. I stroked her hair and watched the hills rise and fall along the interstate.

CHAPTER 64
THE TALK

I told Ailis that, "we needed to talk," a phrase I had sworn would never come out of my mouth because every time I heard it uttered by someone else, it was followed by "I just like you as a friend." She seemed surprised by my statement. Her only response was "okay," but I could hear the questions in her voice.

"I'll be up to the Foleys' house in about ten minutes if that's okay with you," I said.

"Sure, I'll be here. Joe, is everything okay?"

"Yes, very much so, but I'll be there in ten minutes."

It was the longest walk I ever had to Colin's house. Usually, I ran a little in the areas I knew might be an issue. This day I walked slowly and went over what I wanted to say to Ailis. I tried to figure out how she would respond. Would she cry? Would I cry? Tears trickled down my face as I walked. It tore me up to do this, but I knew I had to do it.

Ailis waited for me at the front door. She came out on the steps and hugged me. She started to pull away after a few seconds, but I pulled her closer and buried my head in her shoulder.

"Joe what's wrong?" she asked.

"Can we go out in the backyard and sit down?"

"Sure."

We walked to the backyard and sat in the chairs by the fire pit where I'd drunk several beers while waiting for "Liam from Belfast" to appear. Instead, I got "Ailis from Derry," the best surprise in my short life.

"Ailis, I wanted to talk to you about when you go back to Northern Ireland."

"We still have a week; can't we just enjoy the time we have left?"

"We can, but I wanted to talk about this, set some expectations. Ailis, it's going to break my heart when you leave but I want to make sure we stay connected but not to the point where we bring our lives to a standstill. I would go with you if it was possible. I would do anything to keep you here. The night at my house, after the wedding, I've never wanted anything more than you. I have never been as happy as when you were in my arms."

My voice cracked. I cleared my throat and continued.

"I'm going to college, and you are going back to your life. I think we should write to each other, not every day like I know I'll want to, but once or twice a month maybe. It might be fifty pages long, but I'll only write once or twice a month. I'll agree to whatever you think is best."

"Joe, I don't know," she whispered.

"We don't need to decide right now, don't worry. And we can see what it costs but I would like it if we could talk every now and then. I don't know if I could bear never hearing your voice again."

I stopped and tried to gauge her reaction to my feeble attempt to map out some way to bridge the ocean. I wiped away a tear on her cheek, leaned in, and kissed her cheek.

"And," I continued, "if the fates allow us to be together, it will happen. If we say goodbye at the airport and I never see you again, we will always have this summer. It has changed me forever and I thank you for giving me a chance."

"Joe," she said. She began to cry in earnest and buried her head in my chest.

I put my arm around her and ran my fingers through her hair. I was ready to tell her that I didn't need to go to college. I would move. I thought about begging her to talk to her father and have him sponsor her. I would go to St. Benedict's and then transfer to Fordham or another school near the Bronx. The thought of not seeing her again tore through me, a searing stab wound with no relief. Her crying eased a little.

"Joe, I want to stay. I'll go inside and call my father right now."

"Thank you, but the process takes time. You need to go back to Derry and think this through. You could meet a nice guy once you get back and you'll be like 'Joe who' when I call."

She laughed…well, she tried.

"I know. I should have told you that you weren't my type way back in the beginning. I should have…" I hesitated. "But I'm irresistible, sorry for being that way."

This time, the laugh was genuine.

"Ailis, I loved you from the moment you got out of Big Jim's car wrapped in his coat. I knew it, I don't know how but I did. I'll meet girls at college. You'll meet guys back home. I'll want to kill them, but you will. I'll never forget you, you changed me. Now I'm blabbering like a eejit."

"No, you aren't," she said. The first kiss was light. The second was not. "Are you alone at the house?"

"Yes, my father is staying at Millie's."

Ailis got up and took my hand. She led me out of the backyard and toward my house.

CHAPTER 65
FACING MRS. FOLEY

I woke up before the sun and looked over at Ailis. She lay on her side facing me. I watched her sleep and tried to shut out the thoughts of having to say goodbye. I don't know for how long I watched her.

Her eyes fluttered. When she saw me, she stretched and smiled.

"Good morning," she said. She snuggled closer.

"Good morning, thank you." It was all I could think of saying.

"I think you thanked me enough last night."

"I'm especially happy you didn't say 'wee' when I had my clothes off."

Ailis smiled at me, the wound of her leaving already beginning to shred my heart.

"Well," I said, "then you are really going to have to decide how you'll feel about all the presents I'll be buying for you today. Are you hungry?"

"I'd really like to stay in bed all day."

"Done," I replied without objection.

"But..." She hesitated. "I need to get back to the Foleys' house and face the music then. I'm so surprised Mrs. Foley didn't come down here or at least call."

"I'm not going to let you face her alone. I'm responsible for you staying out all night. I'll take the punishment."

"I can't let you do that," she said.

"I'm going with you. I have to. Let me get you a fresh towel so you can wash up. Do you need anything else?" I asked.

When we were both ready, we walked up to the Foleys' and went inside. Mrs. Foley sat at the dining room table reading the paper, drinking coffee, and smoking a cigarette as always.

"I was wondering when you were going to show up," Mrs. Foley said without looking at us.

I waited for her to throw the coffee cup at me. Maybe the shotgun was beside her chair.

"So, what are youse kids up to today?" she asked.

'We haven't decided yet," I replied.

Ailis shrugged her shoulders; she didn't know what was going on either.

"Ailis, sweetie, I have a roast defrosting in the sink. Can you check it to see if it's thawed out?"

"Sure, Mrs. Foley," Ailis said. She headed to the kitchen.

The second Ailis was out of the room, Mrs. Foley threw down the newspaper and leaned in my direction.

"If we send that girl back home with a baby, I'll personally kick your butt all the way across the Atlantic so her family can kill you."

"I...I..."

"The only answer is, 'We were careful Mrs. Foley and if

I ever do that again I give permission for Mr. Foley to beat me senseless.'"

"We were," I said.

Ailis walked back into the room.

"Still frozen solid, Mrs. Foley. Looks like you just took it out of the freezer," she said. She took my hand.

"Right, right, I did just take it out, sorry I'm getting forgetful in my old age."

"Well..." I said.

Mrs. Foley held up her hand and stopped me.

"Both of you sit down," she said.

We did as she instructed. I held Ailis' hand under the table.

"Youse kids are both almost eighteen. You are almost old enough to know what you are doing. Ailis, I'm going to miss you. I only had sons. It was so nice having a daughter and we protected you like one. But Joe turned up and for some reason you fell for him." Mrs. Foley shot a dagger in my direction.

"So," she said, "I understand what happened and I'm happy for you. There are going to be a lot of tears in a couple days, so I want you two not to waste any time and enjoy the next few days. Just be careful if you know what I mean."

I looked at Ailis. She seemed as shocked as me.

"Thank you, Mrs. Foley, I appreciate you taking the time to let us know how you feel," I said.

Ailis got up and hugged Mrs. Foley.

"Can I hug you too?" I asked.

"Of course not," Mrs. Foley said before she opened her arms and beckoned.

CHAPTER 66
PROTECTING AILIS

The guys finished painting the back of the house and earned the third keg without me. I thanked them for their hard work. They also did a great job of making sure everyone knew about the party. I called classmates who hadn't left for college and went down to the Super Duper to tell my friends there.

"Do you think we need to pitch in for a second keg?" I asked Colin and Lance when they informed me what they had accomplished.

"If we run out of beer, we run out," Lance said. "I've squirreled away a couple of cases in the basement just in case."

"How did you do that?" Colin asked.

"I have my ways," Lance said.

Colin and I looked at each other and shook our heads.

"Only Lance," we both said.

Ailis had been spending the nights at my house since we received Mrs. Foley's tacit approval. I told my father what was happening, and his response was the same as Mrs. Foley's. "Be careful".

Ailis and I were together every day of her last week in Genesee.

The third kegger was scheduled to be the night before Ailis went back to Northern Ireland. We were going out to dinner first with my father, Millie, and the Foleys. Then we were heading to the party for as long as Ailis wanted, so she could say goodbye to everyone.

We got to the party about an hour after they tapped the keg. Every room in the house filled, wall to wall partiers, with the excess spilling out into the back yard.

Ailis was leaving tomorrow. I tried to make myself accept the reality while at the same time desperately searching for a way she could stay.

"She is going back to Derry. She's the best thing that ever happened to me, even if it was for just a few months. I'm going to miss her more than I can imagine," I said to myself.

The party rocked the house. There were my friends from the Super Duper, my high school, and all the people that had been to the previous parties. I saw Gwen come in with some of Andy's friends. She saw me with Ailis and smiled. We went all out for this party and if we killed the keg by midnight, at least we went out in style.

The crush made it nearly impossible to get from the living room to the porch. Lance handed pitchers of beer through the porch window; I walked around to everyone I knew and introduced Ailis to anyone who hadn't met her. We had agreed before the party not to mention that she was leaving the next day. It was a good call. I wouldn't have been able to get those words out without becoming emotional.

All of this, the best party we'd ever thrown, the biggest turnout, and all I wanted to do was be alone with Ailis.

"Can we take a walk?" She couldn't hear me even though I yelled, but she could read my lips.

She nodded. I took her hand and we started pushing our way through the crowd to the front door. We made it outside to the quiet of the front yard. It was like stepping through a time-warp from a raging storm and into a quiet summer evening.

We walked down the street, and I didn't let go of her hand. I wanted to start to tell her all the things I'd rehearsed but I didn't know if I could talk. She sensed my discomfort and squeezed my hand tighter.

She stopped after we walked a block and pulled me to her. We kissed. I wanted the moment to go on forever. I found my voice.

"Ailis, you have made this summer magical. When I find myself missing you, which will be all the time, I'll think of the fun things we did together, the great times we had, and I'll smile. I'll carry your picture with me all the time. I know we have to say goodbye tomorrow, but we *will* see each other again. I promise you we will."

A tear ran down my face and she wiped it away. We kissed again and I held her tight, wishing some miracle would occur and she wouldn't have to leave. We were being pulled apart by going on with our lives and our paths were destined to take us farther apart with each day. I had to be realistic. We were kids. We had a lot of life to live before we could even think about a lifetime together. How could we even know if we were meant to be at this point.

"So," I said, "Monsignor McCarthy is waiting for us down at Our Lady of Sorrows. I have the license in my pocket. Ailis O'Fallon will you marry me?"

She smacked me on the shoulder.

"First of all, you should be on your knee then. Secondly, you should be holding a box with a two, no three-carat diamond sparkling in front of me. And last, yes, I will marry you."

"I knew you would. But I'm joking, no Monsignor and no license. But I do have a ring. I know it's corny since you're Irish and the lady on Liberty Hill assured me that the Irish still give these as presents, but I'm not sure I believe her."

I pulled the ring box out of my pocket and handed it to Ailis.

She opened it up and her eyes moistened.

"Of course, a wee Claddagh."

"Too corny? The lady said she gets the rings directly from Thomas Dillon's in Galway. They've been making the Claddagh since the seventeen hundreds."

She looked at the polished gold ring – a heart clasped by two hands. "No, it's grand. Thank you. Will you do the honors?

"Of course, right hand with the heart facing towards you?"

She looked at me and smiled.

"Yes, that's more than grand."

I put the ring on her finger and hugged her again, tight. I kissed her neck. I was about to kiss her again when I saw a group of guys rounding the corner, maybe ten of them. I knew this was very bad. These guys wouldn't let us pass unscathed.

"Ailis, I need you to do something very important," I said in a slow and deliberate voice.

"What's wrong?" she asked. She stepped back to look at me.

"Go back to the house, get Colin and the guys. Walk for ten feet or so, then run as fast as you can. Do it now."

She turned and looked and saw the group approaching. They were about six houses away.

"Now!" I said.

"But—"

"Now – go!"

Ailis walked away towards Lance's house. She started running after only a few steps. I turned and walked towards the group. The big guy in the center wore a Los Angeles Dodgers cap. He was the same guy I'd managed to avoid months ago. He looked even more menacing up close. I stepped onto a lawn and tried to walk around them, but three of them stepped in front of me.

"Where do you think you're going?" Dodgers cap asked.

"Just walking to my friend's house."

"Where did that fine looking girl go?" He looked at his friends and made a crude gesture with his tongue.

"She had to go home. She was past her curfew and didn't want to get grounded."

"Grounded, what the fuck is that?"

His guys laughed.

I looked around the group for a familiar face, maybe someone I knew from CYO basketball or Little League. It had worked to defuse situations before, but I didn't recognize anyone.

"Maybe, we should bring her back here and ask her

why she ran away from you," he said. He took a step closer and got right in my face.

"No," I said with too much force. I immediately knew it was a mistake.

"Are you telling us what to do?"

"No, I just don't want her to get in trouble."

"She your girlfriend?" Dodger cap asked. "You getting some of that?" He rubbed his crotch.

"No."

"What are you a fag or something?"

"No, she's my friend."

I was pushed from behind, then pushed again.

"It was nice talking to you guys. I have to get home," I said. I tried to walk around them again.

"You're not going anywhere," Dodger hat bumped his chest into mine.

The first punch hit the side of my head, and I stumbled forward only to be hit again. I tried to cover up, but punches came from every direction. I swung my fists wildly; a few of my attempts landed. I caught a set of knuckles square on the jaw and the light started to fade. The streetlight grew hazy as I fell to the ground.

Mercifully I was unconscious before they started to kick me. I didn't feel two of my ribs breaking. I didn't hear my friends from the party, a group of twenty or more, running to my aid. I didn't hear the ambulance or feel anything when they cut off my clothes at the Emergency Room.

CHAPTER 67
BROKEN

They told me I was still unconscious when they finished with me in the ER. My family talked to the doctor in the hallway. Colin, Lance, and Ailis were in the room. The rest of my friends stayed in the hall or the waiting room.

Ailis was leaving that morning to go back to Northern Ireland. There was no way she could change her ticket. She held my hand and cried. Mr. Foley stood in the doorway waiting to take her to the airport.

"Joe, I have to say goodbye." I didn't hear her, but Lance told me she was sobbing.

Colin rubbed her back.

"I'll try to call you once you're awake. I have to hear you say goodbye. You saved me. I'm sorry I didn't get help fast enough."

"There's nothing you could have done," Colin said.

"I could have screamed or stopped a car. Now look at him."

"He'll be okay. He's tough," Lance said.

She leaned forward and spoke into my ear.

"I wish I had the magic to make you better. I will love you forever."

Her tears fell on my face. She kissed me goodbye and stood to leave.

"I'll see you again Joe Di Capra. I love you" she said. Colin helped her out the door.

She was gone.

I awoke a couple of hours later.

Lance was still there. Colin was at the airport.

"Is she okay?" I asked even though it hurt to talk.

"Yes, she's fine," Lance responded.

"Is she gone?"

"Yes."

I tried to move a little, but I could barely move my arms and my head was throbbing. I was about to cry but not from the physical pain. Lance grabbed the call button and pushed it until a nurse finally showed up. The morphine put me under again.

The next time I woke up I felt a little better. The room was empty. I pushed the call button.

"What happened," I asked the nurse when she came into the room.

"You were beaten up," the nurse replied.

"I remember that. How bad?"

"You have a couple broken ribs and a concussion. We had to give you a couple stitches on the right side of your head. The scar will be small and under your hair. We are going to let you go home tomorrow morning."

CHAPTER 68
LAST WEEK

My last days at home were a mix of sadness and pain. Somehow, I found the strength to pack... slowly. My father bought two matching suitcases and a new backpack for me so I wouldn't show up at UVA with all my belongings in Hefty bags.

I wrote Ailis a long letter and took it to the Post Office. I was healing physically but my heart was still lacerated, something a doctor couldn't fix. I asked my father if I could call her, and he agreed but made me promise to keep it under ten minutes. I had her number, the time zone difference, and the times Ailis said would be best to find her at home.

I dialed the long number and heard a few rings then they stopped. A different set of rings started. I let it continue and was about to hang up.

"Hello," she said.

Her voice sounded tinny and far away.

"Ailis, its me."

"Joe, I…" was all she got out before she started to sob.

I don't know how I didn't sob along with her, but I gritted my teeth and tried to breathe slowly.

"I only have ten minutes. I wanted to let you know that I'm okay. I was only in the hospital for a day and I'm feeling much better. I'm still going to school, that hasn't changed at all."

I heard her take several deep breaths.

"I'm sure it's good to be home," I said.

"Yes," she said. She took another deep breath.

"And you got back without any problems?"

"Yes, the flights back were easy, no troubles."

"Have you told everyone about your great summer?"

"I have, and it was great. I miss you, Joe."

"I miss you too. I wrote you a long letter and I'll write again with my address once I get to school."

"Yes, please. Please write whenever you want. I wrote you a letter, but I sent it to the Foleys' because I didn't know if you would still be in your house by the time it gets there."

"I'll check with them then," I said.

I glanced at my watch.

"Make sure you write in a few weeks and let me know if...um...you know, so I can go tell Mrs. Foley we aren't going to be parents and she doesn't have to have me killed."

She finally laughed.

"I will."

The remaining time flew by. I missed her more with each passing second.

"I have to say goodbye, the time is up," I said. "I love you, Ailis O'Fallon."

"I love you, Joe Di Capra."

Then...silence.

§§

I didn't go to Lance's but there was a steady flow of friends at my front door. They kept me company and helped me finish packing. My father wanted me to come down to Millie's, but I preferred to stay in my "home" because these were probably the last days I would get to spend here.

There hadn't been a lot of traffic, but the realtor called a few times saying there would be people coming to look at the house. When they did, I went down to the Super Duper and hung out with the stock boys and joked around with Mr. O about all the crazy things we did after he and Mr. Leonard left the store.

Two days before I had to leave, Mrs. Foley called to let me know that a letter arrived from Ailis. I thanked her and said I would be right up. I sprinted to their house even though my ribs still hurt and went directly to the dining room where I knew I'd find Mrs. Foley.

"You're healing nicely," she said when I appeared at the table completely out of breath.

"Yes," I said. I held my side, "But I'm already starting to regret running the entire way. Thanks for letting me know about the letter. And tell Big Jim I'm surprised the Post Office managed to deliver a letter all the way from Northern Ireland."

Mrs. Foley laughed.

"I'll tell him. Good luck at school if I don't see you before you leave, and I hope they teach you how not to be such a smartass."

"I'm sure they have a class on that." I smiled. "Mrs.

Foley, thanks, I appreciate everything you did for me with Ailis."

Mrs. Foley shrugged. "You're a good kid. Your mother would be proud of you."

I tried to hold in the tears. Ailis's departure, my leaving for school, being beaten up…everything caved in on me at once. Mrs. Foley got up and gave me a hug.

"You're a good kid," she said.

I looked at her. She had tears in her own eyes.

"Okay then, I'm going to head home before Big Jim walks in and sees us hugging and gets the wrong idea," I said.

Mrs. Foley laughed her deep raspy laugh as I headed to the front door.

I walked home holding Ailis's letter, trying to feel her touch.

I ran my hand over the envelope and smelled the faint perfume that had survived the transatlantic crossing. I read the letter quickly, then read it over and over savoring her words. I cried holding a pillow to my sore ribs.

My time in my house was drawing to an end. I saw the ghosts of my memories in each room. I said goodbye to them one by one as I went through the house. I felt my mother's hand on my shoulder.

I thought of the Joe Di Capra who walked into Bishop Slattery nearly a year before, the determined kid, vowing to get himself out into the world. To experience life, break out of my shell. To take charge of his future. To fall in love.

I had not planned on breaking my heart, but I was ready.

CHAPTER 69
HEADING TO THE WORLD

I had healed enough to make it to school in time. I was still very sore but at least the bruises on my face were gone. My preoccupation with leaving for school took my mind off of Ailis – at least partially.

My ribs hurt the most, which made it almost impossible for me to carry all my bags. My father chipped in so Colin could go with me and help me move in. I told Colin I was going to tell people that he was my butler. He was offended for a second. Then thought it was funny and agreed to play along.

My last night in Genesee I spent at Lance's where we quietly drank beer and told stories about our crazy summer.

"You guys have to finish painting the last side of the house so we can have that last keg when I come home for Thanksgiving," I said.

"We'll do what we can with football, school and the weather" Lance said.

"I can't believe we finished three sides," Colin said. "If I had to bet how far we would get back in May, I would have put twenty bucks that we wouldn't get past the front of the house before we called it a day."

"I was tempted," Lance responded.

"We can always say that the summer of 1979 was the summer we almost painted the house." I laughed.

"That's a lot better than the summer Joe got his ass kicked," Lance said.

"It'll go down in history then," Colin said.

"Well, I'm going to scope out the fraternities as soon as I get settled in and you guys have to promise you'll come down for a party."

"I'm looking forward to it," Colin said. "The bigger question is whether me and Lance can save up the money for the bus."

"Well, I might be able to help a little. Even though the Army is paying for everything, I'm going to try to find a part time job for a little extra money, but not until I know that I can handle the classes, ROTC, and the fraternity. That seems like a lot, but you guys know I'll do what I have to do."

"We're going to miss having you around," Lance said clinking my beer bottle with his.

"Aw, man, that's nice," I said.

"Don't get all sappy on me," Lance said. "This is tragic. You buy the beer all the time. Now I'm going to have to get a job to pay for it."

"If I thought you would show up on time, I would tell Mr. O to hire you at the Super Duper."

Lance started to act offended, then stopped.

"That's true," he said. I looked at my watch.

"Let's finish these. We have to be at the bus station at 5:00 AM. I don't think you've been up that early in your life Colin."

"I've been up drinking that long but never woke up that early, even when my dad took us fishing."

"Don't worry, your mother promised me she would have you up and ready. We can go back to sleep once we get on the bus."

We finished the beers and I walked with Colin to the corner where we usually parted. Colin kept walking with me toward my house.

"Forget where you live?" I asked.

"Don't feel like going home right now," Colin replied.

I knew he was lying; he was always a bad liar.

He stopped in the parking lot of Our Lady of Sorrows and watched me walk down the street to my house, just like Sister Catherine all those years ago.

I barely slept. I kept looking at my alarm clock waiting for it to go off. I got up before it rang, showered, and got my things together. My father was sitting in the living room when I came downstairs. He had come over to see me off and say goodbye.

I checked all my bags and then went back upstairs for one last look around my room to see if there was anything I forgot.

"Work hard, study, but have some fun too," Dad said with more emotion than I ever expected. "Always remember that you're a Di Capra. Your grandfather came to this country with sixteen dollars in his pocket, a wife, and a daughter. I grew up in the Depression and saw too much in the war. Di Capra's are tough. You're tough. I'm proud of how hard you worked to get to this point. You are going to do great things."

"Thanks, Dad," I said. Good thing I didn't have anything else to say, because I couldn't talk anymore. This wasn't going to camp for a week when I was twelve. This was leaving.

Mr. Foley showed up early to take us to the bus station. I heard his car out front and extended my hand to my father. He shook it and pulled me in for the first time he had ever hugged me.

I didn't look at my house as we pulled away for the short drive to the station. I sat in the back seat alone, where I sat with Ailis on many car rides. I thought of her and this new chapter in my life. The combination of excitement and sadness was overwhelming. I took a deep breath and fought back the tears.

Big Jim parked the car and helped us with the luggage.

"Thanks, Mr. Foley, for everything" I said. I shook his hand.

"Good luck at school, you have great things ahead of you. You're a good kid."

We paid for our tickets and got on the bus which was already there. Colin and I went all the way to the back. He was asleep before we pulled out of the station. I watched my city disappear out of the back window and stayed awake while we drove through the rolling glaciated hills of central New York and headed to Pennsylvania on Interstate 81.

We changed buses in Harrisburg. We had time to go across the street from the station and get McDonald's. We were in Virginia in just under two hours. It looked a lot like New York.

I was glad.

We had another two hours to Charlottesville. We turned onto Interstate 64 and began the climb into the Blue Ridge Mountains.

It was just over a mile from the bus station to campus. Luckily there was a free shuttle, so Colin and I didn't have to walk. He carried most of my bags. I shuffled along under my backpack. The arrangement would lend credibility to our butler story.

We turned into the University, and I saw the campus in real life for the first time. I realized that I was crazy for choosing a school I had never visited. The panic of being so out of place grew like a summer thunderstorm. I took several deep breaths to calm the beginnings of an emerging panic attack. I fought it off.

We drove past a few houses with Greek letters plastered across the front of pillared porches. The distraction helped me focus. I pointed them out to Colin.

"Toga, toga," he said with a smile.

The bus dropped us off at the dorm. Colin and I walked in, maneuvering the bags around the crowded lobby of students and parents. I went to the front desk and got the attention of one of the people behind the counter. I gave the young lady my name and she handed me a stack of forms.

"Bring them back before five," she said. She handed me a key. "Room 223, take the stairs past the cafeteria. That's the easiest way to get there."

We took the route as instructed and went up the stairs to my dorm room. The door was open and there was already a guy in there with his parents. I knocked for some reason, and they turned to look.

"Hi, I'm Joe Di Capra, it looks like we are going to be roommates."

"Hi, Joe Lane," he said extending his hand. "These are my parents."

I shook everyone's hand and then realized I hadn't introduced Colin.

"Oh, forgive me, this is Colin Foley," I hesitated for a second trying to decide about sticking to our butler story. The Lanes looked like people who might know a real butler; they might have had one. "He's my friend from home; he's helping me out."

Colin dropped my bags and said hello.

"Well, I have to see Colin back to the bus station so he can get the five o'clock bus back to Genesee."

"We can take you; we are heading out to get dinner before we drive back to New Jersey."

Within fifteen minutes, Colin, my new roommate, and I were in the back seat of a huge Mercedes. It was the first time I had ridden in a Mercedes.

We dropped Colin off. I made sure he had his bus ticket and that he found his bus. I hugged him as hard as my hurt ribs would let me and thanked him for helping me out.

"Have a safe trip back," I said. The panic I had suppressed earlier was replaced by a sudden wave of homesickness.

"Have fun finding a fraternity. I can't wait to come to a party."

"Colin...thanks." I swallowed hard and tried to continue. "You guys really helped me in the short time we hung out. You guys mean the world to me. I'm sorry I bust your chops so much, but you know I don't mean it. Well… sometimes I do."

"I know. I have to confess I only wanted you around for the free beer."

We both laughed.

"I do have one regret though," I said. "That night you drank the JD, I regret saving your life, should have let you freeze to death. Every time I got a popsicle out of the freezer, I could have said, look, its Colin."

"I hear ya. Thanks again for that."

"Last year I didn't have any brothers but now I do. See you at Thanksgiving."

"Love you, bro," he said. He grabbed me again in a bear hug.

I watched him get on the bus, then went back to the Lanes.

Dinner was awkward because I had to try very hard to remember all my manners in the very expensive restaurant. I knew Mr. Lane would pick up the tab but I still ordered one of the lowest priced things on the menu.

"Chicken?" Mr. Lane asked. "We are all getting steaks. Why don't you get the New York Strip. I'm sure you'll enjoy it."

When I gave my order to the waitress. She asked how I would like it cooked.

"Medium rare," I said with confidence.

I couldn't believe I had learned something from chain-smoking Carol in Lance's kitchen. After his parents left, my new roommate and I took a walk around campus. The atmosphere was electric. There were students everywhere, music blasting, and signs for parties on every telephone pole. We got to a couple fraternity houses near our dorm.

"I was thinking about pledging a fraternity," I said.

"Me too," Joe Lane replied.

I looked at him and laughed. "*Animal House?*"

"Yep."

CHAPTER 70
PI LAM HOUSE, 1983

It was the spring semester of my senior year at UVA. I was ready to be done with school but couldn't imagine leaving my friends and especially my brothers at the Pi Lambda Phi house. My years in the house were filled with parties, comradery, and friendships I knew would last my entire life.

In a few weeks I would graduate and receive my commission as a second lieutenant in the United States Army. I was lucky. I had received my first choice of Infantry and my station with the 82nd Airborne at Fort Bragg. My fraternity brothers thought I was crazy. In a way so did I.

It was the night of our annual "Pi Lam Slam" – a legend on campus. We were already known as the "animal house" and the movie only enhanced our unruly reputation. For some reason I was not enthusiastic about the festivities and even after the house was full of co-eds ready for the last big blow out party before exams, I sat at the bar slowly drinking my beer thinking about my journey to this point and contemplating life in the real world after college.

"What's got you on the rag?" Joe Lane asked. He was my best friend. We'd roomed together all four years. I was seated at the corner of the bar, peeling the label off my beer bottle with my back to the house full of happy students.

"I wish I knew," I said. "I'm just not into it tonight."

"Stop this nonsense and have some fun, I want to see the old 'Other Joe.'"

Our freshman year after we pledged, someone came to the house looking for me and asked, "Is Joe here?" One of my brothers answered, "Joe Lane?" "No, the other Joe," the guy said. From then on, my nickname was "Other Joe."

"I'm just tired of all the same old girls here. They're looking for rich husbands and I definitely don't meet that criteria. One time a girl asked me what my father did, and I made the mistake of saying he was retired after working at a small retailer that shut down when I was in high school."

"What'd she say?" Joe Lane asked.

"Nothing, she just walked away. It hasn't been easy being here on scholarship with all the rich people like you. You went to Paris over Christmas. I went to Genesee and took my friend Colin to court. When the judge announced his fine, Colin turned to me and asked if I had any money."

Joe Lane laughed; he loved my Genesee stories.

"And you know what else happened in Genesee, that's on my mind all the time. I haven't given up hope."

"Maybe you should, I don't know. What about Clare? You had something with her. She'd take you back in a second. I still don't understand why you guys broke up. You were together most of your middle two years."

"She was too serious; she was planning our wedding at times. Something was missing."

"Is that enough to throw away such a great girl? She's

smart, gorgeous and she's already been accepted at UVA Law so she can support a worthless writer who can't earn enough to keep the lights on."

"I have nothing against being a kept man, but something wasn't there. I can't really explain."

"It can still work out. She goes to law school for three years. You're just down the road at Fort Bragg for four. It's fate my friend. Tell her you're an idiot, you know something she'll believe. You should consider it."

"You're right," I said. "If she shows, I'll talk to her and see if there's any spark left."

"That's a good idea. I understand, you're young, there's still a lot to do and you don't want to be tied down. And I know you want to go back to Genesee someday and hang out with your friends, at least the ones that aren't in jail."

"They are great guys," I said. I started laughing at the memories. "And I'll eventually get used to talking to them through the plexiglass."

"And if none of that works out, I'm sure I'll need a gardener at the estate I'll have after I graduate from business school," Joe Lane said.

"I'll be there. You can call me 'Chauncey the gardener.' Where are you going again?"

"Harvard," Joe Lane said.

"Never heard of it. Good luck finding a job."

"Enough witty banter. Let's get into this party and corrupt some freshman. To the Class of '83, we made it through," Joe Lane said. He held up his beer.

"Class of '83," I said. We clinked bottles.

"Well things may just be changing for you," Joe Lane said with a sly smile.

"What?"

"There's a gorgeous girl standing in the doorway staring at you. She's either smitten or is a process server looking to give you the paternity suit papers."

"I'm going to turn and look, and it'll be some dude or a girl in an Alpha Gamma sweatshirt. It's not Clare, is it?"

"It's not Clare and I'm not kidding; she's staring you down and she's seriously hot."

"Okay, I'll look, but be prepared for me to kick your ass in front of all these people."

I turned around. Every molecule of air left my lungs; electric shocks ran through my extremities. Everyone in the house disappeared except her. I didn't know if I had the strength to stand but I managed to cross the room even though I don't remember my feet ever touching the ground.

I walked to the girl who'd been staring at me, took her in my arms, and kissed her with the trepidation of a first kiss.

EPILOGUE

The rain and gloom of the Genesee November chilled my bones. My knees ached on the way back to Lance's old house. I took my handkerchief from my pocket and cleaned my glasses so I could see my past more clearly.

"Thank you," I whispered. My eyes were moist from the thoughts of my friends from so long ago.

I saw my ride approaching and waved. I turned back to the house and said my goodbyes. Goodbye to the memories and especially to the ghosts filling my vision. They danced around my thoughts, young and so alive, ready for mischief.

"I hope you guys approve of what I'm going to write about us," I said aloud so they could all hear me. I waited for an answer.

A gentle hand rested on my shoulder. I knew the touch. I knew it well. "Who are you talking to?"

"Colin, Lance, and all the guys," I replied.

"You better stop before they put you in a home."

Her Irish accent was undiminished even after nearly

forty years of living in the States. It still made my heart "dance like a cork upon the tide."

"Are you doing okay?" she asked. She put her arm around me. "I know this won't be easy, saying goodbye tomorrow."

"Yes, it's going to be tough and I will miss him dearly, but he lived a good life. I hope you don't mind if I have a pint or two at the reception after the funeral. It's at Quinn's. I can't wait to go back there with you."

"Not at all. It's where we fell in love and I'll be happy to join you in a pint." She smiled.

"And speaking of us," I said, looking down the street where I was beaten all those years ago.

"Yes, that. But it had a happy ending so. Have you been happy?" she asked. I took her hand from my shoulder and squeezed her warmth.

"Yes, absolutely. I asked you to marry me then, any regrets that you said yes?"

"Of course," she said. "I question my decision every day. You know you don't need to ask me. I had no doubts then and I've had none since. I came back, didn't I?"

"Ailis O'Fallon," I said turning to face her.

"Yes, Joseph Di Capra."

"I've been very happy. I'm the luckiest guy in the world. I still intend to find the person who screwed up those plane tickets back in 1979 and kiss them on the lips. Will you be jealous?"

"Depends on how pretty they are." Even after all these years, her eyes twinkled with gold.

"How does it feel to be back here? This is where it all began." I corrected myself. "Where we began."

Ailis looked around and pulled me to her.

"Lovely," she said. "After all, it's where we found our magic."

The End

ABOUT THE AUTHOR

Tom Cosentino lives in Indian Rocks Beach, Florida. He is a graduate of Syracuse University and the Rochester Institute of Technology. He proudly served as an Officer in the United States Army. He has published several short stories and his first novel *The Art of Looking for Trouble* received glowing reviews. This is his second novel.

Printed in the USA
CPSIA information can be obtained
at www.ICGtesting.com
LVHW051321221223
767218LV00063B/1341